THE OFFICIAL MOVIE NOVELIZATION

THE OFFICIAL MOVIE NOVELIZATION

ALEX IRVINE

TITAN BOOKS

Dawn of the Planet of the Apes: The Official Movie Novelization
Print edition ISBN: 9781783292271
E-book edition ISBN: 9781783292288

Published by Titan Books
A division of Titan Publishing Group Ltd
144 Southwark Street, London SE1 0UP

First edition: July 2014
1 2 3 4 5 6 7 8 9 10

A CIP catalogue record for this title is available from the British Library.

Printed and bound in the United States.

To Lindsay, Emma, Ian, and Avi, who are my favorite apes

1

Thunder rolled overhead and a hard rain fell through the upper canopy of the great trees, dripping and sheeting through their leaves into the shadowy space that stretched between the lowest branches—still twenty times an ape's height—and the ground. Caesar sat perfectly still, ignoring the rain and the thunder. Storms had never frightened him, but some of the other apes, raised under roofs and inside walls, had not lost their fear even after all the... years, was the human word... that had passed.

But more and more of them were being born out here in the forest where they were meant to be. Free. His son Blue Eyes—sitting beside him on the branch and trying without success to remain motionless—was one. He looked to Blue Eyes, who felt his father's glance and went still again.

They waited.

A rustle in the trees signaled the approach of a scout. The ape stopped three trunks over, his hunting paint visible in the gloom, and made a series of hand signals.

Caesar nodded and looked down, to where Koba waited at the head of a troop of apes. All were armed with spears or knifes. Koba himself carried a harpoon, brought back from a foraging trip after the humans had died.

Koba looked up, his scarred face and milky eye marking him as a warrior. He had suffered much, and his suffering had made him savage.

Caesar gestured.

Move. That way.

Koba led his troop forward.

Caesar looked to his son again, then looked around. Another troop of apes, waiting in the trees nearby, watched.

He raised an arm and thrust it forward.

Without a sound, thirty apes sprang from their branches, catching and swinging through the treetops. On the ground below, Koba's troop surged ahead, matching their pace.

The hunt was on. His son close behind him, Caesar secured his own spear, leaped, and swung at the head of his apes, a fierce glee building inside him.

None of them screeched or hooted, and to the elk herd that had paused to drink, the sounds of their passage through the canopy were masked by the downpour. The animals didn't react as Caesar's troop slowed and crept along branches toward the edge of the open area near the stream. Across the meadow he saw Koba's apes moving slowly along the ground, up to the edge of the trees.

He waited.

Koba searched the trees, found Caesar, and nodded.

Caesar stood on his branch and let loose a mighty battle cry, a scream that tore through the pounding of the rain as the rest of his apes joined in. The elk panicked, looking up to see the apes coming at them out of the trees. They stampeded across the stream toward the protection of the trees on the other side of the meadow... just as

Caesar had planned.

Koba's apes sprang up in front of them, breaking into small groups to cut off escape and separate the old and the slow from the main body of the herd. Elk could kill apes, but only if the apes did not fight together. *Apes together strong,* Caesar thought, remembering when he had first been able to recognize that thought... before, in the shelter.

Before the humans had died.

The elk began to scatter, the main body of the herd thundering upstream. Several smaller groups were driven into heavy thickets, or water deep enough to slow them down. Apes struck at these first, drawing blood and desperate trumpeting cries.

Caesar swung along the edge of the trees. He looked back to make sure his son was with him. Below them, three elk charged into heavy undergrowth. Blue Eyes let go of his branch, about to drop, but Caesar stopped him with a grunt. Blue Eyes caught the branch again, hanging by one hand, spear in the other. He was too eager, Caesar thought.

Wait, he signaled, and he paused to listen. Rustles and the snap of small twigs came from the undergrowth. He peered carefully into the tangle, trying to pick out where the elk had gone, the better to drop from the trees and finish one of them.

He looked back to Blue Eyes again... but his son was gone. At the same time another smell reached Caesar.

Not elk.

Blue Eyes was on the ground, stalking toward the thicket, body low and spear held ready.

Caesar recognized the scent just as the bear lunged from the thicket. The young ape turned to run, but the bear was too close. With a swipe of its great paw it knocked him tumbling away over the slippery ground. His spear was lost in the frenzy of violence.

The bear stood on its hind legs and roared over Caesar's son, ready to strike the killing blow. Caesar flung himself from the branch, dropping feet-first and hitting the bear high on its back. It weighed as much as ten Caesars, but the force of his falling knocked it to all fours. Before it could react he sprang back up, wheeling around a low branch and throwing himself at it again. This time his feet hit it just as it rose to its hind legs, and again it was knocked off balance.

He landed in front of it, and gestured with one hand for Blue Eyes to stay back. With the other hand he unslung his own spear and leveled it at the bear.

It lowered its head and growled.

Caesar threw his head back and screamed, a challenge to the bear... and also a call for help.

He jabbed at the beast, keeping it away from his wounded son. At the same time he tried to force it toward the edge of a nearby rocky slope, with a smaller stream at the bottom. The bear faced him, swiping every time the spear point came close. Caesar moved to the side, staying close enough that the bear could not go around him and get to Blue Eyes.

If help did not arrive, he would have to try to kill it himself. There had been more bears since the humans died, and Caesar knew killing it was a dangerous task, even for many apes. By himself...

But then there was Koba, bounding along the upper edge of the sloping stream bank.

Caesar glanced away from the bear, and it nearly cost him his life. The animal lunged forward, arms spread wide in the attempt to drag Caesar in. He would not survive that embrace. He leaped back, but the bear pressed him.

There was only one thing to do.

Caesar set his feet and charged forward, spear leveled. The bear reared up to meet him.

At that moment Koba jumped out from the high ground, putting all of his weight behind his harpoon. The steel tip plunged deep into the bear's back, and Koba rocked the shaft back and forth, searching for the creature's heart, his toes gripping the bear's fur. Caesar angled his own thrust upward, driving his spear into its belly.

The beast thrashed in blind agony, crashing over a fallen tree and tumbling with the two apes down the slope to splash into the shallows of the feeder creek below. Caesar's head hit a rock on the way down, stunning him.

When he could look up again, he saw the bear on its side, dead. Its blood dripped from the broken shaft of Caesar's spear. Koba stood near its head, one hand on his harpoon. He looked down at the dead creature with a look of satisfaction.

Chasing elk was hunting.

Facing a bear was *battle*.

Caesar reached out and draped an arm over Koba, who returned the embrace. They had seen many battles together, but none closer than this.

Then Koba bent to pick up Blue Eyes' spear, which had tangled in the bear's feet as it fell. The stone tip was broken off and lost.

Caesar raced up the embankment and went to his son, angry at Blue Eyes' disobedience yet concerned at his wounds. Blue Eyes lowered his head when he saw his father coming. Caesar parted Blue Eyes' fur to see how badly he was hurt. Blue Eyes jerked away, embarrassed, as more apes arrived through the trees and on the ground. His son's behavior angered Caesar, but he held himself back.

The hunt was over. The apes had brought down several elk… and they would return with the bear, as well.

2

Caesar had worried that the bear might have killed the horses. It had happened before.

This time it had not, and he rode now at the head of his troop. They followed the banks of a river, with the giant trees looming in the thick mist on both sides. Around him were other apes on horseback, his closest and most trusted friends. Rocket, who had also survived from the shelter, and who had been Caesar's rival before becoming his friend. Ash, Rocket's son, near Blue Eyes in age. And Koba himself. Next to Koba came two apes who were close to him, Grey and Stone. They dragged a sled made from boughs.

It had taken several apes to drag the bear to open ground and onto the sled, but it was not a prize they would leave behind.

They had brought down five elk before Caesar's call for help had drawn the troop away from the herd. Those lay across the backs of horses, which were led by apes. The rest of the troop stretched out behind, walking on two legs.

Caesar watched his son touch the ragged gashes that ran across his chest. Sensing his father's attention, Blue Eyes looked up.

You must learn to think before you act, Caesar signed.

Blue Eyes looked away. Again Caesar was angry, and again he held it back. The boy had learned, or he had not. If this lesson had not taught him anything, neither would his father's anger.

Caesar turned away, his watchful gaze sweeping the tree lines on either side of the river. They were about to pass a human ruin—the one closest to the apes' home. On top of a tall steel pole, entwined with vines, was a large orange ball. It had numbers on it. Caesar had learned his numbers a long time ago, in Will's house: 76, the ball said. He had seen many places like this one, where humans brought their cars. Will had brought him snacks from inside them, but those snacks had all been gone for a long time. Now the inside of that...

Gas station. That's what Will had called them.

The inside of that gas station would not even keep out rain anymore. Apes avoided it, as they avoided most other places where humans had once gathered in large numbers. The forest was their home.

The troop crossed a shallow, rocky stream that fed into the river just beyond the gas station. Then the ground started to rise. Ahead of them, wreathed in fog, was the base of a high ridge. Caesar rode a little faster, but not so fast that the walking apes had to drop to all fours. It was important to them that they were able to stay on two feet.

They climbed through the fog. It swallowed the world, baffling the apes' ears and filling their noses. The ground beneath their feet and the closest boulders and trees were the only things they could see. The rain stopped when they turned away from the river, and around them the forest was quiet... until he heard the sound of a small waterfall ahead. That low rumble, signaling the approach to home, was one of Caesar's favorite sounds.

Cornelia would be there.

The fog began to clear as they climbed the base of the ridge and felt a wind coming down from above. It always did, late in the day. Caesar tilted his head back and sniffed. The wind brought the smell of just-after-rain, and with it the scent of their fellow apes. His horse clip-clopped out of the fog and Caesar smiled.

He always did when he saw what the apes had built together.

3

Their home, which lay behind a wall of timbers and a heavy gate, spiraled around the flanks of the mountain. It was a place made for them.

Apes looked over the walls and hung from the timbers higher up the mountain, hooting out excited welcomes as they watched the troop approach. The noise increased as news of the hunting party's return spread.

Caesar and the other older apes had spent their lives in human cities, human buildings, human laboratories. This place was unlike any of them. There was a central open area anchored by a large fire pit. Around it scattered clusters of huts and lean-tos followed the natural shape of the mountain's slopes, continuing along the edge of a steep canyon bridged by fallen trees. The sound of the river rushing through the bottom of the canyon rose and fell with the seasons. The torrent was high now, too high to cross even on horseback, the rocks on either side slick with spray and moss.

The village was united by a network of paths along the ground and timbers in the air, running from higher slopes to the branches of larger trees that grew within the walls.

Those trees, which served as lookout posts and homes, were connected to each other by woven grass ropes and swinging bridges.

As he always did when he surveyed the village, Caesar felt a quiet pride at what the apes had done together. Chimp and orangutan, gorilla and bonobo and gibbon, all turned to see what their leader had brought them. The younger apes ran and scampered in excited circles, dodging too close to the horses until Koba signed and shouted for them to get back. Then they chased each other, the thrill of the occasion too much for them to handle.

The troop arrived in the center of the village, near the fire pit. Gorillas knuckle-loped over, seeing the elk and the bear. Two of them could carry an elk or a full-grown brown bear. Once, on the other side of this mountain, Caesar had killed a smaller black bear. The gorilla with him had draped the dead creature over its shoulders and walked back to the camp as easily as if it had been carrying a baby. Caesar was stronger than most chimps— and any human—but a gorilla could tear him limb from limb. They were fearsome when their tempers were hot, though that seldom happened.

Maurice hooted and grumbled at the scrambling children. They looked over at him, standing next to a stone wall, and the old orangutan gestured for them to come back and pay attention. The young ones did so, then settled down and picked up flat stones and pieces of charred wood. Maurice pointed at the wall, picking out each letter of the words carved there.

To help the children, and those of the older apes who had never learned to read, pictograms accompanied the words. In the first, two apes faced each other, teeth bared. A harsh diagonal line slashed through both of them. The translation was written next to the picture.

APE WILL NOT KILL APE.

Caesar had not wanted to use so human a symbol, but it was better than any he could think of. An open book with the alphabet showing on its pages appeared to one side of the second line, and on the other side there was a clenched ape fist.

KNOWLEDGE IS POWER.

The same symbol was repeated at the end of the third line, but below the open book lay a careful carving of the four kinds of great apes, arms linked together.

APES TOGETHER STRONG.

Every young ape learned how to write. It was another human thing Caesar had not wanted to copy, but writing was a powerful tool no matter who it came from. Apes were stronger for it. Maurice, a natural teacher, kept the children focused on each letter in turn. The older ones, impatient, were given whole words to copy.

Caesar thought back to the first time he had seen Maurice sign. At that moment he realized he wasn't the only one in the shelter who could do it, and knowing it had given him hope. More than any other ape who had fought with him in those days, Maurice was his trusted friend.

Two gorillas pulled the bear off the sled. Near them, Blue Eyes got down from his horse, slowly, watching the gorillas carry the bear away to be butchered. Ash skipped through the crowd and grinned at Blue Eyes' wounds.

He never would've gotten me, Ash signed. *But I'm quicker than you.*

Blue Eyes shoved him away, but he too was smiling. Ash

shoved back, playfully—then both of them stopped when Rocket came around from the other side of the sled and signed at them.

What are you standing around for? Go help with the horses.

Ash ducked his head and hurried away. Caesar watched his son, trying to judge how badly he was hurt from how he acted when he didn't know his father was watching. It looked as if he would be all right, but someone would have to see to his wounds to clean them, at least.

Past Blue Eyes, Caesar saw a female chimp named Sparrow come from deeper in the village, rushing toward the hunting party. She was plainly alarmed, pushing other apes aside in her hurry. Caesar's own alarm grew. She was headed for him. He flipped the reins of his horse to a waiting gorilla and was moving toward her before she reached him.

Follow me, she gestured.

Cornelia, Caesar thought.

4

A path along the edge of the canyon led up to the base of a massive oak tree. Beyond it lay an open grassy area enclosed by a timber wall, and beyond that a high meadow spread along the mountain's upper flank. From the head of the path, an ape could look down on the village, and even further down to the bridges spanning the canyon and the rushing water below.

The oak marked Caesar's home, which was built into its branches. Its lower part faced the canyon, overhung by a roof worked into the branches and braced by a timber floor just barely too high for an ape to leap up and grip. Ascending through the tree were other parts of Caesar's dwelling, but it was to the lower section he ran now, ducking from the path into the tunnel dug among the tree's roots. He came out of the tunnel and climbed the trunk, then swung around and landed on the floor inside.

All the while the sound of Cornelia's screams spurred him on.

Other apes followed him. He could hear them in the tree's branches, too, and see their anxious faces peering through the walls and roof. Many of them were children, running away from Maurice's lesson to see what this new excitement was about. Now they were frightened by the sound of Cornelia's pain.

So was Caesar.

His eyes adjusted to the gloom in the deeper part of the room, against the trunk. Cornelia lay on the bed he had made for her, years before when he had selected this tree for his own… and hers. Other female apes surrounded her, stroking her forehead and grooming her hair.

She shrieked, longer and louder than before, the sound digging into Caesar's ears until he wanted to hit something. He held himself still, watching her bare her teeth and draw another breath to scream again. He was more frightened now than he had been facing the bear. There he had looked an enemy in the eye, but here there was no enemy to fight. She would either survive the birth, or she would not.

Caesar could do nothing.

Cornelia drew a series of whistling breaths. If she knew Caesar was there, she gave no sign. None of the other females looked at him, either. She breathed in more deeply and shrieked one more time, even longer than before. Two of the other females moved to shield her from Caesar's view.

So they do know I am here, he thought in the midst of his anxiety.

The scream went on, becoming a growl and finally trailing off into shallow panting.

In the sudden quiet Caesar heard a tiny squeak. His heart jumped. He took a step forward as the females parted, and he watched one of them place the tiny newborn on Cornelia's chest. It was slick and wet, all fingers and toes. She gathered it in and brought it to her breast to nurse. It squeaked again, twice, and then grew quiet as it found the nipple and began to suck.

Caesar took another step. The attending females

groomed the blood and fluid out of Cornelia's fur and cleaned the bed around her. She looked up at him, then down again to the newborn. He approached and settled next to her, stroking her head. When he bent to kiss the tiny newborn, its fingers spread and then clenched into fists again, holding tight to Cornelia's hair.

From outside came the grunts and hoots of the children. Their light steps pattered back and forth across the roof. He heard the news of the birth relayed through the camp, followed by an outbreak of excited shrieking. Every birth was celebrated.

Movement from the open side of the dwelling made Caesar look up. He saw Blue Eyes, hesitant to enter, and beckoned him in. He came slowly to join them. Cornelia hooted a quiet greeting and smiled at him. His answering smile was nervous and wondering as he saw the newborn. Caesar saw him again for what he was: a child still, and growing into himself. The anger he had felt in the forest left him.

He rested a hand on Blue Eyes' shoulder. The three of them breathed together, and realized they were breathing in unison with the newborn. They looked at one another, and smiled.

5

Later that night, the celebration had taken over the entire village. The birth brought joy to the apes, as did all births, and especially that of a strong healthy child born to their leader.

They also celebrated the hunt. Haunches of elk roasted on spits over the fire as the sun set. Apes drummed and danced, the sound of the beats echoing from the canyon walls. Caesar and Cornelia sat on a ledge looking over the fire pit and the gathering, Blue Eyes and some of their closest friends nearby. She wore a crown of wildflowers picked by her midwives, and cradled the newborn, who slept the way only newborns could sleep.

Beside them was a tribute pile, offerings from the rest of the troop—flowers to adorn, pelts to warm, food to enjoy and sustain. Caesar looked at Cornelia and smiled. He had been unable to stop smiling all day. The tension and anger from the end of the morning hunt was all but forgotten.

Below them the gathering parted and three apes appeared, bearing to Caesar yet another gift. They carried the head and pelt of the bear, walking slowly through the crowd and up to the proud parents. Caesar watched them approach. Out of the corner of his eye he saw Blue Eyes' expression change. The young ape touched his wounds, and looked away.

The three apes laid the pelt before Caesar and set the head next to it. They knelt and lowered their heads, extending one hand each, palm up. He answered the supplication, swiping each of their palms with his own. Then, as they stood, he embraced all three, one after the other. His leadership was unquestioned, but these were more than his subjects, and he was not just their leader. Every ape in the village—brown, black or orange, young or old—they were all his family.

He picked up the bear pelt, felt its weight. A pelt like this was a rare treasure. Caesar stood and carried it to the other side of the fire, where Koba sat with Grey and Stone and others close to him.

Koba saw him coming and rose to meet him. Caesar ducked his head briefly, showing respect but not supplication, and offered Koba the pelt. He saw the emotion on his friend's scarred face. Affection was still strange to Koba, who had seen so much cruelty. The two apes looked at each other for a long moment. Koba took the pelt and they embraced. Every ape in the village watched.

Caesar broke the embrace and picked up a branch from the kindling piled at the edge of the pit. He held it up and broke it. Then he broke the two pieces into four. Holding the four pieces in both fists, he raised them above his head.

"Apes... together... strong," he said.

There was a moment of absolute silence from the assemblage, broken only by the crackle of the fire and the distant rush of the river. Then the apes erupted in a thunder of screams, cheering Caesar and themselves. Together, yes, they were strong. Amid the cacophony,

Caesar could hear some of the other apes doing what many of them found so difficult.

"*Ape*," they said. They grunted it, shrieked it, growled it. "*Ape. Ape. Ape.*"

6

Late in the night, most apes were asleep. The drums had gone quiet. Blue Eyes and some of the other young ones were tamping down the fire. They packed earth over it rather than drowning it, wanting to keep coals alive for the next day.

Koba watched Caesar's son. A strong one, but Blue Eyes did not know how strong he was because he saw himself as nothing but a weak shadow of his father. Koba knew what it was like to be in Caesar's shadow.

He went to Blue Eyes, who looked up at his approach. When Blue Eyes saw the bear pelt under Koba's arm, he looked down and away, shamed all over again.

Koba reached out to tap the youngster, and get him to look up again.

I know he is hard on you, Koba signed. *But only because he must be.*

Blue Eyes frowned at this. Koba knew that frown for what it was—a young ape feeling sorry for himself. While he understood the pressure of being Caesar's son, Koba did not believe in pity. Not for himself, and not for others. He grunted sternly, and then signed again.

Your new brother will need you. To lead him. And someday so will the others.

At that Blue Eyes looked uncertain. Still not fully meeting Koba's gaze, he looked up from beneath a lowered, sullen brow.

What if I'm not ready? he signed.

You will be, Koba answered.

The dying flow of the fire caught all the warring fear and hope, shame and frustration, in the young ape's face. He looked much like his father. But he had not yet learned his father's unshakable resolve. He still had need of guidance.

Koba grinned at him, feeling the time had come to ease the youngster's mind.

Maybe next time you hunt with me, he signed. Blue Eyes looked uncertain, as if he might not have understood what Koba meant. Koba touched the raw gashes on Blue Eyes' chest, then signed again. *Don't feel bad. Your scars make you stronger.*

As the idea sank in, Blue Eyes smiled a little, and looked down at himself.

Yes, Koba added. *Females see scars, and they see a warrior.*

Blue Eyes looked at him then, studying his face and the other scars splitting the thick hair of his shoulders and chest. Koba had earned them all, and he carried them proudly. Even his dead eye was a source of pride to him. He had fought, he had survived.

Now he saw what he had wanted to see from the beginning. Blue Eyes admired him.

Yes, Koba thought. *Admire your father because he is your father. Admire Koba because Koba is strong.* He turned and walked slowly away toward his dwelling, keeping his body turned so the bear pelt stayed in the firelight, visible to Blue Eyes for as long as possible.

Caesar led the apes. It was right that Caesar led the apes. But it was also right for apes to see Koba as strong. He could also lead.

7

The village was quiet the next day, as it always was after a celebration. Apes slept and rested, their bellies full and their minds at ease.

Cornelia, exhausted, slept most of the day, the newborn cradled to her breast. Caesar stayed near enough to hear them but not so near that he would disturb her. In his hand he held a pair of stones, using one to carve the other, then smooth its rough edges.

He found himself thinking of the years just past, the desperation of their escape from the human city and then the slow disappearance of the humans themselves. It was natural to think about the past when a child was born, he thought. The past had brought them to where they were, to this moment where he had two children whose future would be his greatest concern, for as long as he lived. All apes were his family, but only Cornelia, Blue Eyes, and the new son were his blood.

Caesar had gotten them off to a good start. He would lead the apes until he was no longer able, and then his children and their children would spread over the world.

Perhaps someday they would return to the city where

they had come from. He looked over it now from the upper part of his house, the side that faced away from the canyon and toward the jumbled hills and the ocean, far away, gleaming orange under the setting sun. Caesar remembered the first time he climbed one of the great redwoods and looked at the city, back when Will was alive. There had been so much motion then—cars on the roads, ships on the water, planes in the sky. The air had been brown over the city.

Now he saw the city from much farther away. The air was clear and nothing moved. In the shadows among the buildings, no lights came on as the sun sank into the ocean.

He worked a piece of stone in his hands, needing something to do other than sit and stare and wait for time to pass. A rustling in the branches behind him drew his attention away from the darkening city. He looked to find Maurice clambering over the edge of his perch. Maurice paused with his head, shoulders, and one foot over the edge, waiting to see if Caesar preferred solitude.

Caesar waved him up. Together they moved higher in the tree, to avoid waking the new mother.

Maurice settled next to him and patted his back.

Another son, he signed.

Caesar nodded and smiled.

Makes me think how far we've come.

Nodding back, Maurice traced Caesar's gaze and looked out over the humans' city. After a silent moment, he signed again.

Seems so long ago. After another, he added, *Do you still think about them?*

Humans? Caesar signed. *Sometimes.* His expression betrayed his mixed emotions, though. One open hand wiggled back and forth, a human gesture they had adopted to mean uncertainty.

Maurice looked at his old friend and replied, *I didn't know them the way you did. Only saw their bad side.*

Good and bad, it doesn't matter now. We watched them destroy each other. It was their nature.

It was Maurice's turn to wiggle his hand.

Apes fight, too, he signed.

But we are family, Caesar answered firmly. *All of us.*

Maurice considered this. He nodded, but Caesar could see he was being agreeable, rather than agreeing. Considering what that meant, he looked back toward the city. The sun was almost gone into the ocean. Streaks of orange and pink in the sky reminded him of a flavor of ice cream Will had gotten him once after a trip to the woods.

I wonder if they really are all gone, he signed.

Ten winters now, Maurice signed. *And for the last two, no sign of them.* He shrugged. *They must be.*

Caesar wasn't so sure. Humans had been strong enough and smart enough to create great cities. They had made roads across the world. They had built machines that could fly. Will had told him once that humans had even walked on the moon. If they could do that, what could kill all of them off? He knew some of them had been sick when the apes had escaped after becoming smarter, but apes got sick sometimes, too.

Yet no sickness killed them all.

The last of the sun's rays glowed on the high parts of the orange bridge that crossed the narrow water separating the city from the land where they now lived. Looking at that bridge took Caesar back, as it always did, to the day ten years ago when he had led the escaping apes across that bridge to...

He had not known then what he was leading them to. Only that he was leading them away from cages and pain. The images from that day would never leave Caesar's mind.

Riding a horse for the first time.

The gorilla, Buck, sacrificing himself to bring the—helicopter, that was the word—crashing down out of the sky.

An even darker memory, of the human, Jacobs, pleading for mercy as Koba tipped the broken helicopter off the edge of the bridge.

Will saying goodbye.

The troop charging across the land on the other side of the bay, through the streets that wound up into the hills, over the hills and into the woods. The humans had chased them, of course. Men with guns and trucks and more helicopters hunted them. Then they stopped. Caesar did not know why, but when the sickness began to spread he guessed that they were turning on each other.

Those first years were hard. Apes died from the cold and from starvation, before they learned what foods grew in these woods and which animals could be hunted.

Now, ten winters since the day they had broken free, the woods belonged to the apes. As Maurice said, they had not seen a human in two winters.

So many of them, Caesar thought. *Can they really all be gone?* He wished for it, and at the same time the idea made him sad. Humans had been cruel to him, and kind. He was proud of what he had done, but he also missed Will. Other humans, too. Will's father, some scattered few others who had treated him well. But it was hard to think of many. Most of them had feared him, caged him, tried to kill him.

Maybe it was better that they were gone... but still it made him sad.

He watched the sun vanish into the ocean, dragging the last light out of the sky. The city vanished, too, slowly fading into the darkness. He did not see a single light.

Perhaps one day they would return to the city and see what the humans had left behind. Caesar had talked about this with Maurice, who said it would be dangerous. What if the sickness could spread to apes? The orangutan's caution made sense to Caesar, and the apes stayed in the mountains. They had everything they needed here. Caesar's children would live in a world without cages, without needles, without humans in masks making soothing words while they caused apes pain.

If the humans all had to die to create that world, it was worth it.

8

Maurice yawned and waddled to the edge of the floor. He stretched. Something popped in one of his arms. *Sleep,* he signed, and dropped out of sight. Caesar listened to him swinging down through the branches and walking away down the path. He sat for a little longer, looking at the stars. Humans had told each other stories about the stars. Caesar did not know any of those stories. Maybe they were in books somewhere. Or maybe apes could make up their own stories. The shapes in the stars did not have to be human shapes.

He stood and walked quietly down the sloping catwalk that spiraled around the trunk of the tree, linking the different parts of his shelter. At the edge of the sleeping room, he paused and took a deep breath of the night air. He smelled the remains of the fire, the richness of the meadow soil, the mossy scent of the wet rocks at the river's edge far below.

Apes had done well.

He went inside, rubbing his fingers over the stone he had been carving before Maurice joined him. On the trunk side of the shelter, away from where Cornelia and the newborn were sleeping, was a table with a chessboard. Caesar had made both himself. He set the stone in its place on the board, among the other pieces he had fashioned. They were not the same as the pieces on Will's board, but they would do the same things. Small pieces in front, to march forward and protect the more useful pieces behind. He thought of all the different ways the pieces moved. Will had taught him that.

He picked up his new piece and moved it, up two and over one, as Will had shown him when he was barely grown. Then he put it back. He had not yet taught Blue Eyes to play, but he should begin. Then Blue Eyes would teach the new child. Ape would pass knowledge to ape, and knowledge was strength.

He stood over his mate and baby, just looking at them. No thinking now, just feeling. Caesar crept quietly around to the other side of the bed and eased himself down next to Cornelia. He felt good. It was time to sleep.

As he closed his eyes, he heard something change in Cornelia's breathing. She wheezed and shifted, turning a little more on her side and settling the baby against her again. Caesar lifted his head and listened. The motion woke her briefly. She saw him there, and smiled as her eyes closed again and she grew still. Caesar could tell she had never really been awake.

He started to lie back, then paused as the wheezing started again. The talk of sickness was fresh in his mind. He leaned his face close to her, listening and trying to decide how serious this sound was. The newborn made a small sound and opened his eyes. Caesar felt again the emotion he had experienced the first time Blue Eyes had looked him in the eye. A new life, seeing the world around it. Seeing him.

He reached over Cornelia and gently stroked his tiny

son's hand. The hand turned over and gripped Caesar's finger, startling a smile from him. He stayed like that, looking into his son's eyes and feeling the grip of his son's fingers, until both of them were asleep.

9

Blue Eyes and Ash stood in the shallows of the river early the next morning. Mist still drifted in the high valleys, and the sun had just risen high enough to shine down on the river. The gashes from the bear's claws the day before were still raw, but they were starting to scab over. More than anything else, Blue Eyes was still embarrassed because he had gone after the elk too fast. He had ruined his father's plan, and almost gotten himself killed. That felt worse than the tears in his skin.

He was also angry at his father for not trusting him. Who could have known a bear would be there? If he wasn't stuck to his father's side, Blue Eyes knew he could have led one of the hunting groups. He could have brought down an elk himself, or been part of one of the groups that had divided the herd.

Ash had done that. He'd talked about it all the way from the village down to the river. His father, Rocket, let Ash do things that Caesar would never let Blue Eyes do. It drove Blue Eyes crazy that Caesar treated him like a baby. And it was Koba—not his father—who had tried to make Blue Eyes feel better last night. All Caesar thought about was Blue Eyes' new brother.

All of this went through his mind as he stood, cold water rushing around his feet and spear poised, looking down at the water and waiting for a fish to move so he could see it. The trout in the river blended into the rocks, and when the sun got higher they would move to other parts of the river to hide from birds. It was hard to get them, but worth it when you were sitting around a fire eating them.

There. Blue Eyes saw the flick of a fin, and all of a sudden the shape of the fish was obvious. He stabbed down and missed, the spear point grating on a rock. As fast as he could, he stabbed again, but the fish was long gone. Ash laughed from his spot just upstream.

Let's see you do better, Blue Eyes signed.

Ash took a step into deeper water, up around his thighs, paused—and struck. He hooted with delight, drawing his spear back and holding it level with the water. A trout thrashed and wriggled on the end of it.

That's how you do it, he signed with the hand not holding the spear. Blue Eyes couldn't stand it. Ash did everything right. Everything was easy for him. And his father let him hunt. Blue Eyes could feel his temper rising. Caesar had taught him control, but it was hard. He got his spear ready again, looking from the water to Ash, who set the butt of his spear into the riverbed so he could reach the fish he'd gotten.

Ash caught the fish and dragged it off his spear, looking smug—and then the fish flipped out of his grasp. He dropped his spear and snatched at it, catching it by the tail for a moment. But it was too slippery. It wriggled free and dropped back into the water.

Now it was Blue Eyes's turn to laugh as Ash charged through the shallows after his quarry. Blue Eyes saw it go past him. He slapped the water, trying to catch it, but missed, still laughing. Ash bounded along the rocky riverbed. Blue Eyes followed, splashing him on purpose. The fish was gone, he knew. They would never catch it now.

Ash headed for a rocky overhang on the inside of a river bend, as if the fish might hide there. Blue Eyes caught his eye as they stomped through the water.

You're supposed to hold it by the gills, he signed. He laughed harder as Ash splashed him, then shoved him out into the water.

Blue Eyes tripped over a rock and fell. He sprang back up and went after his friend, who had splashed around the rock, and then stopped short. Blue Eyes swatted at the water again, but Ash didn't move. Blue Eyes called out to him and churned his way over.

Then he, too, froze.

From where they were standing next to the rock, shallow rapids spread out into the middle of the river just downstream, with the deeper, quiet water at the outside of the bend on the other side. The overhung rock formations created another slow-moving eddy, with a sloping open bank.

On that bank, squatting with his hands in the water to fill some kind of container, was a human.

Blue Eyes had never seen a live human. He'd seen a dead one, once, on the road that crossed the river. He had been very young and only remembered being surprised that the corpse had so little hair. And he had seen pictures, had heard stories, and this definitely was a human. Male, skin the color of wet sand, a little patch of fur the color of a young chimp's. Blue Eyes did not know how to read humans' faces, but if he had seen this expression on an ape, he would have thought the ape was scared.

Very scared.

The human stood up, his round bottle dropping onto the bank and spilling its contents. He took a step back and grabbed at something on his belt. It was dark and made of metal. He held it in both hands, his arms straight. A small hole in the tip of the metal thing was pointed right at Blue Eyes and Ash. Blue Eyes felt like he knew what the metal thing was, but it took a moment for his mind to start working again after the shock of seeing a human, alive, almost within shouting distance of the ape village.

Gun, he thought. That was the word. He remembered the sign, a wiggle of the thumb with a finger pointed out.

The sound of the gunshot was the loudest thing Blue Eyes had ever heard.

10

Caesar heard the gunshot and was racing toward the village gate before the echoes had died away down the canyon. He gestured as he ran, signaling his apes to arm themselves and follow, but he did not wait for them. He ran. The sound had come from the river below. The canyon broadened into the wide valley where they had hunted elk the day before.

Blue Eyes and Ash had gone fishing down there.

His mind raced faster than his legs and arms. Just last night he and Maurice had talked about the humans. Now this morning, there was a gunshot. Some of the apes believed that dreams could see what would happen. Some of them believed that certain apes could do the same. Caesar believed none of it, but still... Last night he had wondered if the humans were gone. This morning he had heard a gunshot.

Only a human would have a gun.

He skirted the edge of the canyon, following a steep path and using the trees where the aerial passage was faster. Behind him, he heard the rush and rustle of his troop. Most of them knew the sound of gunshots, from the day they gained their freedom. Even those who did not—the youngest Caesar would allow to fight—could see how their elders were reacting. They hurtled through the trees and along the path as if they were going to battle.

Caesar was first to reach the barren ridge above the river's edge, between the meadow where they had caught the elk and the wider, slower water downriver, where an old bridge crossed not far from the gas station. He halted on the ridge, looking down the slope as the rest of the apes gathered on either side of him. Koba, as always, was close by his side.

At the edge of the water, across the river, Ash lay against the sloping face of a rock. Blue Eyes crouched over him, protecting him. Both of them were looking at the human, who stood a short distance away on the same bank, his gun still pointed at the two young apes.

Crashing sounds came from the trees beyond the bank, and more humans spilled from the forest. Caesar counted them. Altogether there were five grown males, one female, one young male. Several of them carried guns. The first human pointed up in Caesar's direction and the humans stared in shock at the massed apes on the ridge.

Yes, Caesar thought. *If you are not gone, it is good that you should fear us.*

Koba, too, was surveying the scene. Rocket, on Caesar's other side from Koba, saw that Ash was wounded. He started to scream with rage and anguish, and signed furiously.

Humans shot Ash!

Caesar nodded, holding out an arm to keep Rocket from charging down and across the river. They did not want killing here. He watched the humans react to Rocket's sounds. One of the males pushed the young male behind him. A father, Caesar thought. So the humans had children still.

Hold, Rocket, Caesar signed.

I will kill them, Rocket answered. He bared his teeth at the humans and screamed again, shaking his spear.

Hold, Caesar repeated, with more emphasis. He looked back to the humans, focusing on the one who had protected the young male. That was the one to whom he would need to speak.

Everything was different now. If apes were not alone, Caesar would have to decide whether human and ape would both live, or whether there would be killing.

He held the gaze of the male human.

Your move, he thought.

11

Leave it to Carver, Malcolm was thinking. *He goes to the river to fill his canteen, next thing you know we're looking up the ridge at a million pissed-off apes with spears.*

He couldn't believe it. Everyone in San Francisco had heard the stories about the cover-up, right before the Simian Flu had scythed through humanity and left the survivors scrabbling in the ruins. But this? An organized group of apes, with weapons they had to have created themselves, rallying to defend two others. Yet not just charging down to kill them. Malcolm's head spun at the implications of it.

He stepped forward, both hands out in front of him, making sure to keep Alex behind him. The apes had stopped at the top of the ridge, but one of them was still making a hell of a racket, and spears could start flying at any moment.

Malcolm saw the one in the center of the group, his face streaked with red paint of some kind. The others looked to him. He was the one who had stopped the screaming chimp from coming after them. He must be the leader. And he was looking right at Malcolm, as if he recognized his human counterpart.

Okay, Malcolm thought. *Chief to chief. Let's talk.*

"We don't... we don't mean any harm," he called, loud enough for his voice to carry over the sound of the river, but not so loud—he hoped—that he sounded threatening.

Ellie spoke just behind him, her voice a terrified whisper.

"Malcolm, what are you doing?"

"They're apes," Carver said, louder than Ellie. He was waving his gun around, from the two apes in the shallows near them to the dozens on the ridge. "You think they understand what you're saying?"

Idiot, Malcolm thought. "They look like just apes to you?" he responded quietly.

They sure didn't to him. All of them stood looking down on the group of humans with what could only be intelligence. They were assessing the situation, waiting for orders. Next to the one Malcolm took to be the leader, an older chimp—with graying fur and a dead eye—looked at Malcolm with an expression of hate. Not animal, predatory hunger. Not the anger an animal felt toward a rival. Hate. It—*He?* Malcolm thought—was also staring at their guns.

Malcolm fumbled for what to do or say next.

"Dad?" Alex said.

"It's okay," Malcolm said automatically. The next step was clear. If they started shooting, they would never survive the apes' attack... and Malcolm did not for one minute believe that the guns would scare these apes off. They had heard Carver's shot and responded in force with arms of their own. That could only mean they knew what guns were. The one-eyed chimp's glare made Malcolm even more certain.

There was only one way out.

"Lower your guns," he said, keeping his voice low and even. "*Everyone.*"

Carver looked at him like he was nuts. Malcolm couldn't see the others, but he figured they were doing the same.

"Do it," he said.

They did. Malcolm kept his eyes on the leader, the one right in the middle. They sized each other up. *This was what it must have been like for explorers,* he thought. *Thing is, I've got no empire backing me up.*

The chimp planted the butt of his spear in the ground.

"Go," he said.

None of the humans moved.

"Holy shit," Carver breathed. Malcolm amended his previous thought. This wasn't like being an explorer. This was like meeting aliens for the first time. The chimp talked.

He slammed his mind back into gear.

"Okay, okay," he said. He took a step back, motioning for the rest of the group to do the same. "We're leaving right now! Just—"

The one-eyed chimp leaned forward, out over the ridge crest.

"GO!" it roared.

The other apes—*Damn,* Malcolm thought, *there are even gorillas*—started to shriek and roar. They were working themselves up to something.

"Come on," he said to the others. He turned Alex around and gave him a push. "Now."

They started to run, propelled by the rising hysteria of the apes' screaming. Alex's satchel slipped off his shoulder and fell down the rocks to the riverbank. He stopped, turning back for it. Malcolm reached out to keep him with the group.

"Alexander, leave it," he said. Ellie tried to catch him, too, but he was panicking a little, and he didn't have much. The satchel was important to him.

Not as important as staying alive, though.

"I said leave it!" Malcolm shouted, dragging the boy up the bank to the trees. "Come on!"

They ran. He just hoped they would get back to the trucks before the apes caught up to them.

12

Caesar watched the humans go. Around him, the rest of the apes quieted and looked to him for guidance.

He waited until the humans were gone. But where were they running to? Would they return with more humans, and more guns? Everything he had thought yesterday was suddenly uncertain.

Right now he had to take care of his son and see to Ash. He moved down the ridge, keeping a careful eye on the spot in the trees on the other side of the river where the humans had disappeared. The rest of the apes followed him down the rocks and across the river, wary and unsettled. Rocket ran ahead to Ash, lifting him to his feet and helping him out of the water. Ash sat on the bank. The hair on his arm was wet with blood from a wound on the outside of his shoulder. Caesar saw at a glance that the wound was not bad. He left Ash to Rocket, and motioned Blue Eyes to him.

What happened? he signed.

We were chasing a fish, Blue Eyes replied. *When we came past the rock, the…* He stumbled over the sign. *The human was there. He…*

Again Blue Eyes paused, not knowing the sign for what he wanted to say.

He shot at you, Caesar said. Blue Eyes nodded.

Caesar patted his son's shoulder. They had been lucky. The shot could have killed one of them. Still, this was bad enough.

Go to your friend, he signed. Then he moved over to the bag the young male had dropped. For a long moment he looked at it. He prodded it with the tip of his spear. Then he picked it up.

With the humans gone—at least for now—there was time for questions. What were they doing here? Where had they come from? No ape had seen any sign of humans living in the mountains, not in several winters. And the city was dark and quiet. Could these humans have come from somewhere else, over the mountains or the ocean? Had the sickness not been able to cross the water?

Too many questions.

They needed answers.

Caesar turned to Koba, who was still watching the woods. He grunted, and when Koba turned to him, he gave a sharp signal.

Follow them.

13

They made it to the trucks at a dead run, throwing their gear into the backs, and grinding gears in their terrified haste to get the hell away from the spear-wielding apes. Malcolm drove one truck, with Ellie and Alexander. Carver drove the other with the rest of the crew. Malcolm had already decided that he and Carver were going to straighten a few things out when they got back to San Francisco.

What the hell was he thinking, shooting at a pair of chimps before he even told anyone else they were there?

That was the problem. Carver *wasn't* thinking. He wasn't much of a thinker. He was good with his hands, but he'd absorbed the legends about wild apes killing and eating people in the mountains, back in the days when the Simian Flu had thrown everyone into a panic. Apes had spread the disease to humans, sure. Fine. But shooting them wasn't going to make the flu any less contagious— and in any case, if Carver had been vulnerable to the flu, he wouldn't have lived long enough to be at that river and see those chimps in the first place.

Stupid.

Malcolm's truck bounced off the dirt road and onto the

highway, following it down out of the mountains toward the city.

"What do we tell Dreyfus?" he asked. "You think he'll believe us?"

"I'm not even sure *I'd* believe us," Ellie said. "Are we certain that wasn't some kind of weird echo?"

"I heard it," Alexander said. "The chimp talked."

14

Koba led Grey and Stone through the treetops, following the sound of the trucks. He didn't need to keep them in sight. He knew where they were going. Trucks couldn't go through the forest, so they had to be heading for the big road. If the apes got there first, they could see which way the trucks turned, and then they would know whether the humans had come from the city or somewhere else.

They reached the edge of the forest and listened. Koba stilled himself, learning everything he could about the humans by watching closely as the trucks rolled slowly down the last stretch of the dirt track. When they got to the edge of the road, they turned toward the city. Koba saw the humans' leader driving one truck, with his female and boy. In the other truck were four men. The one who had shot Ash was driving.

You, Koba thought. *You shot an ape, and you will die.*

He would not tell Caesar that he thought this. Caesar was powerful and a good leader, but he thought too much. Thinking weakened apes sometimes. Koba did not think. He planned.

They will have to use the bridge, he signed to Grey

and Stone. *We must get there first.*

As soon as the trucks were out of sight around a bend, the three apes dropped from the trees, ran across the road, and leaped into the forest canopy again, making a direct line for the orange bridge that glowed like fire every sunset. Koba's anger grew hotter as they got closer to the city. He had never wanted to return to it. It held for him only memories of bad smells, cages, and pain.

Koba, Grey, and Stone reached the orange bridge, and then swung along the underside until they reached the first pillar sunk into the water. They climbed up to the road level. The trucks were still coming down through the hills, slowed by damage to the road. Koba led the way up the pillar, climbing all the way to the top, where the thick cables rested in steel brackets. They found secure places to stay, on the side of the bridge away from the open ocean, and settled in to wait and watch.

The bridge was not completely broken, but pieces of its surface had fallen away. Wrecked and abandoned cars clogged the pathways, leaving only one open. Koba thought it seemed like humans must have cleared it. All those cars would not have died or crashed in every path but one. He decided to include this in his report to Caesar. It meant the humans had been organizing and working here for some time.

That meant there were many of them.

And *that* meant they were a threat to apes.

He looked toward the city. Below the other end of the bridge was a large ship, damaged and partly burned. Perhaps the humans had fought each other on that ship. It rested at anchor near a heavy stone building, four stories tall, a long rectangle that reached under the curved steel supports holding that end of the bridge up.

Beyond it, the city looked quiet. Koba could not see any more humans.

He heard the trucks approach, and shifted around to watch them. They drove slowly across the bridge, coming to a stop at the far end. Koba squinted. His eye was not good enough to see what they were doing. He poked Stone, who saw farther, and signed.

What are they doing?

More humans are meeting them, Stone signed. *Five. With more guns. They are talking.*

That made twelve humans. Ten men, one woman, one boy. If there was only one woman, they would not let her go into the mountains. She would be too precious. So there must be more women as well… and if there were more women, there would be more children.

They all have guns?

Stone nodded.

This was enough, thought Koba. He signed to Stone.

Look over the city. Tell me if you see smoke.

Stone shifted around on the pillar to get a better view. He gazed out. Koba looked in that direction, too, but all his eye saw were buildings. Tall buildings, short buildings, made of stone or glass or steel. Some looked unfinished. He wished he could kill the human who had blinded him.

He grunted at Stone.

Well?

Stone eased himself back around the pillar, hiding himself from the distant humans at the other end of the bridge.

Yes, he signed. *There is smoke.*

Koba nodded. He signaled to the other two.

Back under the bridge. We will see what makes this smoke, and how many humans there are.

They dropped down the pillar, using it as cover to avoid the gaze of any human who might look their way. Caesar would learn much when they returned to the village, Koba thought. The apes could no longer go on believing they were alone, and humans had already proved they would use their guns first, and talk later. There would be no lasting peace between human and ape.

All that remained was to plan for the war.

15

Malcolm eased up to the security checkpoint on the San Francisco side of the bridge, and saw Finney coming out to meet him. Right behind him came Dreyfus.

The man himself, Malcolm thought. *The whole colony must be on pins and needles waiting to see what we found up there.*

Boy, were they going to get more than they anticipated.

Watching Dreyfus approach, Malcolm pondered the irony—was it irony?—of bringing this kind of information to a checkpoint that had been built during the desperate days when the Simian Flu was killing a million people a day. It was almost as if he was bringing a new panic, and once again it was apes that would be infecting the human survivors. Only this time the contagion was fear.

If anyone could handle it, though, Dreyfus could. He'd been police chief, and then briefly mayor in the last moments before the Simian Flu had destroyed human civilization. As more and more people died, the survivors looked to whatever authority was still there—and Dreyfus had been up to the challenge. He'd held them together through the plague and its aftermath, and through the spasms of violence that had threatened to tear the survivors apart.

Along the way he had put a lot of people in the ground. Maybe too many. But the Colony, their settlement in what had once been San Francisco's downtown, was there because he had kept them together, and done what needed to be done.

Now he was expecting Malcolm's report on an old dam up the valley. Malcolm had news about the dam… and a whole lot more. He wasn't sure how to handle it.

As Dreyfus came around the front end of the truck, Malcolm rolled the window down.

"So? Did you find it?" Dreyfus asked.

"It's up there," Malcolm said. *So are a bunch of pissed-off apes*, he added mentally. "Right where the records said it was. The dam looks more or less intact. It could probably start generating power for us within a week… once we get a crew up there working on it."

"That's great," Dreyfus said. He broke into a broad grin, and Dreyfus wasn't a man who smiled that often. Then he caught something in Malcolm's demeanor. He leaned a little closer to the window.

"What? What's the matter?"

Malcolm cut his eyes at the sentries. Good people, but he didn't want to spread this revelation too far, too fast.

"I need to talk to you," he said.

Malcolm needed the group together to figure out how they were going to handle this situation. He left Foster to drive the second vehicle and the rest of the group jammed into his truck, along with Dreyfus. They drove along the Presidio Parkway and into the city as Malcolm filled Dreyfus in on what they had seen.

"It was right after we found the dam," he started. "We checked it over from the outside first, then went in and found a way to access the control room. There wasn't any damage, just ten years of rust. Assuming we can replace corroded wiring and run it from the generators at first, it ought to be functional. Most of the transmission wiring is intact, but until we try to get power throughput, we won't know if there are problems there. Oh, and we'll have to clear the logjam at the intake, but that's just labor. So yeah, I think—"

"You didn't bring me on your tour so you could give me a report I could have heard back at the Colony," Dreyfus said. "What are you avoiding?"

Malcolm slowed and navigated around a block of storefronts that had collapsed in the earthquake that had struck a couple of years after the plague. By then, too many people were dead for there to be any kind of restoration effort. They'd abandoned most of San Francisco, leaving it to fall into ruin, and that's exactly what had happened. Everything was overgrown, parks turned to pockets of wilderness and gardens spreading out to take over sidewalks and streets. It had happened with incredible speed, Malcolm thought. Without a million people making daily efforts to hold it back, nature took over.

"Apes," he said. "We saw apes."

He could feel Dreyfus's gaze as he skirted another spill of bricks and masonry that was blocking part of the intersection at Lombard and Van Ness. He turned south.

"Apes," Dreyfus repeated.

"On our way back after we inspected the dam. Carver went down to the river to fill his canteen, and two of them were there. He shot one of them."

Dreyfus looked back at Carver.

"Damn right I did," Carver said. "If either one of 'em

had taken another step, I'd've shot 'em both."

Malcolm was accustomed to Carver's coarse bravado. So, he saw, was Dreyfus, who looked at the man a moment longer before turning to face forward.

"Go on," he said. He was already thinking, planning.

"We heard the shot, and we came running," Malcolm said. "One of the chimps was trying to take care of the one Carver shot. Then…" He took a deep breath, and let it out. "Then a lot more of them showed up. All at once. They had weapons they'd made themselves. Spears, clubs…" Malcolm trailed off, remembering the sight.

Dreyfus let him think for a moment, then prompted him.

"How many were there?"

"I don't know," Malcolm said. "Eighty? Ninety?"

Dreyfus shifted in his seat to focus on Ellie.

"Is there a risk of contagion?"

She shook her head. "For one thing, we're all immune, or we wouldn't be here. For another, we're not sure the apes spread it."

"Sure," Kemp said. "It's a total coincidence that the flu hit right after all those apes broke out. And for all you know, we could be infected again right now. You weren't a doctor, you're a nurse."

Ellie bridled at the insult, but tried to keep her cool.

"I worked with the CDC," she reminded him. "Before… everything collapsed… we were isolating the disease vectors. The flu started in a lab, that much we know. But the lab was working with a number of strains of different microorganisms. One of them could well have started the flu."

"I don't want to argue about the flu," Dreyfus said. "Ellie, if you say we're immune, I believe it. Malcolm, finish the story. Tell me everything."

"Not much more to tell," Malcolm said. "The apes

showed up—mostly chimps, but there were some gorillas and orangutans, too. They looked at us. We looked at them. Then one of them, the leader, told us to get the hell out. They were... they were organized, Dreyfus. They looked to their leader, they took their cues from him, they..."

He stopped the truck so he could look at Dreyfus.

"They were intelligent," he said. "You could see it in their eyes."

Dreyfus stayed silent. Outside the truck, three coyotes loped across Van Ness in the direction of Lafayette Park. They had the run of the city now. There were mountain lions and bears in the Presidio. Only in the Colony did humans still hold sway... and Malcolm could almost read Dreyfus's mind.

If there are that many apes out there, how long will it be until they decide to finish what the plague started?

"Sorry, I don't know if you heard what he said," Carver said. "They spoke."

Dreyfus nodded. "Everyone, just, please... I'm trying to process this. Give me a second to process this." After a beat, as if thinking aloud, he said, "I thought they were all dead? There were air patrols, fire bombings..."

There had been. Large swaths of the forest at the edges of Muir Woods National Park had gone up in smoke. Malcolm didn't know the details, but patrols of armed mercenaries had gone after the apes, too—at least until the Simian Flu took priority. Dreyfus had been in charge. If he was confused, the apes' survival must have been incredibly unlikely.

The image of the apes strung along the ridgeline over the river came back to Malcolm. However unlikely it might seem, they were there.

"Fire bombings, huh?" Carver said. "Mission *not* accomplished."

In the truck behind them, Foster honked. Malcolm looked out the window and saw Foster waving him on. He was in a big hurry to get out of the abandoned city to the safety of the Colony. Malcolm put the truck in gear again. They couldn't just drive around the city forever.

"What are we going to do?" Ellie asked.

"I don't know," Dreyfus said. "We need that dam running. Without power... oh, crap."

They drove for a while in silence. Carver sulked and muttered back and forth with Kemp. Malcolm couldn't hear the conversation, but he knew the man well enough to figure that they were griping about the failure to exterminate the apes, ten years ago. In the rear-view mirror, Malcolm saw Alexander scoot away from Carver. The boy didn't like aggression, and it came off Carver in waves. Whatever happened, Malcolm thought, they would have to keep him away from the apes, or somebody would get killed.

"All right," Dreyfus said. "Let's not tell anybody about this. Not until we figure out what to do." Malcolm started to argue, but Dreyfus went on. "I don't want to create a panic. We're barely holding things together as it is."

He didn't like it, but Malcolm nodded. A few minutes later they arrived at the Colony.

16

The Colony was built into the lower levels of a skyscraper that had been in progress when the plague struck, and still stood unfinished, its upper floors a steel skeleton with cranes still braced against the clusters of girders that framed elevator shafts.

The lower twenty floors or so had flooring, and had been turned into housing for the few thousand people who, for all they knew, were the last surviving humans on earth. The bottom six floors occupied the entire block, and enclosed what had been envisioned as an upscale mall and luxury office complex.

Dreyfus had chosen the location carefully. The triple arch of the building's main gateway was easily defended, and other entrances had been blocked for years. At first they had built defenses against gangs and loose militias that had ravaged the city during the plague's first years. As time went on and more and more people died, however, many of those marauders "came in from the cold," as it were, joining what came to be called the Colony.

Now they all had to stick together.

Part of the mall was open to the air. Its roof had fallen in during the earthquake and they had never had the resources to spare for repairs.

An open area on the other side of the building had once offered parking and delivery space. The Colony's mechanics and engineers had taken it over, and their meager supplies of fuel were stored there. Long lines for fuel were a fact of life. There was very little of it, and as the years passed, they were able to find less and less in sealed tanks throughout the city. Much of what they *did* find went to power the generators that gave the interior of the Colony power for a few hours a day.

Inside the ground floor of the Colony, where there were supposed to be salons charging sixty bucks for a haircut next to boutique clothing stores and gelato stands, they had established a bazaar where time was the only currency, and barter was the general rule. Every morning, groups went out into the city, ranging as far as they could while making certain they could return to the Colony by nightfall. Occasionally Dreyfus authorized longer expeditions, but some of those didn't come back.

There were animals. There were accidents. What they *didn't* have, Malcolm thought, was enough people.

A broad outdoor staircase led from the entrance to street level. Barricades and sentry platforms lined it and covered two of the three openings. The third had a reinforced gate. It had been a while since they needed to hold the Colony against any violence, but Dreyfus insisted they maintain the defensive measures. He called it—to anyone within earshot—a "better-safe-than-sorry" approach to the security of the Colony.

"You never know what's coming," he told everyone. "We can't assume we're the only ones left, and we can't assume the next people we see will be friendly."

Assume nothing... but if you're going to assume something, assume the worst. That was Dreyfus.

They got out of the trucks and headed in. On the way, Malcolm dropped a hand on Alexander's shoulder.

"Hey," he said, noting his son's morose demeanor. "I'm sorry you lost your bag back there."

Alexander shrugged. That was his response to lots of things lately. Malcolm tried not to let it get to him. Fifteen was a tough age, even when you hadn't grown up during the collapse of human civilization.

"You okay?" Ellie asked on his other side.

Alexander nodded after a moment. Malcolm focused on that moment. His son wouldn't have given it to him. Ellie could get through to the boy, even though she wasn't his mother. She made no effort to replace Malcolm's mother. She was just there. She had made a point of being there until he trusted her. Also, she was a better listener than Malcolm, which meant she picked up on things he didn't.

Right now, however, he exchanged a look with her and saw that they were both thinking the same thing. Behind Alexander's hesitation was something that they all would have to talk about sooner rather than later. Call it fatherly instinct, call it something else, he knew something was on his son's mind... and he had a suspicion that it had to do with the apes.

Alexander seemed on the verge of opening up to Ellie, but he never got the chance because Foster jumped out of the second truck and came storming over to Malcolm.

"Hey, man, I just talked to Carver," he said. "We're not gonna tell anybody what happened up there?"

"Not yet," Malcolm said. "Dreyfus has a plan. We need

to stick to it. That's what's gotten us this far."

Foster shook his head. Malcolm could already see him lining up with Carver and Kemp, who would want to go right out and slaughter the apes. Malcolm had no problem with eliminating the apes, if they were going to be hostile—but that wasn't what had happened. If anything, Carver's itchy trigger finger had set things off. Maybe it was up to the humans to make sure tension didn't escalate.

"Foster," Malcolm said. "This isn't the time to go off half-cocked. We need the dam working. That's more important than anything else. Right?"

"Right," Foster said, but it took him longer than Malcolm would have liked. Then he walked off to rejoin Carver and Kemp.

"Is this going to be a problem?" Ellie asked as they watched him go.

"I hope not," Malcolm said.

"Maybe we should tell Dreyfus," she said.

"I think he already understands that he needs to keep an eye on Carver," Malcolm replied.

"Maybe, but you should tell him anyway," Ellie said.

Malcolm nodded. "I will. But let's get inside. Whatever happens, it isn't going to happen today."

17

From the highest floor of a building, across an open plaza from the human camp, Koba, Grey, and Stone watched the humans until the sun was level with the top of the bridge towers. During that time, Koba saw them recovering fuel for their trucks. He saw them making food, and trading cloth for pieces of machinery. He saw them argue, waving their arms and shouting.

It was remarkable, he thought, how much they looked like apes. Sometimes.

It looked to Koba as if they all lived inside the big building whose bones reached toward the sky. There were… he counted windows. If each was a room, the building could hold more humans than there were apes in their village.

They had machines that used gasoline to make electricity. Apes could make use of those. He saw trucks come and go. Stone followed one of them far enough to come back and tell Koba that it had gone to the boxy building by the bridge. Other humans were there. Stone did not know what they were doing.

It was time to return to Caesar, and tell him what they had seen.

And soon it would be time for war.

It was evening by the time they reached the village. Caesar and Maurice and Luca the gorilla—along with several other veterans who formed Caesar's council—stood and sat before the large stone wall inscribed with the laws. Koba joined the group, as was his right. He, too, had fought with Caesar from the beginning. Grey and Stone waited nearby, watching from the main body of apes. As he approached Caesar, Koba saw that they were looking at him.

The bag dropped by the young male human lay open on the ground, its contents scattered in front of the ape leader. Koba recognized some of the things he saw. There were thin books full of pictures, with few words. He could not remember the word for them. Maybe he had never known it. There were pencils in different colors. He had used pencils like that before, long ago, when he still trusted humans. They were used to draw.

The young human had made many pictures in another book. Maurice turned the pages, seeing drawing after drawing. He held the book so that the apes nearby could see the drawings.

Koba moved closer to get a look.

In one of the pictures, houses were burning. Human figures ran from the fire. Other humans with guns chased them. The boy had drawn much blood. In another, buildings fell and humans ran in the street. In another, humans hid behind a wall that had monstrous shapes lurking on the other side. In yet another, rows of dead humans lay in the street in front of a building with a large red plus sign. This made Koba remember when a human had taught him to count.

In another, a dead human woman lay with light shining

through a window, and onto her face. Around her stood other humans with masks over their faces.

The watching apes were jumpy, shoving and signing at each other in their nervousness. Koba had to remind himself that many of them had never seen a human... and all of them, including himself, had believed they were gone. The pictures told a story that none of them had heard before.

He saw now that the human survivors had suffered. And he knew that if they all felt the boy's fear, they would be dangerous.

Maurice was fascinated by the images. He turned through the pages several times. *The plague almost ended them,* he signed. *The boy told the story in pictures.*

Koba grunted to get their attention. Both Maurice and Caesar looked to him.

We must attack them now! he signed angrily. *Before they attack us!*

Maurice set the book down and signed back.

We don't know how many there are, he said. *How many guns they have.*

Luca, who spoke rarely, added another question.

Or why they came up here.

Questions, questions, Koba thought. He had answers, but not for all the apes—not yet. Caesar had to hear them first.

He tried to catch Caesar's eye, to let him know that they needed to talk, and alone. Before he could do so, however, Caesar picked up the book. Something stuck out between two of the pages. Caesar opened the book there and a picture fell out. It showed a woman and a small boy.

Koba guessed the story. The boy who had made the drawings had a picture of his mother. His mother had died of the sickness. On the page marked by the picture was a drawing of the same woman. Koba saw the resemblance between her and the dead woman on another one of the book's pages. The one who lay in the light.

His mother...

He looked back to Caesar, and saw that Caesar was staring at the drawing. He looked sad, as if the human's story meant something to him.

Enough of this, Koba thought. *Are we going to be sad for humans, who caged us and cut us and killed us?* Koba would not. He signed angrily.

Look what they did to Rocket's son! He turned to Rocket, who squatted at the edge of the council group. *Don't you want to fight?*

Now all eyes turned to Rocket, who shifted on his feet, as if he was considering how to reply. Koba saw his anger, and saw him contain it. He raised his hands, paused, and then signed.

I want what Caesar wants. A murmur swept through the assembled apes. Many of them signed their agreement.

No! Koba thought. *You have not seen them! Caesar has not seen them. We must act, or they will.* But he said none of this. It was not the time to challenge Caesar, and Koba did not want that challenge at all. What he wanted was for Caesar to see the truth. But instead of signing, he clenched his fists, and clamped his mouth shut instead of speaking.

Then Blue Eyes, standing at his father's side, stood and spoke out loud.

"Koba... right!"

Silence fell in the village. Caesar's own son, lining up against his father—and standing with Koba? They were stunned. Every ape assembled saw Caesar turn away from the book, saw the anger on his face.

Blue Eyes saw it too, but he did not stop.

Humans tried to kill Ash, he signed. *They*—

"Enough!" Caesar growled. Again silence fell. For a long

moment Blue Eyes held his father's gaze, stubborn and angry. Then he lowered his head and stopped signing. Koba, amazed at this show of rebellion, took a new view of the young one. He had a strength Koba had not seen before, together with anger toward his father. Koba would not rebel openly, but Blue Eyes had. It would not be the last time, Koba thought… and within him a small flame began to burn.

If Caesar could not control his own son, perhaps he was not fit to control the apes.

Just as quickly as he had the thought, Koba banished it. *Apes together strong.* He believed those words. Now, of all times, there could be no arguing. The human problem had to be solved first… and to do that, apes had to act together. Koba would not be the ape who broke them apart.

Caesar turned to look at the faces of his council, gathered around him. He signed carefully, slowly, making sure every ape in the village understood.

If we go to war, we could lose everything we've built. Our homes, our families… Our future.

He stood, looked from face to face, and Koba saw fear among the apes. They needed Caesar to lead them, and they would follow where he led. Still, they also needed a decision they could believe in.

I will let you know my decision, Caesar signed, and with that he walked away. Koba watched him go, and watched the other apes watching Caesar. They would not be able to wait for long. But they would have to wait at least a little time. Big decisions could not be made in a hurry. Koba understood this.

He also understood that Caesar did not yet know how great the human threat might be. He, Grey, and Stone had not yet had a chance to tell him. Now was the time, when the report would have the most effect on Caesar's decision. Koba believed in Caesar… but he also believed in himself.

Caesar had not suffered at human hands the way Koba had. He needed Koba with him constantly, to remind him that for every generous human, there were ten cruel ones. Or a hundred. A thousand.

He gave Caesar a moment to get clear of the gathering. Then he followed, slowly, thinking of what to say and the best way to say it.

Caesar had too much in his head. It was hard enough to think of humans, spreading from the city again, crossing paths with apes and bringing their guns and their science.

He walked alone up the path to the great tree where he and Cornelia made their home. He climbed into the lower branches, then swung himself higher, as if he would think more clearly the closer he got to the stars.

From below he heard his name. He looked down and saw Koba, who bowed and held his head low, peering up from below his brow. Caesar gestured for Koba to join him. He asked for no obeisance, but Koba's approach was humble, anyway. It was difficult, being leader of apes like Koba. Caesar knew he hated humans, and knew that he would resist any effort to live with them—or even *near* them. He had good reasons. Humans had taken his eye, and crushed out of him any belief in kindness.

But Koba's experience was not the only experience. Apes could not be driven by hate and fear. Whatever else the humans had done, they had also given apes the gift of intelligence. They might be enemies, they might be friends, and they might choose to live separately from apes. The world was large.

But those decisions could not yet be made, and while they were being considered, Caesar had to lead. He could not be seen as weak.

Koba settled next to him, high in the tree. They both looked in the direction of the city, now vanished with the fall of night.

Blue Eyes is struggling, Koba signed. *It is hard on him to be in your shadow.*

It is natural, Caesar signed. *He likes you, Koba, because you want to act. He is young and angry, so he also wants to act.*

Maybe he is right, Koba signed. Caesar gave him a hard glance, and he added, *I do not challenge you, Caesar. But let me tell you what we saw today.*

Caesar nodded for him to go on.

We followed the trucks to the city, Koba signed. *Other humans met them there. We followed them to see where they would go, and see how many of them there are.* He hesitated, and then continued. *There was war in the city. Parts of it burned. Many buildings have fallen from the…* He did not know the word for what he wanted to say, so he held out both hands and shook them.

Earthquake, Caesar signed.

Koba nodded. *Earthquake. But they fought each other. The humans who still live built a wall around their village. Grey and Stone and I watched them, tried to count them.*

How many? Caesar asked.

Hundreds.

Caesar considered this. *More than us?* he signed.

Maybe.

Do they have many guns?

We saw humans with guns, but not that many. They have more trucks. They go through the city looking for things to use. They are… again Koba paused. *They are like us. They survive, and they are growing. There were children.*

The forest is large and the city is far away, Caesar signed.

Not that far. They found us. They will find us again.

We must discover what they were doing here, Caesar signed.

How? Should we go and ask them, so they can shoot us? Koba started to become angry. Caesar knew what he was thinking—to Koba, thinking often seemed weak. Caesar knew he had to be careful. He and Koba were brothers. They had fought together, they had built this ape village together, they had saved each other's lives... but Caesar led the apes. He did not want to provoke a challenge, but he also could not tolerate Koba—or, for that matter, Blue Eyes—turning other apes against Caesar's leadership.

Koba gathered himself and signed again.

For years I was their prisoner. They cut me. Tortured me... Koba looked Caesar in the eye. *You freed me. I would do anything you ask.*

Caesar nodded. He grasped his friend's shoulder.

We would not have survived without you, Koba.

But we cannot forget what they are, Koba added. *We must show strength.*

Caesar considered this. How did they show strength without starting a war they might not survive? The ape village was healthy and growing. In ten years, they had learned where to find food, how to prepare for the winters, how to keep themselves safe from the animals that hunted them, mountain lions and wolves and bears... but they lived on a thin edge. Winters were still times of hunger, especially hard on the orangutans, who needed fruit that did not grow in the winter and had to be dried. They were still learning to grow food themselves, and keeping the orangutans alive meant long trips on horseback down into the warmer valleys, where fruit trees grew wild.

Then he stopped himself. He was becoming distracted. The problem before him—right now—was what to do about the humans. And Koba was partly right. They needed to show the humans strength, but they needed to do it without provoking the humans into a fight.

We will, my friend, Caesar signed. *We will show the humans our strength. Here is how.*

18

Finney was dreaming. In his dream he was at the movies, watching spaceships dart through a field of asteroids, shooting lasers at each other. Then he was on one of the ships, shouting commands and wisecracks at his crew. Then he was riding his motorcycle up in Napa, a woman's arms around his waist and big plans for later that night.

Living in California, his dreaming self thought. *Can't beat it.* Then he and his girlfriend were at a steakhouse down on the waterfront, spending money they didn't have and enjoying the recklessness. The steak was perfect, hot all the way through but still a little bloody in the middle. She'd even talked him into drinking wine instead of beer. Then they were riding again, but this time horses, on a ranch up in the wine country, headed for a lodge where they would spend the night with nothing for company but a roaring fire and another bottle of wine.

Horses.

Finney had never ridden a horse in his life. That thought intruded on his dream and he started to drift toward wakefulness, reconnecting with the real world even as he clutched at the beautiful vanished world of his dream.

Clip clop clip clop. The sound of horses' hooves on pavement stirred him all the way awake. It was dawn. He was at the checkpoint at the south end of the Golden Gate Bridge. He hadn't had a good steak in ten years, and the girl in his dream was dead, like all his other girlfriends, none of whom had survived the Simian Flu. All of that fell into his awakening consciousness as Finney registered the heavy fog that obscured most of the bridge. The horse sounds were coming from that direction, or that's what it sounded like. The fog made it hard to tell.

He leaned closer to the window of the guardhouse. Was there something out there?

"Damn," he said softly as a chimp on horseback rode out of the fog.

Was he still dreaming? What kind of chimp knew how to ride a horse? Hell, where had the chimp come from? They'd all been killed right at the beginning of the Simian Flu outbreak. He'd seen it on TV, walls of fire scouring the forest where they'd run to hide after breaking out of their lab. Finney hadn't thought about that in years. He'd been too busy surviving the flu, the gangs, all the other hellish times that had killed just about everyone he knew before Dreyfus got them all together and kept them alive.

He grabbed his gun. Its stock was cold. Now he was all the way awake. He stepped out of the guardhouse and raised the gun. Nobody was supposed to go through the checkpoint without Dreyfus's okay. Especially not chimpanzees on horses.

Then a second ape appeared.

Then a third.

Then a dozen more, all on horses, and around them God only knew how many walking and jumping.

Finney turned and ran. His motorcycle—not the sweet tricked-out Harley Electra-Glide from his dream, but a battered Honda dirt bike he wouldn't have given a second look back in the pre-flu world—was just behind the guardhouse. If he could get on it and get it started before the apes knew what he was doing...

As fast as he'd started running, Finney skidded to a halt. There was his bike, all right, but it wasn't parked. It was in the air, held six feet off the ground by a *gorilla*. The gorilla threw the bike off the bridge. Almost immediately it was swallowed up by the fog, then there was the splash.

The gorilla dropped back to all fours and growled at him. Finney froze. It could have stomped right into the shack and torn him apart while he was sleeping. But it hadn't. It had gone right to his bike and gotten rid of it. Finney wasn't a genius, but neither was he stupid. He put two and two together and came to the inescapable conclusion that the gorilla was trying to stop him from getting away—without killing him.

Right on the heels of that thought came another. If they'd wanted to stop him, the apes didn't want anyone at the Colony to know they were there. That meant they knew about the Colony. They must have been watching—

Chimps on horseback rode past Finney. One of them, a mean-looking sucker with one eye, glared at him in passing. Finney looked down at the ground. He dropped his gun. He closed his eyes for good measure. Apes ran past him, softly grunting and hooting to each other as they went. He heard them in the bridge cables, too, hundreds of them, it sounded like. But no way was he going to look.

If they wanted to get into San Francisco, Finney wasn't going to stop them... and he damn sure wasn't going to die for no reason. He kept his head down and his eyes closed as the apes went by, and all the while he tried to wrap his head around what he'd seen.

They planned this out. It couldn't be true, but it was.

When the noise died down, he opened his eyes again and looked around. The bridge was quiet again, the fog as thick as before, blanketing the city. The apes could be anywhere.

Finney started walking. Whatever the apes were going to do, he didn't want to be alone when they were on their way back. And now that they were gone, some of the paralyzing fear left him. Maybe they didn't know exactly where the Colony was. Maybe all of his suppositions were wrong. Maybe the gorilla had thrown his bike off the bridge just... well, it *was* a gorilla. Who knew why they did anything?

He walked fast, then broke into a run, heading across the bridge approach and along the road toward downtown. Maybe he could get to the Colony before the apes did. Even if not, he sure as hell didn't want to be alone right now.

19

Caesar led the apes through the park called the Presidio, now its own forest within the city. They emerged in an area he remembered. Will had lived near here somewhere... he looked up and down the streets, trying to locate himself. The earthquake had torn this part of the city into pieces. The streets were cracked and split, with rusting cars lying at angles in the wider holes. Houses had fallen into the earth, and fires had burned block after block down to the foundations. A few chimneys, wrapped in vines, still stood. Other parts of the area—Pacific Heights, Will had called it—were not as damaged, but even there, windows were broken and roofs caved in. Some houses were untouched except by the years of emptiness.

They kept going, toward the tall buildings of downtown. Caesar sent scouts up to rooftops, including Grey and Stone, who had been this way before. He made sure they reported back to him, rather than Koba. When they reached the humans, every ape needed to know who spoke for them. If they did not speak strongly and together, the humans would know this. And if the humans thought the apes could not control themselves, a war would come.

From the tops of buildings, the scouts had a view over the hills that lay between the troop and downtown, yet they reported seeing no humans. The fog here in the city was not as thick as it was out on the water, and they could see that some of the tall buildings had fallen. Others still stood, but were partly broken—their lower floors overgrown. If there were humans, there could not be many, Caesar thought as he digested each new piece of information. They would have brought order. There would be cars. But they did not see any cars, or hear any.

They did see a tunnel leading under the hills. Caesar led the apes to it, and then into it. He signaled for them to stay quiet, and as they moved through the darkness the only sounds were the horses' hooves and the soft scrape and shuffle of a thousand feet, moving together. In the darkness they wove among abandoned cars, some damaged, some with barely visible bones lying across their seats. Soon they were through, standing again in the soft early morning light. Caesar paused at the mouth of the tunnel. They were deep in the city now, and much closer to where Koba had reported the human settlement to be.

He looked out at an open area surrounded by buildings. It, like everything else, was overgrown by young trees and clusters of weeds, with ivy and other vines tangled over everything. He saw the movement of small animals— squirrels, rabbits, and raccoons. The trees were thick with birds. There was no sign of living humans.

There was ample sign of the dead, however. Most of the open space was closed off behind a fence, with signs hung on its wire. Caesar read them.

FEDERAL EMERGENCY MANAGEMENT AUTHORITY
QUARANTINE AREA. NO ENTRY.
UNAUTHORIZED PERSONS PROHIBITED.

Bullet holes punched through the signs and pockmarked the nearby buildings, where other signs read CURFEW LIMITS STRICTLY ENFORCED. The gate was open, but inside the fence were only bones and the shredded remains of what must have been tents. Caesar counted skulls, and stopped when he realized that to count them all would take too long.

Other signs on the fence, pieces of paper in plastic covers, showed smiling pictures with words below them— MISSING PLEASE HELP—over and over, with name after name. Bits of paper, pulped by ten years of rain, still clung to the wire around them. On the buildings, more signs were plastered on the few unbroken windows and doors.

Many of the buildings had burned.

The fence line had once extended into the tunnel, Caesar saw. Now the poles were fallen down and the wire trampled mostly flat, but he knew there would be more bones back in the dark parts of the tunnel. San Francisco was full of bones now, many more bones than people.

Caesar gestured, and the apes moved out, skirting the fence. He saw messages painted on walls: MONKEYPOCALYPSE and THIS IS THE END and MOTHER EARTH FIGHTS BACK and 7 BILLION AND COUNTING. There were pictures here, as well, on long stretches of wall without windows. Even as they died, the humans made pictures. Apes dancing along the lit fuse of a bomb. Ape heads on the bodies of monsters. Burning buildings, skulls and bones, clenched fists, strings of letters that made no words Caesar knew...

One of them he did remember. ALZ113. He remembered Will saying it, but not what it meant.

He lingered over one long wall, painted from side to side with a series of images.

Koba saw it, too. He caught Caesar's eye and Caesar

was certain he knew what he was thinking. *You see? This is what humans will do to us if we give them the chance.*

Caesar nodded without speaking. They would not give humans that chance. But neither would they seek a war, if it could be avoided.

He motioned the apes forward. It would be best if they reached the human settlement before all the humans were awake.

20

Malcolm snapped awake at the sound of pounding on his bedroom door.

"Dad! Dad!" Alexander was shouting from the other side. Ellie scrambled out of bed and started getting dressed. Malcolm did the same, pulling on yesterday's pants and hurrying to the door. "Alexander, what is it?" he said as he opened it.

Alexander looked scared.

"There's something going on," he said.

"What do you mean, something going on?"

"Dad, if I knew more I'd tell you—come on." Alexander looked ready to run out the door. Malcolm could hear the sounds of a crowd gathering in the market.

"All right, give me a second," he said, irritated at being rushed right out of bed. He turned back into the bedroom to grab a shirt, and without thinking opened the door, presenting Alexander with a view of Ellie just putting on her shirt. She shot him a glare, then looked awkwardly at Alexander.

"Hey," she said.

"Hey," he answered, just as awkwardly.

Malcolm grabbed his own shirt on and headed past them.

"Come on, then, let's go," he said. It was getting louder outside.

"Smooth," Ellie muttered to him as he passed. There was nothing Malcolm could say that wouldn't either make the situation worse or delay them getting out the door, or both, so he didn't say anything. As he passed through the kitchen, he heard the rising whine of the Colony's air-raid siren.

Uh oh, he thought. *Ellie's pissed, Alexander's embarrassed, and the whole Colony's been put on alert. This is a hell of a way to start the day.*

By the time they got out into the plaza, just inside the Colony gate, they were fighting through a crowd the likes of which Malcolm hadn't seen since the early months of the Simian Flu, when San Francisco had seemed like one great panicked mob surging from hospitals to police stations to grocery stores... Eventually that mob had turned on itself, and the city had burned for more than a year, until there were no longer enough people to carry on the looting and violence.

Now the survivors jammed their way through the gates, some with guns, trying to shout at each other over the sound of the air-raid siren. Malcolm looked up onto the platform built above the arched entrance, where a sentry named Leonel was cranking away at the siren while looking back and forth from the crowd to something outside. He was clearly terrified.

Where was Dreyfus? Malcolm pushed forward, trying to get to the scaffolding that led up to the platform. Then he caught sight of Dreyfus, reaching the platform and pushing through to stare out into the city.

The look on his face was one of… fear?

Malcolm got to the stairs. Dreyfus had left guards to stop the crush of people from flooding up, but the first man recognized Malcolm and let him through.

"Stay together!" he called to Ellie and Alexander as he climbed up.

It was crowded on the platform, but nothing like down below. More and more people were screaming questions up at Dreyfus, demanding to know what was going on. *Good question,* thought Malcolm. *I'd like to know myself.* He got next to Dreyfus and looked out into the street beyond.

What he saw stunned him absolutely.

"Oh my God," he said.

Dreyfus signaled the sentry to stop cranking the siren, and it cut off abruptly. But it was far from silent—the crowd was in full voice, hundreds of people calling out questions and demands.

Malcolm looked back to the street outside, where hundreds and hundreds of apes stood in perfect silence, massed along the entire block facing the Colony gate. In the center were several dozen on horseback, with the leader right up front. Gorillas loomed, flanking the horses, with chimpanzees ranked beside and behind them. All of them were armed. A forest of spears stood upright, and those without spears held clubs and stone axes. Malcolm also saw the gleam of steel. The humans weren't the only ones who had scavenged the ruins for weapons.

"This is a hell of a lot more than eighty," Dreyfus said. Malcolm nodded. What he had seen on the ridgeline up in the mountains was a hunting party. This was an army.

It was an impossible sight. How had this many apes stayed completely out of sight of humans? More importantly, how had this many apes come into the city and planted themselves at the Colony's front gate without anyone knowing? Malcolm had a bad feeling about whoever had been standing guard at the bridge.

He fought down an urge to panic. If the apes had come to kill them, they would already be fighting... or so he hoped. The truth was, he was still thinking of them as apes, when they clearly were more. Rumors had flown in the months after the outbreak of Simian Flu— conspiracy theories about top-secret military projects to create ape super soldiers, and other ridiculous fever dreams. Some of the scientists from a biotech lab where apes had broken free hinted at experiments to increase their intelligence.

But Malcolm hadn't believed any of it. That was the stuff of pulp science fiction, not reality. He'd always figured that some enterprising microorganism had made the jump from ape to human, and biological incompatibility had done the rest. But now he had to face facts. He'd heard two of the apes speak. He'd seen them organize themselves. Now he was looking at an ape army.

And unless he was mistaken, they hadn't come for battle. From the look of things, they wanted to parley.

"I'm going to talk to him," Malcolm said.

"Him?" Dreyfus said. "Who's him?"

Malcolm pointed at the chimp on horseback, front and center.

"See the one with the red on his face? That's the one who spoke before."

"Spoke, like said words out loud," Dreyfus said.

"That's what I told you before," Malcolm said.

"I know you did, but I didn't believe it."

"You believe it now?"

Dreyfus, still looking out at the ape army, replied, "I don't know what the hell to believe. You want to talk to him? You sure?"

"I have a feeling that's why they're here," Malcolm said.

Behind them, one of the sentries said, "I got a feeling they're here to kill us."

"If that's what they wanted, you'd already have a spear in your gut," Malcolm said. "Look at them. You think they couldn't get in if they wanted to?"

The sentry didn't answer.

Dreyfus leaned in close to Malcolm.

"You think you can talk to them, go ahead," he said. "I'll even come with you. But they make one move, and we're going to protect ourselves."

Malcolm looked the chimp leader in the eye. He was met with a steady gaze.

"Don't be in a rush to start a war," he said to Dreyfus, quietly. "Let's see what they have to say."

21

The Colony gate made an ear-splitting metallic screech as they swung it open. WD-40 was hard to come by these days. Malcolm took a step through the entryway, keenly aware that what he did in the next moments could make the difference between a conversation and a bloodbath.

He walked forward with Dreyfus right behind him, and a dozen armed men with Dreyfus. The crowd massed in the doorway and on the parapets built above the arches, hundreds of people taking in the sight and telling those behind them what they saw. Malcolm heard people swearing, some angry shouts, isolated crying from children who had grown up hearing stories of the simian flu. Apes were their boogeymen, the monstrous villains of stories told to keep them from ranging too far into the city when the Colony gates were open.

The ape army was a terrifying sight, even from the relative safety of the parapet. On the ground, out in the open, it was overwhelming. The sound of maybe a thousand apes shifting their weight, softly grunting to one another, was like nothing Malcolm had ever heard before, or imagined hearing. The thick smell of them hung in the morning air.

Malcolm took ten steps out from under the arch and stopped, waiting to see what the apes would do. After surveying their lines, he kept his eyes on the leader, who made a sign to the apes on either side of him. One of them, Malcolm saw, was the other chimp who had spoken up in the mountains. The angry, scarred one missing an eye. The leader tapped his horse's flanks and rode forward, followed by three others. One was an orangutan.

The watching crowd fell dead silent.

The leader stopped halfway between the ape lines and the small group of humans. He looked at each of them in turn, lingering on the armed men behind Malcolm and Dreyfus. There was no trace of fear on his face. The one-eyed ape at his flank gripped his spear and glared pure hate. Malcolm felt Dreyfus shift next to him. He looked over and saw Dreyfus drop a hand to the gun holstered at his belt.

Malcolm shook his head.

He looked back at the apes and saw the leader staring at him. *Okay,* he thought. *I get it. You came this far, now it's my turn.*

He started walking toward the apes.

"Malcolm," Dreyfus said. Malcolm ignored him, keeping his eyes on the leader. He stopped in front of the small group, just out of range of a spear thrust, or so he hoped. Then he waited.

The leader regarded him for a long moment. Then he spoke, slowly.

"Apes… do not… want war."

Reaction swept through the human crowd, disbelieving gasps at hearing a chimpanzee speak. The chimp looked up at the crowd, observing the reaction—and, Malcolm thought, enjoying it a little. What should he say in return? *Neither do we? Then why did a thousand of you show up with spears?*

The chimp saved him the trouble of a response by speaking again.

"But we will fight," he said. "If we must."

Malcolm did not like this turn in the conversation at all. He wanted to run, to gather up Alexander and Ellie and make a break for it, south all the way to Santa Cruz, or hell, San Diego. But he stood his ground. If the apes were there for a show of strength, humans needed to return that show.

The chimp glanced back and from within his ranks, another chimp appeared. As he came out into the open, he raised one arm, showing the assembled humans Alexander's satchel. Malcolm couldn't believe it. The apes had mustered an army and marched down the mountains and through the city, to give them back a bag Alexander had dropped? This was a more sophisticated gambit than Malcolm would have believed them capable of planning, even knowing what he knew from seeing them yesterday and this morning. They had combined a ferocious show of strength with a good-will gesture, exactly the way a head of state would do when initiating diplomacy with a rival.

Malcolm realized he wasn't looking at just a general, or even a king. This ape was a statesman.

It boggled the mind.

He stepped forward and reached out to accept Alexander's satchel from the chimp. Was it the same one who…? He saw the wound on its shoulder and was stunned all over again. Not only had the ape leader brought the satchel back, he had deputized the wounded ape to make the gesture. This demonstrated a grasp of symbolic nuance that Malcolm wouldn't have believed, if he hadn't been right there to witness it.

When the bag was in Malcolm's hands, the young chimp turned and rejoined the ranks. Malcolm followed its progress for a moment, and then looked back at the leader. He nodded his thanks.

The chimp, holding Malcolm's gaze, pointed at the Colony.

"Human home!" he said, loud enough for everyone to hear. Then he pointed in the other direction, arm lifted at an angle to indicate that he meant the distant hills and mountains beyond the bay. "Ape home," he said.

He dropped his arm and said, more quietly but still loud enough for Dreyfus and the nearer humans to hear, "Do not come back."

Malcolm said nothing. A moment passed and then the chimp signaled to his army. Slowly and purposefully they began to retreat, first the infantry—that was the only word that fit, even though Malcolm was astonished to find himself applying it—then those mounted on horses. He stood and watched them go. The leader did not look back.

The grizzled, one-eyed ape did, though. Malcolm saw him, looking long and hard at the guns in the humans' hands. On his face was an unsettling combination of hatred and desire.

I hope you keep a handle on that one, Malcolm thought. *He wants trouble.*

He stepped backward, watching the apes until they were gone and he was back in the company of humans again.

22

Maurice and Caesar rode together back through the city, returning along a different route than the one they had used to approach. Caesar had no desire to see the fence and bones again. Nor did he wish to view the image of hate on the building near the mouth of the tunnel. Everything he had seen worried him. He thought of the ape village and the human settlement. The apes seemed more settled, happier. Every moment he had spent in the presence of the humans stank of fear.

It was natural for them to be afraid, he thought. So few of them were left compared to before the sickness. But natural or not, their fear was a danger to apes.

Caesar thought about what he and his troop had done. He wondered whether it would be enough.

Maurice, next to him, hooted—a soft questioning sound. Caesar looked at him, and then glanced over his shoulder. Koba was riding a short distance behind with Grey and Stone. Caesar signaled to Maurice, making sure Koba could not see.

They are desperate, he said. *This may not be the last we see of them. We must prepare.*

Maurice nodded solemnly. *But for what?*

That was the problem. Caesar did not know.

Koba watched Caesar and Maurice, and knew they were signing. He also thought he knew what they were saying. Caesar had done exactly what he had wanted to do, just as he had told Koba the night before. *We will go to them in strength,* Caesar had said. *And while we are strong, we will give them a gift.*

A gift? Koba had said. *We pay* tribute *to humans?* His outrage had nearly made him say something unforgivable.

No. Not tribute, Caesar responded. *We give them a gift that means much to them, but costs us nothing. From this they will know that we understand them and that we do not wish for war. But showing them our strength will let them know that we also do not fear them. We will meet as equals.*

But we are not equals, Koba had protested. *The humans scavenge the ruins of their city. They are rats. We are* apes.

Whether we believe we are equals or not, Caesar had signed, *we will tell them that. If we appear weak, they will try to kill us because they think they can. If we appear strong and wanting a fight, they will fight because they think they have no other choice. If we meet them face-to-face, strength-to-strength, they will respect us.*

Koba had considered this then, and thought it might work. But he was disappointed. What he had wanted was a reason to kill every human that survived. Caesar would not give him that reason. He had left angry, though he had not told Caesar that. Now, this morning, he was riding angry because he had hoped to make a show of strength involving human blood, instead of hard looks and gift-giving.

Caesar led the apes, but he did not have the only good ideas. Koba watched him and Maurice. The orangutan was very smart, but lacked the stomach to fight. Maybe that was because he ate only fruit. Whatever the reason, he always counseled patience, patience, patience. Koba believed there was a time for patience... but he also knew that one of the times patience was most important was during a hunt, when the hunter had to wait for the prey to make a mistake.

The humans would make a mistake, he thought. He had seen their fear and their hate, just as they had seen his. They would strike at the apes, Koba was sure of it. When that happened, the apes would strike back. He would make sure of that.

23

The noise inside the Colony at dawn had been nothing compared to the din now. Every single citizen, every surviving human being in San Francisco who was able to walk, was crushed into the space just inside of the gate.

There was an almost palpable air of panic. Knots of people shoved and grappled to get closer to Dreyfus, shouting their questions and venting their terror. Dreyfus himself stood with his back to the gate, holding a battered police megaphone to his mouth and raising his other arm in an effort to calm people down. Malcolm watched from the edge of the crowd, with Alexander and Ellie right with him. Alexander clutched his satchel. Both of them looked scared, and they had every right to be. This crowd was a bomb, and the appearance of the ape army had lit its fuse.

From the barrage of questions, a few were repeated enough that Dreyfus made an attempt to answer them first.

"We're all immune!" he shouted through the megaphone. "We're all immune or we wouldn't be here!" He cut his eyes at Ellie as he said this, and Ellie in turn looked to Malcolm. She had said this to Dreyfus the day before, and if it turned out not to be true… well, that didn't bear thinking about.

"Now please, try to—*try to calm down*," Dreyfus said. From somewhere in the crowd a man shouted.

"How did they find us?" Several other voices took up the question. Dreyfus waved the megaphone, trying to settle them enough that they would be able to hear his response. There was a brief pause, or at least a slight lessening of the general pandemonium.

"We, uh… we found them," Dreyfus said. "Just yesterday. There was—"

He didn't get a chance to go on. The crowd exploded. From the uproar came a dozen variations on a single question, given full voice by another man, right in the front. He shoved forward, until he was up against the cordon of Dreyfus's unofficial police guard.

"You *knew* they were out there, and you didn't tell us?" he shouted at the top of his lungs.

Malcolm gathered Ellie and Alexander closer to him, trying to protect them from the sudden surge and crush of the crowd as people jammed forward, their furious panic abruptly redirected from the apes to Dreyfus's failure. Dreyfus's guards held their rifles across their bodies and forced the crowd back, but the circle of space around the Colony's leader was getting smaller by the moment.

This is going to turn violent, Malcolm thought. *Any second now.*

Dreyfus seemed to be thinking the same thing. His voice pitched higher as he shouted into the megaphone.

"I was only waiting to—"

"What if they come back?" a woman shouted between two of his guards. They shoved her back, but the crowd was on the verge of clawing its way through the cordon. Malcolm started to look around for the best way to get the hell out of there if the situation really spiraled out of control.

Dreyfus climbed part of the way up the scaffolding

that supported the parapet. He waved for silence, but the crowd's panic was a feedback loop. They were almost beyond any one person's ability to keep them from rioting.

"If they come back," he began, and realized not enough of them could hear him. Malcolm saw him frightened—maybe for the first time ever—and he began again, louder this time. "*If they come back, they're gonna be sorry they ever did!*"

This got the crowd's attention. They wanted a rallying point. They needed someone to focus their attention and their emotions, to give them a place to displace their anxiety about this new... threat?

Were the apes a threat?

Malcolm wasn't sure.

The crowd settled down somewhat. They were still rowdy, still shouting, but Dreyfus saw that he had a chance to make a point.

"We may not have the manpower this city once did, but we have the firepower. Those stockpiles left behind by FEMA, the National Guard, we have it all." He let that sink in, gauging the reaction of the crowd. They continued to be restive, still on edge, but for the moment most of them were listening.

"Look, I know why you're scared," Dreyfus continued. "I'm scared, too, believe me. But I recognize the trust you all placed in me, I do. We've been through hell together. When we settled here, it was because we'd had enough of living in fear, living like animals. We spent four years fighting that virus, then another four fighting each other after the city came apart.

"It was chaos—worse than anything I'd seen in all my years on the force, and I want you to know, there's not a day that goes by when I don't think about that. It wasn't until we came here—and started working together—that we finally started to live again, like human beings. And I would never do anything to jeopardize that, I promise you."

Malcolm could only admire the skill Dreyfus was demonstrating. He'd taken a sliver of a chance to turn back the tide of panic, and now he was already rallying everyone together by recalling their common experience. A master of his craft, the man looked from face to face in the crowd, making eye contact with the people who moments before had been ready to lynch him.

His tone changed a little, now that he'd brought them back from the brink.

"But you all know what we're up against. We're almost out of fuel. Which means no more power—which means we could slip back to the way things were. That dam up there was the answer. We just had no idea... they were up there, too."

"So what do we do now?" someone cried. It was the same woman who had asked what they would do if the apes returned. Dreyfus had turned her attention toward the future, toward action rather than reaction.

Malcolm had always taken Dreyfus's leadership for granted. The survivors of the flu had fallen into place around him because he had been the police chief, and then the mayor as the entire world sneezed blood and died. But now Malcolm saw that there was a reason for that. Whatever intangible characteristic it was that defined a leader, Dreyfus had it.

Maybe Malcolm had a little of it, too. He wondered about that. At least the ape chief seemed to think so.

"We will find another way," Dreyfus said. "You all know Malcolm," he added, pointing him out. Heads turned to look. "He's not just a brilliant architect, he cares about the future of this community as much as I do. And I've already spoken to him about finding an alternative power source."

Just like that, Malcolm's opinion changed. He kept looking at Dreyfus, not trusting himself to stay impassive—much less hopeful—if he had to interact with the crowd at that moment.

Because there was no alternative power source. Dreyfus had suddenly gone all politician on the crowd, and on Malcolm in particular, waving a sign of hope that only Malcolm knew to be false. If they didn't get the dam running, there would *be* no power, except what they could keep squeezing out of the generators. That would only last as long as they could keep finding drips and trickles of fuel, which were growing scarcer and scarcer.

That son of a bitch, Malcolm thought. What Dreyfus had done, more or less, was take the bull's-eye off his own back and put it on Malcolm's. It was one thing to lie in a political speech, but it was another entirely to tell a bald-faced lie in a life-or-death situation.

Especially when it was Malcolm's death they were talking about. If they couldn't get the dam operational and there was no other power option, the Colony would blame him. It wasn't just possible, but *probable* that someone in the Colony would be so desperate and angry about the failure of the power project, that he would put a bullet or a knife in the person he blamed for it.

The crowd now focused on him. First Dreyfus had shifted their attention away from the apes. Then he'd shifted it away from himself. Dreyfus had made Malcolm the fulcrum of their hopes. And now he swung into full-on rallying mode.

"Because power isn't just about keeping the lights on. It's about giving us the tools to reconnect to the rest of the world. To find out who else is out there, so we can start to rebuild—and reclaim—the world we lost." He paused for a professional beat, bringing the crowd back to him. "We *will* get there. You have my solemn promise."

By which, Malcolm thought, he meant they had Malcolm's promise.

Dreyfus wrapped up his speech by exhorting the assembled citizens of the Colony to return to their necessary business. They still had machines to repair, fuel to find, food to cook, children to raise.

"This is our home," he said. "Nothing will take it from us, and nothing will stop us from rebuilding our civilization and reclaiming what was once ours. Now let's get to it."

The crowd started to break up, encouraged by Dreyfus's guards spreading out and moving them along. Malcolm, Ellie, and Alexander stayed where they were, near the base of the stairs leading to the top of the parapet. A few people looked their way, but none approached them.

"That was quite a performance," Ellie said.

"Yeah," Malcolm said, watching the passers-by and keeping his voice low. "It sure was." Then he looked straight at her. "I'll catch up with you in a bit. Right now I have to find out what the hell he thinks he's talking about."

24

He caught up with Dreyfus as the crowd dispersed, waiting while he had exchanged a quiet word with one of his lieutenants. Then Malcolm approached him and spoke, trying not to sound angry.

"There is no alternative power source," he said, keeping his voice low. "That dam's our only option."

"Fine," Dreyfus said. "Then we'll do what we have to do." He started walking, and Malcolm went with him under the parapet and through a hall that led to his office. Maps of San Francisco covered the walls, each heavily annotated with information about earthquake damage, the location of resources that might not yet have been recovered, previous sites of fighting with long-gone gangs. Other maps of the Bay Area highlighted places they were planning to search. There were farms to explore so they could perhaps start growing more food, marinas to search for fishing boats that might still float… even other dams to assess, in an effort to get the lights back on.

As Dreyfus's security entourage began to leave, Malcolm lingered over the circled spot on the map marking the dam he and his team had seen the day before.

He mentally added a note: *Here be apes.*

"What does that mean, 'we'll do what we have to do'?" he asked when they were alone.

"I meant what I said back there." Dreyfus looked at the regional map and put a finger right on the spot Malcolm had pegged as the apes' location. "If we have to fight them, we fight them."

"You can't be serious," Malcolm said. "Did you see them? That's an army. They showed up to let us *know* they have an army. We can't fight them. You think we can just hand out a bunch of guns and go after them? We'll be massacred."

Dreyfus turned away from the map and pointed back in the direction of the Colony plaza.

"You see what's going on here," he said. "These people are going to turn on each other. On me!" He brought himself up short. "But this isn't about me. That power is everything. I'm not giving up on this."

"Neither am I," Malcolm said. "But you know you just put a big target on my back, right?"

"I had to do something," Dreyfus replied. "You saw that crowd. They were this far from turning into a mob." He held up one hand, thumb and forefinger an inch apart.

"So you pointed them at me instead of you. Thanks."

Dreyfus sat and rubbed the bridge of his nose, closing his eyes and sinking into his chair.

"Listen," he said after a moment. "You can hate me for it if you want. But if the power doesn't come back on around here, the next thing that's going to happen is these people are going to turn on each other. I'm trying to keep that possibility as far away as possible."

"By turning them on me instead," Malcolm said.

"Would you rather I let them work themselves up to riot and start killing each other?"

If that keeps Alexander and Ellie out of it, Malcolm thought, *then yes, that's what I would rather have happen.*

But it was done now, so all he could do was figure out how to make it work. They had tried getting the power plants at Potrero and Pittsburg back online, they had tried rewiring old solar panels... they had tried everything. Too much time had gone by. There was no fuel to run the big power plants, and the kind of delicate equipment needed to generate power with the solar panels had long since corroded to junk. Dams were much simpler, their basic technology unchanged since the invention of the steam turbine.

If Malcolm was going to keep Dreyfus's promise, he was going to have to figure out a way to get that dam running again. And now he was going to have to do it even though the apes' leader had made it very clear that he didn't want to see the humans again.

Devil and the deep blue sea, Malcolm thought. But hey, as long as he was reciting proverbial expressions, might as well add in the old saw about necessity being the mother of invention. He sighed, trying to let go of the impulse he was feeling to punch Dreyfus in the mouth. It didn't completely go away, but throwing punches wouldn't solve anything. Malcolm had never been much for fighting. No point in starting now.

"Okay," he said. "I think I have an idea."

"You do?" Dreyfus looked dubious.

"Well, I better. You made sure of that." Malcolm paused for a moment, getting himself the rest of the way under control. Dreyfus needed him to get the power going, but he needed Dreyfus on his side, too. It wouldn't do anyone any good for the two of them to be enemies. "Here's what I think I can do," he went on, and started to lay out his plan.

25

An hour later Malcolm was at the garage in Fort Point. He watched as two mechanics poured dirty liquid out of five-gallon cans. The flow went through a jerry-rigged set of multiple coffee filters, and into funnels positioned over another set of cans. They poured slowly, and the purified fuel dripped through the filters just as slowly. After every couple of pints, the mechanics had to stop and scrape out the gunk. After every couple of gallons, they had to throw the filters away and replace them.

This was what happened, he mused, when you were down to scavenging gasoline—or any hydrocarbon—from the bottoms of sealed tanks. What was left there had to be purified before it could be used. Before the flu, no gas station would have sold it.

But thanks to human ingenuity—specifically, in this case, Carver's ingenuity—their trucks could run on it. Whatever Carver's other character flaws, and they were many, he was very good with internal combustion engines. While the mechanics repeated the laborious filtering process, over and over, he was giving the run-down FEMA truck a tune-up. At least, that's what it looked like to

Malcolm. He was an architect, not a mechanic.

"This is crazy, if you want my humble expertise," Carver said from under the hood.

Malcolm agreed, but he wasn't going to tell Carver that.

"Just tell me how long you need to get us moving again," he said.

"At least an hour." Carver stood up and showed Malcolm what appeared to be a fuel filter. "I'm still replacing the filters and flushing out the shit from our last trip." He looked over to the other end of the garage, where Alexander sat reading a graphic novel. "Gonna take your kid up there again?"

"He's safer with me than he is down here," Malcolm said, although he didn't know if it was true. The real truth was he couldn't stand to have Alexander out of his sight, knowing how precarious the situation was with the apes. For all he knew, their leader might already have changed his mind, and turned his army around to destroy the Colony.

He didn't think that would happen—something about the ape had struck him as trustworthy, maybe even noble in a way. But when it came to his son, Malcolm didn't believe in taking chances.

"I don't know," Carver said. "Seems like he's got enough problems."

Guys like Carver, who lived through their hands, never understood kids like Alexander, who lived through their minds. Malcolm bridled at Carver's attitude.

"Do me a favor. Just get the damn trucks working. We have to get up there before dark."

"We?" Carver said, looking alarmed. "Oh, no. No way."

"I don't like it either, but you're the best mechanic we've got. Dreyfus said you were going."

"Crap," Carver said. But he kept working.

* * *

Alexander was a strange kid. Malcolm could hardly blame him, after all he'd been through. He was just learning how to read when the Simian Flu killed his mother, and now he was in the throes of adolescence as human civilization seemingly gasped its last breath.

Malcolm knew his treatment of Alexander was full of contradictions. He wanted humanity to survive and thrive, at least partly because that would mean Alexander would live to see a better world again... but he wanted to take Alexander up into the mountains again. That was on Malcolm and no one else. He had lost his wife to the flu. He wasn't going to lose Alexander by not being there when his son needed him.

Alexander had started drawing a lot when he was eight or nine, as the plague wound down for lack of remaining available vectors. Then they'd had to deal with the violence and wars of the next four years. He'd seen a lot of things no kid should have had to see... but that was always true, wasn't it? Maybe Alexander's experience wasn't that different from a kid in the Sudan in 2012... or Bosnia in 1993... or Leningrad in 1942. And there were a lot of damaged kids who had come out of those times and places, too.

Not that Malcolm thought Alexander was damaged. He was just... quiet. A little introverted. Preferred drawing and reading to most forms of human interaction. An arty bookworm coming of age in the ruins of one of America's great literary cities, home to Jack London, Mark Twain... Twenty years ago, Malcolm thought, this would have been the perfect place for a kid like Alexander. Even twelve years ago.

But things were different now, and they all had to do the best they could.

Even Dreyfus, who had forced Malcolm's hand. The last thing in the world any of them should have been doing at that moment was preparing to head up to the dam again. The apes meant business. What drove Dreyfus was the beautiful dream of electricity—and the dark side of that dream, which was the knowledge that without it, the human survivors in San Francisco were destined for a slow, ugly slide into barbarism.

That barbarism might be closer than any of them thought, Malcolm mused, thinking of the mob in the Colony. They prided themselves on keeping civilization alive, but that was starting to seem like an illusion. They were treading water... maybe. More likely, they were sinking so slowly that they would be able to pretend it wasn't happening, until they began to drown.

"Alexander," he said.

His son looked up. For the thousandth time Malcolm wished he would let people call him Alex. Four syllables were way too many to say every time. But when you were a kid who had lost so much before you'd reached your tenth birthday, you held tight to the things you still had. And Alexander had his name. His mother had named him. Malcolm had been thinking Justin or Henry, but fifteen years after Alexander's birth, Malcolm thought she had been right. The name fit. Maybe not in the leader-of-men sense, but still, he was an Alexander.

Whatever that meant.

"Dad?"

Malcolm caught himself. "Yeah. We're going to head out pretty soon. Get your stuff together."

"Didn't the chimp tell us to stay away?" Alexander didn't look too scared. He seemed more curious about why his father was turning right around the same day, and doing exactly what a thousand armed and intelligent apes had just told him not to do.

Malcolm nodded.

"He did. But I think I can talk to him. He needs to see that we need certain things… and then maybe we can offer him certain things, too. I don't think there's any way we can avoid each other forever."

Ellie came in from outside, where she had been checking over the supplies before Carver's guys loaded the truck. She'd heard the last part of their conversation.

"Talk to him, huh?" she said.

"I don't think we have a choice. If I don't try something, Dreyfus is going to go up there with a bunch of guys with guns." Malcolm looked in Carver's direction as he said this, making sure Carver was otherwise engaged. He was, scrubbing the truck's spark plugs at the other end of the garage.

"Maybe you ought to let him," Ellie said. "If that's the way things are going to go anyway. Why put yourself out front? You have him to consider." She glanced at Alexander. "And I'd just as soon you stuck around, too."

"Believe me, we're on the same page there," Malcolm said.

"Then let Dreyfus be the big chief."

"Oh, I am," Malcolm said. "But you heard that speech. Basically he pointed the crowd at me and said I was going to fix the problem. So either I fix the problem, or the Colony…"

"The Colony what?" she prompted.

"I don't know," Malcolm said. "That's the problem."

"You don't know what the chimp will do, either," Ellie pointed out.

"This is going to sound nuts," Malcolm said, "but I think I trust him a little more than I do most of the people down here."

"Based on what? You looked him in the eye and he

brought your son's comics back?"

"That's part of it. He didn't have to do that. He was making a good-faith gesture. There's… he wouldn't have done that if he really didn't ever want to see a human again. You know?" Malcolm watched Ellie think this over. She didn't like it, but he knew her well enough that she wasn't completely convinced he was wrong.

"This is a lot riding on a snap judgment," she said.

"I know," Malcolm agreed. "I wish I had a better idea."

26

Two hours later, the truck was back at the turnoff from the highway. It passed through Muir Woods, onto the dirt fire road that led up the valley toward the dam. Carver was driving, nursing the truck over the ruts and boulders while the engine belched and stuttered from the poor quality of the fuel.

"Sooner or later, I'm gonna have to do a complete rebuild on this pig," he muttered. "My guess is sooner."

"As long as it gets us home today," Malcolm said.

"Oh, it'll get me home. You, I don't know about, if you're seriously gonna go flirt with the monkeys."

"For a policy advisor, you make a great mechanic," Malcolm replied. Carver snorted and eased the truck down a steep cut in the road, where a flash flood had started to carve the course for a new stream. Everyone held on and waited for the sound of grinding metal—if the truck bottomed out and tore off the oil pan, say, they'd all be walking home.

But that didn't happen, and Carver worked the truck up the slope. Behind them came the second truck, with Kemp at the wheel. The dam-repair crew was ready to go, depending only on Malcolm's ability to reach some kind of arrangement with a tribe of fully sentient talking apes.

No biggie, Malcolm thought wryly.

As the road leveled off slightly, they arrived at the clearing where they'd parked the day before. Malcolm figured it was fifty-fifty whether or not the apes would be watching the spot. It didn't matter, really, since his plan didn't call for secrecy. A few hundred yards up the valley was the ridge that formed one wall of the dam. A few hundred yards down the valley was the shallow crossing where Carver had gone to fill his canteen.

Carver killed the engine. Malcolm turned so he could see everyone.

"Nobody gets out of the trucks," he said. "No one." To Carver specifically he added, "If I'm not back in two hours, get everyone back to the city as fast as you can."

"You got it. Two hours, we're gone."

Malcolm looked at Ellie and Alexander. Now that they had come all this way, he realized what a risk he was taking. He'd known it before, but suddenly it seemed clearer, the way bad decisions always did as soon as they were irreversible. But it was done now. He hoped it was the right thing to do.

Ellie looked scared. Alexander looked as if he was trying not to look scared. Malcolm started to say something to them, but he'd already said it all. Repeating it in front of Carver wouldn't make it any truer. He opened the door and started to get out.

"You don't want me to come with you?" Alexander called.

Malcolm leaned back into the truck. He felt a rush of love and pride for his son, trying to be brave when in fact he was utterly terrified.

"I need you to stay in the truck," he said. "It's going to be okay."

Alexander's nod was the last thing he saw before he shut the door and started walking.

He worked his way down the slope toward the river and paused at the shore below the rapids, re-envisioning the events of the previous day. The damp sand near the water's edge was trampled, with hundreds of ape footprints clearly visible. Where the wounded ape had been, Malcolm thought he could still see faint bloodstains on a rock face. He walked along the shore, pushing through tree branches that leaned out over the water.

Farther downstream, the water was quieter and deeper. This was as good a crossing as any, he thought, unless he wanted to go all the way back down to the highway bridge, and that would take too much time.

Splashing out into the shallows, Malcolm stepped from rock to rock as far as he could. Then he had no choice but to drop down into thigh-deep water and wade the rest of the way. It was freezing, and he didn't like the feeling of being exposed out in the middle of the expanse. He pushed hard to the opposite bank and paused, looking around on the off chance he might spot one of the apes, watching. Did they usually post sentries this far from their camp? That was a tough question to answer, since he didn't know how far the camp was.

He climbed the ridge, wet boots squeaking on the rocks, and reached the top where the apes had lined up the day before. He saw prints here and there. Some of them looked strange to him, not like feet, and then he figured out they must have been left by the knuckles of gorillas. Once he was over the ridge, the ground was fairly level. He followed what looked like a path and was surprised, a few minutes later, when he came out onto a road. He was even more surprised to see an abandoned gas station, its sign overgrown, its parking lot thick with weeds and saplings.

The plate-glass windows that had formed the front wall were long gone. The inside of the station was empty, looted years ago. Three rusting cars sat on flat tires at the side of the building. Malcolm didn't stop to look through them. He walked up the road a ways, and turned back into the woods when he saw clear evidence that apes had passed by. Small broken branches dangled in the tree canopy, and there was a scattering of freshly fallen green leaves.

Hiking uphill through the woods again, Malcolm started to feel as if something was watching him from every direction at once. Every rustle of a breeze in the leaves brought him up short. Twice he saw animals moving in the undergrowth, and froze until they were gone. He glanced at his watch, which he'd made sure to wind that morning. Thirty-five minutes since he'd left the trucks.

Was he going in the right direction? Ahead of him there was a heavily wooded ravine. If he was an ape, he'd want to be on high ground, but not above the tree line. They were around here somewhere. At the head of the ravine, where it narrowed into the flank of the mountain, might be a good spot.

He started up the center of the ravine, looking up into the trees and trying to keep an eye out for poison oak and the brambles that grew in impenetrable shadowy thickets along the ravine's walls. It was slow going. Finally he decided he'd be able to move faster if he climbed up out of the ravine, and worked his way up the mountain along its edge.

Just as he was about to do that, he saw a path ahead... and at the same moment, a structure that definitely had not occurred naturally. It was a tripod, made of three tree trunks bound together with rough rope. At the top, in the notch created by the crossing of the trunks, was an eyrie of sticks and brush, decorated with carved totems and a single antlered skull. It had to be an ape nest.

The woods were quiet around him, except for the ever-present sound of birds in the trees and small animals in the brush.

He was getting close.

Past the nest, he climbed toward the head of the ravine, climbing a steep rocky slope with a clearly worn path ascending it. And at the far end of that slope, there was an open gate.

It, too, was made of tree trunks and festooned with various totems. Beyond it was a well-worn path, almost like a dirt street. Malcolm approached it and saw carvings on the posts. Some of them were letters, some glyphs he couldn't interpret. In several places he saw the word APE.

My God, he thought. *They can write, too?*

He almost turned back then, feeling that he was getting in way over his head. He had a son to consider, and Ellie. There had to be another way to bring electricity to the Colony.

Didn't there?

Malcolm took a deep breath. No, there did not. This was the only way. They had tried everything else.

He passed through the gate, feeling as he did that he had committed himself to some inevitable series of events, the outcome of which he couldn't predict. More totems stood on posts near the street... and now he could hear apes in the branches that overhung the street.

They were getting closer. And there were a lot of them. He kept his hands visible and his eyes front, and he kept walking. The apes' noises were all around him now—behind him, on both sides, and above him. He couldn't help it. He started to scan through the branches, and he saw a chimp looking back at him from just above his eye level. Malcolm raised his arms, palms out, like he was being arrested.

The ape vanished.

At the same time, a series of alarms sounded, the cries of apes echoing in a chain upward through the trees and away into the forest ahead of him. Malcolm kept walking, half-convinced he was about to die, but fully convinced that if he ran now he wouldn't get ten steps before a spear punched through his lungs. He kept his hands in the air, walking nice and slow, determined but non-threatening.

Apes began to emerge from the trees. Malcolm kept walking until they appeared in front of him. Then he stopped. They circled him and he started to turn, keeping as many of them as possible in view. He started walking again as he completed a full turn. Then he stopped dead.

Right in front of him, within arm's reach, stood the chimp with the blind eye. It held a harpoon twice its height, both hands on the shaft, the steel point gleaming in the sun. The other apes stopped moving, waiting for their cue. Malcolm knew this was one of the leaders. Both times he had seen this ape, it had been right next to the one who first spoke, whose eyes Malcolm had first met.

And both times, seeing this one-eyed chimp, Malcolm had thought the same thing.

This one really doesn't like people.

None of the apes were moving now. The one-eyed ape could almost have been a statue, if its good eye hadn't moved up and down. Malcolm remembered how it had looked at the guns held by Dreyfus's guards. He was glad he hadn't brought a gun.

"Listen," he said. "I—"

Before he got another word out, the one-eyed ape brought the butt of the harpoon up and around to crack into the side of his head, just over his left ear. Malcolm's legs went out from under him. His ears rang and he couldn't see. He had a sense of the ground hitting him, and then everything faded to a dim gray. As it did, he had one last coherent thought.

Well, there was a chance.

27

He never quite made it to unconsciousness, but for what must have been several minutes Malcolm was drifting. He had the sensation of moving, and of something wrong with one of his feet. Briefly he put those two things together and realized he was being dragged somewhere. He tried to speak but couldn't figure out how. All around him was an overwhelming wave of screeching. *Apes*, he thought as his head started to clear. He blinked and his eyes started to focus. At the same time the pain from the side of his head hit him again, and he grimaced.

He was on his back, being dragged along the muddy path. Above him he saw an arch, with wooden walls extending away into the woods on either side. Along the tops of the walls, pointed timbers stuck out. Apes were everywhere, running along the walls, swinging down from the outthrust timbers, dropping from the top of the gate, running out from huts on either side of the path. Huts! They had built *houses*…!

They came close, peering down at him and signaling to each other as they screeched. He was amazed how loud they could be.

The sound changed as his body was dragged. Without warning he was on harder, packed earth—and stone, he realized as a protruding rock gouged its way up his back and dug into his shoulder blade. Still there were apes all around, and ape houses everywhere… it was astonishing what they had done.

Abruptly the ape that was dragging him flung him around. Malcolm got to his hands and knees, not sure if he could stand. But when he saw the point of the harpoon in front of his nose, he decided to try. He managed, although his head still spun, and the one-eyed ape gestured with the harpoon, nudging him forward.

Malcolm turned around and was amazed all over again. Before him was an immense crowd. Chimps, gorillas, orangutans, all watching him. Some of them looked curious, some angry, others laughed and joked with one another. He saw young apes ducking and weaving through the group to get a better look at him, and it occurred to him that he was probably the first human they had ever seen.

The butt of the harpoon prodded him in the back and Malcolm started walking. The sea of apes began to part, leaving him a narrow path forward. He walked, hearing them sniff at him as he passed, seeing the intelligence in their eyes as they watched him watching them. Most of them looked hard and hostile.

He didn't maintain eye contact for very long with any individual, remembering a movie he'd seen once where a biologist stayed alive by lowering her head. He wasn't going to do that. These weren't just apes. They were rational—something had been done to them. The jungle rules of submission didn't apply here, in a village built by their own hands.

The body of apes finished dividing in two, and ahead of him Malcolm saw the leader, standing alone before a stone wall. On the stone wall he saw words. APE SHALL NOT KILL APE jumped out at him. Then he saw APES TOGETHER STRONG. There was a third line he didn't catch because the one-eyed chimp shoved him forward again and then cracked him across the backs of his legs with the harpoon butt. Malcolm dropped to his knees. He was about eye level with the chimp leader.

"Please," he said. "Please don't kill me until you hear what I have to say."

The chimp said nothing. He stared stone-faced at Malcolm. Whatever understanding he had thought they shared that morning, it was gone. Malcolm thought again that he might just have gotten himself into a hole way too deep to climb out of.

"I know you said not to come back," he said. "I get it, I understand why... what you've been through. It's just..." He got one foot under him and started to stand. "I wouldn't be here if it wasn't absolutely—*unh*!"

The one-eyed chimp smashed the harpoon shaft down on Malcolm's shoulder, driving him back to the ground.

"Please!" he cried. His arm was numb. "There's something I need to show you, it's not far, if I could just—"

"Human lies," the one-eyed chimp said.

"No, no, I swear—"

Stepping past Malcolm, the one-eyed chimp signed to the leader. Malcolm didn't know sign language, but he recognized the violence of the gesture. One-Eye wanted to kill him, and was asking permission. He'd bet... well, he'd bet his life on it.

"Please," he said again. "If I could just show you why we came up here. Then you'll understand."

The leader had not moved. His expression had not changed. The orangutan that had ridden next to the leader outside the Colony hooted softly, but the leader did not look at him. One-Eye dropped the point of his harpoon until it was level, pointed straight at Malcolm's sternum. Malcolm held the leader's gaze. If he was going to die, he was going to do it with a little dignity.

The leader raised one hand. Nothing else about him changed. One-Eye paused, his harpoon still leveled at Malcolm and his face a mask of frustrated hate. A long moment passed. Malcolm looked steadily at this chimpanzee that held Malcolm's life in his hands.

"Show me," the leader said.

28

They cut along the canyon's edge, Malcolm on a horse led by an ape who appeared to be one of the leader's inner circle. When they reached the base of the canyon, Malcolm spoke up.

"We should walk from here," he said. The ape leader nodded, and they dismounted—he and a group of apes including One-Eye, who still looked like he wanted to dig his harpoon around in Malcolm's guts. He led them down the face of the canyon to a logjam choking the river, with the roar of a waterfall just beyond it. Soon it was too loud to speak and be heard, so Malcolm waved everyone forward and started working his way out across the logs.

It was a tricky scramble, slippery with a long drop on one side and rolling water on the other that would trap you under the logjam long after you'd drowned. Mist from the waterfall swirled all around them. Malcolm picked his way to the middle of the jam, and looked down.

Here's where I start to spring my own surprise, he thought.

He jumped… and landed on a catwalk six feet below the logjam. He looked up to see the apes' heads appear, puzzled at first and then surprised as they saw Malcolm standing unharmed.

He waved for them to join him. They climbed down and looked over the dam's vast spillway and the concrete retaining walls built to anchor the structure. Surely the apes must have seen this before, thought Malcolm. But if they had, they'd never been on the catwalk—at least not this group. They looked around in wonder and stuck close to Malcolm as he led them to the far side of the walkway, with a hundred-foot slope of concrete below them and the mossy face of the dam above. Water surged down the front of it. In its ruined state, it was a spectacular sight—maybe even more spectacular than it would have been when it was in good repair.

They reached the end of the catwalk, where it seemed to dead-end into one of the retaining walls... until you noticed the rectangular outline and the stainless steel door handle sticking out like a bent finger. Malcolm wrapped his shirt around it to get a better grip, and twisted, then pulled the door open with a squeal that cut through the roar of the falls.

Inside, he led the apes down a cement staircase into the mechanicals room of the dam's powerhouse. The room was maybe three stories high, with overgrown windows on one side admitting dim light. Immense pipes and valves dominated an end of it, and on the ground floor below these were the control panels, gathered around a central console with an array of knobs and dials. The rest of the room was given over to worktables and tool lockers.

"It's what we used to call a small hydro," Malcolm explained as the apes descended the staircase behind him, looking in wonder at the building they had never noticed so close to their village. "It was built to service areas north of here, but we've been working to re-route the necessary lines in the city to, um…" He cut himself off. "Sorry, I'm getting ahead of myself. See, the city, it used to run off nuclear power, but that gave out years ago. We've been running diesel generators, gasifiers—but we're almost out…"

The ape leader stood before the console, looking at the panels and gauges.

"If we can just get this dam working again, we have a shot at restoring limited power to our…" Malcolm trailed off as he saw the ape leader looking hard at him. He got nervous again, his initial flush of excitement disappearing as he was put in mind of One-Eye's harpoon. "Is any of this… making sense?" he asked.

The leader held his gaze a few seconds longer.

"The lights," he said.

Malcolm realized he'd been holding his breath. Now he let it out and smiled. "Yes. The lights. Listen, I know this is your home up here. And we're not trying to take it away from you, I promise. But if you could just allow us to do our work, please—"

One-Eye cut him off.

"You brought others?" he growled.

Very carefully, Malcolm measured his reply.

"Just a few." He hoped that would satisfy them. "Look… if you still think I'm a threat, then I guess you'll kill me. But I swear, I wouldn't have come back up here if I didn't have to. I have a son…" He thought this seemed to get through to the leader, and he kept talking. "We're just trying to survive down there. All we need is a few days, and I give you my word.

"You will never. See us. Again."

29

The waiting was killing them. If it had been up to Carver, he would have started the truck and gotten the hell out of there the minute Malcolm was out of sight. But that wasn't really possible with his woman and his son sitting right there. So he and Foster sat up in the front and Malcolm's little family sat in the back, Alexander reading the same comics over and over.

Weird kid. Carver didn't like him. He didn't like Malcolm either. Ellie was all right, easy on the eyes and pleasant, but he'd have been just as happy to never see any of them again. What he wanted was a wrench in one hand, a beer in the other, and the sure knowledge that they'd come up here with every gun in Fort Point, then used them to put those apes in the ground.

Instead they were sitting in a truck up in the mountains with pine needles raining down all over them. At least he had a cigar. It was hand-rolled in the Colony from lousy tobacco they'd grown themselves, but it was a cigar.

Pine needles. Why were there so many…?

"Oh, shit," Foster said, as Carver heard rustling in the trees. He pitched the cigar and rolled up the window.

"That's it," he said. "We're gone. It's probably two hours anyway." He locked the doors and reached for the ignition as the trees around them were suddenly full of apes.

"It hasn't been two hours," Ellie protested. "You can't—"

"The hell I can't," Carver said. "You see what's out there? Probably one of them brought Malcolm's head to show us." He started the truck and jammed it into gear. Around them, the apes drew closer. They were in the mirrors, too, coming around behind the truck. Carver figured he'd have to run over some of them to get out, but that was fine with him.

"Wait! Stop!"

It was the kid. Carver looked back out the windshield and saw Malcolm being marched out of the woods, flanked by two mean-looking chimps. He thought fast and then made his decision. "Nope. We're gone."

But when he looked in the mirror again, the path back down the mountain was blocked by a bunch of chimps on horseback.

"Shit," Foster said again. "We're dead." Carver killed the engine as Malcolm and his escorts came to the driver's-side window. Malcolm motioned for him to roll it down. Carver hesitated, but he did it. Hell, if the apes wanted in the truck, they could get in the truck.

"Give them your guns," Malcolm said as soon as the window was down. "That was the one condition."

"The one condition of what?" Ellie asked.

Malcolm nodded toward the ape leader. The chimp with war paint was watching them from across the clearing, near the second truck. "He says we can stay."

"Great," Carver said. He wished he hadn't tossed his cigar.

* * *

They marched up the slope toward the dam, carrying their gear and watched closely by a heavy guard of apes. Some of them rode horses, more were on foot. Kemp, Foster, and Carver stuck close together and tried not to look the apes in the eye.

Malcolm couldn't quite believe he'd pulled it off. Well, he hadn't—not yet. The dam wasn't running. But he'd come back to the apes and managed not to get harpooned. That was a pretty good first step, all things considered. It was late afternoon and it looked like they would live through another day. Probably. But they still needed to be careful. There was no telling how long the ape leader's goodwill would last, or how long One-Eye would contain his temper.

"Stay close to me," Malcolm said to Alexander, but meaning it for both him and Ellie.

The sun was low over the ridge when they got to a clearing at the edge of the river. The ape leader signaled a halt and pointed at the ground. Malcolm looked at him, uncertain for a moment… then he figured it out.

"You want us to camp here?" he asked. The chimp nodded. Malcolm looked to the others, who started to drop their gear and make what preparations they could before it got dark. He looked over at One-Eye, who was watching the humans with what seemed like disgust. A thought occurred to Malcolm, incongruous given the circumstances. But he thought he'd give it a try.

He walked up to the ape leader's horse.

"Thank you," he said. Then he placed one hand flat on his chest and said, "Malcolm."

The chimp looked surprised. He considered Malcolm, deliberating over something. Then he tapped his own chest.

"Caesar."

Well, of course, Malcolm thought. *The leader of a*

renegade band of genetically enhanced apes is named Caesar. What else would it be?

Without another word or gesture, Caesar wheeled his horse around and rode off. The rest of the apes followed.

"Looks like we're here until morning," Malcolm said. "Let's get some sleep."

30

They could not burn the metal parts of the guns. Those they smashed with rocks next to the fire pit, all under Caesar's direction. Maurice and Rocket did most of it, with Koba glowering across the fire pit. As Rocket tossed the wooden parts of the last gun into the fire, Koba stood abruptly and loped around the pit to where Caesar sat watching.

This is a mistake, he signed. *Why help them?*

Caesar nodded. *Helping them could be dangerous. But not helping is more dangerous.* Koba grunted, acknowledging this without agreeing. Caesar saw Blue Eyes looking at them.

They're trying to save themselves, Caesar signed, making sure Blue Eyes could see. *If we force them to leave, we give the humans no choice. They will attack.*

Let them! Koba thumped his chest.

And how many apes will die? Caesar put an edge on his signs. *We will let them do their human work. And then they will leave.*

Koba grunted again, this time openly scoffing.

"Human work?" he said. He turned sideways to Caesar

and gestured at the scar that ran down the length of his spine. "This human work."

Koba's defiance began to attract attention from the other apes gathered to watch the fire. He pointed to the scar across the base of his skull. "Human work…?" Then he stabbed a finger at his blind eye and growled, louder, "*This* human work!"

More of the apes were staring now, uneasy at the challenge to Caesar's authority. *Enough,* Caesar thought. He would not have this. He stood and stepped to Koba, so close that their faces almost touched, locking eyes and silently daring him to continue his defiance.

Silence fell, broken only by the crackle and hiss of the fire. Then Koba took a step back and looked down.

Forgive me, he signed.

Caesar did not move.

Koba kept looking at the ground. After a hesitation, he extended a hand, palm up. Caesar looked at Koba's hand for a long moment before he brushed his own palm across it, accepting the supplication.

Koba glanced up at Caesar, then back across the fire at Blue Eyes and the other watching apes. He looked back to Caesar and dropped his gaze once more before turning and walking away out of the firelight. Caesar watched him go, glad that Koba had not pushed him to a fight. *Apes together strong,* he thought. It was more important than ever now that they had the humans to think about as possible rivals, or even enemies.

Blue Eyes, too, watched Koba go. Turning back to his father, he approached.

Koba says humans are to be hated, he signed.

At last, Caesar thought. He had expected this. *That is because from humans Koba learned only hate,* he signed.

Blue Eyes considered this. He was torn, and Caesar could

understand why. Young apes felt a powerful drive to supplant their elders. Blue Eyes felt this without understanding it. Caesar had to make sure he learned to understand it before his son's youthful energy led him to rebel.

Without another word, Blue Eyes left. Caesar wondered if he would seek Koba. They both needed watching, and control, but for different reasons. He looked up to see Maurice, who gestured that they should walk together. When they were out of the firelight and away from the gathered apes, Maurice stopped.

Koba's anger is strong, he signed.

His loyalty is stronger, Caesar answered. *He is an ape.* They stood looking back at the burning guns, knowing the problem was more complicated than what he had said. *But he must not be left alone with the humans. He may not be able to stop himself. We can't let him start a war.*

Maurice nodded, understanding that Caesar had set him this task. Yet it would take more than one ape to ensure Koba did not cause a war that only he wanted.

Caesar yawned. The guns were destroyed. Sentries watched the humans. It was time to rest. He signed *good night* to Maurice, who ambled back to the fire as Caesar went up the path toward his tree. He climbed up to the sleeping room and stepped softly to the bed, where Cornelia lay looking at their newborn.

Barely two days old, Caesar thought, *and so much happening around him. What story will we tell of these times when he is old enough to hear it?*

Cornelia smiled up at him. Her breath rattled still, maybe worse than it had been the day before. Worried, Caesar stroked her face. Her skin felt warmer than it should have... but perhaps that was because she had been tucked down into the bedding?

Blue Eyes will watch the baby tomorrow, he signed.

You need rest.

She shook her head.

I'll be fine, she signed. *You're worried. About the humans?*

He looked from the baby back to her and nodded. She knew him, and would know if he tried to pretend otherwise. But nothing could be done about the humans tonight, Caesar told himself. He also needed rest. He lay down beside her and drifted off to sleep, hearing the wheeze and rattle of her breath in the darkness and thinking it was not just the humans he worried about.

31

They put up their tents quickly, before dark, and gathered wood for a fire. The six of them sat together to eat, but it was clear that Foster, Kemp, and Carver considered themselves a group within the group.

From up the canyon, they could hear distant ape noises—the occasional call, and as dark fell a long series of smashing noises.

"Listen to that," Kemp said.

"Damn, take a look. See that glow?" Carver said, pointing into the darkness. "The apes have fire."

"They have our guns, too," Kemp said. "Don't know about you, but I am *not* getting any sleep tonight."

Malcolm heard all this while he sat in front of his tent, studying schematic diagrams of the dam. Dreyfus had helped him find them in a room full of filing cabinets down in the basement of San Francisco City Hall. Nobody had bothered to loot it. He'd looked at them before, but now he was making a real study of the wiring in the pump house, and how it connected to the transmission grid.

He noticed Ellie sitting next to him, but was so deeply

engrossed in the schematics that he didn't hear what she said at first. She nudged him.

"You have to eat," she repeated.

"In a sec," Malcolm said.

She waited until he picked up the corner of a page, then said, "That was brave. What you did today."

Malcolm nodded, registering the compliment and appreciating it, but not wanting to break his concentration on learning the dam schematics.

"You're so hard on yourself," she went on. "I know everyone's depending on you, but—"

He looked up from the drawings.

"I don't care about any of that," he said, more sharply than he'd intended. "Any of it. I just care about him. He's the only reason I'm doing this."

Alexander sat near the three mechanics, intent on whatever he was drawing in his sketchbook. Whatever happened between human and ape, Malcolm reflected, he would always give Caesar the benefit of the doubt for returning Alexander's satchel. The boy identified with his art. He needed it. Malcolm wondered if Caesar had understood that, or if the satchel was the item that presented itself as a way to make a good-faith gesture.

"There were things he saw that no kid should ever have to see," Malcolm said. "There's no way I'm ever letting us go back to that."

"You're not the only one responsible for everyone's well-being," she said. He felt her hand brush down the back of his head and come to rest on his nape. He looked away from Alexander, and toward her. It might have been the end of the world, but there were things to be thankful for.

Malcolm leaned into her.

"I don't mean I'm not doing it for you, too," Malcolm said, probably way too late.

"I know what you mean," Ellie said. "You know I've been trying to get closer to him. But he…"

"It's not you. He has a hard time trusting people."

Ellie nodded, understanding.

"I can't say I blame him."

"Let's join up with the group," Malcolm said. "Make sure everyone's on the same page."

"You know the scariest thing about them?" Foster was saying. "They don't need power, lights, heat… nothing. That's their advantage. That's what makes them stronger."

Malcolm privately thought this was bullshit. Humans didn't need any of those things, either. They wanted them, they benefited from them, but *Homo sapiens* had existed for a long time before electricity.

As they approached the three men, an ape called through the trees, answered a moment later by another, quite a bit closer. Malcolm had a paranoid moment, wondering if Caesar was allowing humans to fix the dam so he could use the power himself…

"Maybe one of us should stand guard?" Kemp suggested.

"With what?" Foster asked. "They took our guns."

"If they wanted to kill us, we'd be dead already," Malcolm said, as he and Ellie joined the group at the fire. He leaned over to see what Alexander was drawing—it was a portrait of Caesar on horseback.

Interesting, Malcolm thought. *That's one charismatic chimpanzee.* In the picture, Caesar looked fierce and also noble, posed the way a medieval artist might have staged a painting of a knight on horseback. *Caesar as crusading knight,* Malcolm thought. Only drawn graphic-novel style. Not manga—that wasn't Alexander's thing, really—but more heroic and gritty. Malcolm considered Alexander a pretty talented artist. Too bad he lived in a world where art was a complete luxury.

"Maybe they're just taking their time," Carver offered. "They already wiped out most of the planet."

"Oh, come on." Ellie rolled her eyes.

"What?"

She looked at Carver like she couldn't believe she actually had to spell out what she was about to spell out. "You can't honestly blame the apes."

"Who the hell else am I gonna blame? It was the Simian Flu. Si-mi-an."

"The virus was engineered by scientists, in a lab," Ellie said. "The chimps had no say in the matter—"

Carver snorted. "Spare me the hippie-dippy bullshit, okay? You're telling me you don't get sick to your stomach at the sight of them?" Seeing Ellie's scorn, he narrowed his eyes and took another shot. "Didn't you have a little girl? How'd *she* die?"

Ellie's face went slack from shock and then closed off. Boom, just like she was made of stone. Alexander watched it happen, and looked from her to Malcolm.

"That's enough, Carver," Malcolm said.

Apparently it wasn't, though, because Carver looked him straight in the eye and continued.

"Or your wife, for that matter."

Malcolm knew he wasn't going to get the better of Carver in a fight. But he also knew he couldn't back down in front of everyone. On top of that, he wanted Carver to *know* he wouldn't back down. But before he could say anything that would escalate the situation, Foster jumped in.

"Carver, you better shut your mouth before I beat the shit out of you," he said. "I mean, what the fuck? Talking about people's kids and wives?"

Carver looked from Foster to Kemp, who shook his head.

"I'm with them, man," Kemp said. "What's your problem?"

Malcolm kept glaring at Carver. At this point he was hoping the man would come after him. Now that he knew he had Foster and Kemp on his side.

Carver seemed to know it, too. He turned down the aggression a notch.

"I'm just saying…" He broke off and stood up. "Yeah, okay, all right. I'm the asshole." Shaking his head, he walked away to the tent he was sharing with the other two. In his wake was an awkward silence.

"Carver doesn't like the apes too much," Foster said. It was obvious, but Malcolm appreciated the effort to break the ice.

"Yeah," Malcolm said. "I got that impression." He leaned over to Ellie. "You all right?"

Ellie nodded. "I'm fine."

Foster poked at the fire. Everyone paused as the hooting of a pair of apes carried down the canyon.

"Pretty damn spooky, you have to admit," he said.

"No argument here," Malcolm said.

Alexander looked up from his drawing.

"I think they're amazing. I mean, dangerous, yeah, but think about it. Apes who can talk? They escape the city and spend ten years hiding in the mountains? Pretty badass."

It was as many words as he had spoken in the last two days.

"Don't say that when Carver's around," Kemp said. They all laughed, except Ellie. She was looking at Alexander, and Malcolm wondered if when she saw him she also saw the ghost of what her daughter would have become.

32

A rustling outside of the tent nudged him to consciousness.

Malcolm would never have guessed that he would need to be awakened on a day when he was going to be escorted by armed chimpanzees to work on a dam to bring electricity to San Francisco. But that's what had happened.

At the end of the previous evening, Kemp and Foster had argued halfheartedly about whether or not to post guards. When it became clear that neither of them wanted to take the first shift, everyone gave up and went to bed... And, judging from the fact that neither Alexander nor Ellie seemed to be awake, they all must have slept like the dead.

Clean air, Malcolm thought. The air in San Francisco was clean compared to what it had been ten years before, but still not like it was up here.

Alexander had fallen asleep with a comic spread across his chest. Now, starting awake, he looked at something out the tent flap. Still lying down, Malcolm leaned to see out, and found himself peering straight into the wrinkly, bemused face of an orangutan.

Not ten feet away, the creature sat observing them. It was the one Caesar always kept close.

Alexander sat up, and the comic fell to the ground next to his sleeping bag. The orangutan watched it. Alexander saw this, and Malcolm could see him trying to decide what to make of it. Beyond the orangutan there was a cluster of chimpanzees. Malcolm thought he recognized one of them, another of Caesar's confidantes.

He flipped the flap of the sleeping bag back, and ducked out into the camp, nodding to the apes. There were maybe twenty of them, armed and watchful.

"Morning," Malcolm said, *because why not.*

Foster, Kemp, and Carver had exited their tent, and were standing in a tight knot. Carver looked jumpy and ill at ease. No surprise there.

Foster and Kemp didn't look happy, either. Malcolm thought he understood them. They were the kinds of men who were a little too easily led, not because they were stupid but because they were ever so slightly lazy, and thinking for themselves took too much work. They were both good mechanics, and generally good people, but Carver was a bad influence on them... and, it had to be said, an influence they too easily accepted.

He was thinking all this when he walked over to them.

"Well," he said, "if everybody's up, let's go."

"Hell, yes," Carver said. "Get this over with."

It took only twenty minutes or so to hike from the campsite directly to the logjam, even with packs full of gear. Malcolm had gathered everything he thought they could possibly need to get the dam working again, from electrical tape right on up to explosives. He hadn't told Caesar about the explosives. Better to let their use explain itself later, when he could show that they had not endangered the apes, rather than promising that they wouldn't. *Better to ask forgiveness than permission,* as the old saying went.

The apes did not go with them across the logjam. They crowded the lower branches of the trees on either side of the slot canyon, and took up stations on the ground where the path snaked back up toward the village. Malcolm led the way to the point where they could drop to the catwalk. He stopped there to help each of the others get braced and make a clean drop. A broken leg would throw a serious monkey wrench—so to speak—into their plan.

First Foster dropped. Then Malcolm lowered their packs to him, one by one. Then Carver, Kemp, Ellie, and Alexander jumped down to the catwalk. None of them bothered to talk, since the waterfall's thunder was louder than any of their voices. As Alexander dropped, he was looking back at the apes, both nervous and curious.

That right there is why Caesar's demand was never going to work, Malcolm thought. *Once we knew the apes were here, how could he think we wouldn't come out here to take a look?*

It was a philosophical problem for later, he decided, and he made the jump to the catwalk.

From above, near where Malcolm had dismounted and led them down to the logjam the day before, Caesar and Blue Eyes sat on horseback, and watched. Soon it would be their turn to assume guard duties. For the moment, however, Blue Eyes held his baby brother.

Caesar watched the humans cross the logs, so awkward on their long legs and their arms that hung only to mid-thigh. They tripped and fell much more easily than apes did, especially when they carried heavy loads. Caesar did not laugh often, but at times he wanted to chuckle at humans when they did things like struggle across slippery logs. What stopped him was knowing how chimps felt when humans laughed at them.

Clinging to his older brother's hair and peering over his shoulder, the youngest member of their troop took in the world, wide-eyed and round-mouthed. He scrambled up and down his brother as if Blue Eyes was a toy like those they'd had in the animal shelter—wood or plastic carved in the shapes of trees, rope ladders and swings, and from the top arc of the swings you could see the rows of steel cages…

Caesar shook off the memory. He looked at his sons. They and Corneila gave him joy. He could ask no more of life than for them to survive.

Rocket and Maurice rode out of the forest, joining them at the lookout over the logjam.

Do you think they can do it? Caesar signed.

Both Rocket and Maurice shrugged.

If they do not do it, what will happen?

Rocket didn't try to answer this question. Maurice did.

They will go away and leave us alone for a while, he signed. *Then either they will return because their leader has decided to fight, or they will die out, or they will return because their leader wants to make peace…*

I understand, Caesar signed. There were too many possibilities.

I think they will keep coming back no matter what, Blue Eyes signed.

Caesar and Maurice responded simultaneously.

Why?

Because humans will not be able to stand knowing they do not control us.

"Blue Eyes," Caesar said. "Take…brother. Play."

"I am fighter," Blue Eyes said. "Not child."

Caesar stared at him. Blue Eyes stared back. Caesar

saw something in his son's expression that he had never seen before, and he realized with a shock that there was now a shadow of Koba cast over Blue Eyes' face. He did not let Blue Eyes see his emotions, nor Rocket or Maurice. He held his son's gaze until Blue Eyes swung down from the horse, the tiny baby squeaking in surprise. Blue Eyes flipped the baby over his shoulder and cradled it in one arm, then scooted off into the trees.

He will be a good brother, Caesar thought. *And a good son.* The only danger was that Blue Eyes would travel too far and too fast down the rebellious path, and then find himself stuck there. It would be up to Caesar to prevent that.

Then Caesar noticed that he had not seen Koba, Grey, or Stone that morning.

Where is Koba? he asked Maurice.

Grey said they were going hunting, Maurice signed. *Probably for the best.*

Caesar nodded. It might well be for the best, if Koba's temper was going to get the better of him, and start something with the humans... but Koba's absence concerned him. Koba would not lie, Caesar thought. At least he never had before. But hunting was a broad word. Many ideas fit inside it.

What quarry, exactly, was Koba hunting?

And where had he gone to find it?

The last of the humans dropped over the edge of the logjam.

Now what? Rocket signaled.

Caesar shifted his weight in the saddle. *Now we wait.*

33

Koba, Grey, and Stone swung along the underside of the orange bridge. They had left at dawn, not telling Caesar because he would have forbidden what they were planning to do. They stopped and settled themselves against the great steel beams, looking down at the square building under the bridge, with heavy stone walls and small windows. Near it was a giant steel ship, its top like a table with a building and airplanes on it. The ship was damaged and partly sunk.

The night before, after nearly baring his fangs to Caesar, Koba had gone away to think. Much later, after everyone else but Grey had gone to sleep, Koba had returned to the fire pit, accompanied by Stone.

The wood parts of the guns were gone, ashes and embers. The metal parts lay near the fire, bent and dented by Maurice and Rocket. Koba touched one of them. It was still hot. He used a stick to push it away from the coals and waited patiently for it to cool. He picked it up and looked closely at it. It was a tube of black steel, with a long slot near one end. Another part of it, rectangular and with a spring, had been broken off and was in the coals somewhere.

"Without these, they are nothing," Koba had said, quietly. Then he had noticed marks on the tube. He turned it toward the dying glow of the fire, but could not read it. *Stone,* he signed. *Read this.*

Stone took the metal tube and held it at different angles over the fire pit. He signed the letters and Koba put them together into words:

PROPERTY OF U.S. NAVY.

There is also a picture, Stone signed. Koba put his head close, looking hard at the part of the barrel Stone indicated… Yes. He could see it. Barely.

An anchor, with rope twisting around it. Koba thought. He had seen that sign before. He thought harder, and remembered.

Now he was looking down at that sign, visible through the streaks of rust on the side of the flat-topped ship.

So. There would be guns here.

He was committing a grave offense against Caesar. Apes together strong… but knowledge was strength. Koba was here for knowledge. He was here to keep humans from killing apes. If Caesar could not see that, then his two eyes did not see as clearly as Koba's one.

Even so, Caesar would never agree. Neither would many of the other apes. Koba understood this. He was prepared to accept the consequences of it. The one thing he could not do was allow Caesar to make apes forget what humans would do to them, once they had the chance.

If it was up to the humans, apes would be dead. All of them.

Grey and Stone looked over at him. *What do you see?* Koba signed.

Koba himself saw a fenced place outside the building… he remembered the word. Strong buildings with small windows like that were called *forts*. Outside the fort, but inside the fence, were trucks, cars, and larger vehicles. He could see humans, but not how many.

Count the humans, he signed.

Stone nodded and looked back down to the fort. He counted and signed.

Twenty-three. More inside.

Koba pointed at large metal boxes, big enough to put trucks inside. *What is in those?* he asked. But neither Grey nor Stone could see.

Then we must get closer, Koba signed. They moved in, slowly. From the closest pillar they dropped to the deck of the ship. Chimps and orangutans could swim, but Koba did not know how. Even if he had, he did not trust the water swirling through the narrow gap between the bridge pillar and the fort. They crept along the railing, and then climbed a metal frame tower coming up from the top of the building on the ship's deck. They moved slowly, to avoid drawing attention, and watched from the top of the tower.

Just inside the fence, near enough that the apes could hear their voices, two humans were talking while six others used metal bars to pry open crates.

"Bottom line," one of the humans said. "How much of it still works."

"We're still taking inventory," the other said, "but so far most of the arsenal seems functional."

The first human nodded.

"Good. Because we may have to go up there, if Malcolm

and the others don't come back down. Deal with those animals ourselves."

Animals, Koba thought. *So be it.*

As the tops came off the crates, Koba saw guns. One of the crates held guns like the ones they had burned... yet not the same. They had no wood parts. They looked new. Koba thought about this and decided they must have been in those boxes for ten winters. So the humans were not just taking care of guns they already had.

They were looking for new weapons... and finding them.

The second crate opened. Inside it were long metal tubes with bulbs at one end, shaped like the bulb of a flower just before it bloomed. What were those? On the side of the crate were letters, roughly painted over older, smaller letters.

RPGs

What are RPGs? he signaled to Grey and Stone. Both shook their heads. Koba did not know either. But he intended to find out.

His focus was broken by the sound of gunfire. Many shots, in a burst. He looked across the open area to the fence line on the other side. A large warehouse stood there, built onto one side of the fort itself. The gunshots came from that direction.

The sounds drew Koba. He could not resist them.

They worked around the fence and along the steep rocky bluff separating the fort from the overgrown area at the base of the bridge. The bluff ran under the bridge and the apes followed it toward the area from which they had heard the gunshots coming.

Koba sped up when they got under the bridge again, unable to stop himself. They got to the corner of the fence and peered through it, around the side of a metal building. Two humans stood with a crate of guns, near a pile of sandbags in a narrow space between the metal wall of the building and another wall inside the fence. One of them removed a curved part of one of the guns, and put it on another. He squatted behind the pile of sandbags and aimed the gun at an old car, out under the bridge on the shore.

Grey and Stone were tense on either side of Koba. He was just still, watching as one of the humans fired many shots, at least ten, the bullets punching holes in the metal body of the car and breaking its windows.

The sound was deafening. Koba loved it.

His hands ached to hold a gun.

We must get closer, he signaled. Stone began to motion as if he might argue, but Grey grabbed his hands and pushed them down. The three apes watched again.

There was a fence in the way. How did they get closer? Koba could be patient when he had to be, especially if he could pass the time watching the two humans firing. One of them was big and hairy, wearing a black leather vest. His chin fur reached over his chest. The other was stringy, with very short hair and no beard. He looked, Koba thought, like any ape could break him in half.

Another burst of fire chewed at the car. Then the firing stopped.

"Terry!" the thin human called. "Jammed."

The large bearded human took the jammed gun. Koba watched. He would need to know everything about the things. The bearded human, Terry, removed the curved bullet box. Then he pulled on a little lever on the gun. It wouldn't move.

"Damn," he said. "I'll take it inside."

Inside, Koba thought. He looked at the warehouse wall, seeing the door that until then had blended in. Terry opened it.

"Hold on," the other human called. "It's your turn to shoot, man. I don't want to bogart the AKs."

"Square deal, McVeigh." Terry walked back out and took a new gun from the crate. He put the bullet box in it and pulled the little lever. The gun clicked. Koba imagined making that click. He imagined the fear on the face of the human at which he pointed the gun.

When Terry began to shoot at the car, Koba jumped from the rocks over the fence. Grey and Stone came immediately after. He motioned them to stay back, near the fence while he scooted toward the door which Terry had left open.

Terry fired and fired.

Koba got to the door and looked in.

He could not believe what he saw. Crate after crate after crate, all like the gun crates and the RPG crates. They were stacked higher than Koba's head, higher than a human's head. Rows and rows, hundreds of crates... *thousands* of guns. Koba moved into the warehouse, unable to resist. He came closer to the nearest crate and reached out.

"What the—?"

Koba spun around to see the spindly human, McVeigh, pointing a gun at him. Not the jammed one, a new one.

"Don't you move. Understand me? I know you can talk." He called out over his shoulder. "Terry! Get in here quick!"

Koba did not move. He showed the human no fear, but neither did he show aggression. He had not yet decided what to do.

Terry came through the door.

"Holy shit," he said. Koba didn't know the word holy,

but he knew shit. Terry pointed his gun at the ape.

Behind the two humans he saw Grey and Stone, peering in. Koba made a small sign, as small as he could possibly make it. *Back*. They eased out of view, but he knew they would stay close by. Then he studied the humans again, deciding what to do next.

34

McVeigh and Terry looked at each other, then at the chimp. Then back out the door.

"What do we do?" McVeigh asked. Terry might look like a meth-head but he wasn't stupid.

Terry shrugged, but the barrel of his AK didn't move.

"Where'd he come from?"

"I just found him," McVeigh said.

"Should we shoot him?" Terry asked.

McVeigh didn't know what to say about that.

"Maybe," he said. "Yeah. I mean, no. I don't know."

"Dreyfus should know about this," Terry said.

That was for damn sure. But McVeigh didn't want to leave this ape here while they went and got Dreyfus. He was leaning toward killing it, especially since it just stared at him. Didn't move, didn't blink, no expression on its face.

Don't borrow trouble, he told himself. *Apes show up in the fort, the day after they make a big deal about not getting in each other's space. That happens, apes get shot. Simple.* His finger tightened on the trigger. "You are one ugly sonofabitch, aren't you?" he said, working himself up to it.

The truth was, McVeigh liked shooting guns, but he didn't like shooting people. Or animals, for that matter. He liked the swagger of guns, the feeling they gave him. But he'd killed a man when he had to, in the second year after the plague had petered out. A bandit, caught breaking into the Colony. *Bam*. No second thoughts. He had to go down.

This situation didn't feel like that. But McVeigh couldn't put a finger on why.

"You gonna do it?" Terry asked, looking freaked out. McVeigh figured he probably looked pretty freaked out, too. He sure as hell felt that way.

"I don't know. Do you? Shit. One of us should go get Dreyfus." McVeigh wanted to be the one, but he knew if he suggested it, Terry would want to do it instead, which would put McVeigh on the hook if he stayed here and the chimp split. Nope, he didn't like that idea.

"Let's just shoot it," Terry said.

The chimp, which throughout their conversation had not moved so much as a whisker, suddenly stuck its tongue out and let go the longest and wettest Bronx cheer McVeigh had ever heard. He looked at Terry, just to make sure his friend had seen it, too. Both of them quickly looked back at the chimp, AKs still leveled at it. But now it started prancing around, and making faces like it was...

"Damn," Terry said. "You think maybe it used to be some kind of circus chimp?"

"I thought they didn't have chimps in the circus anymore," McVeigh said. "I mean, anymore before the flu."

Thinking of the flu made him want to shoot the chimp again. But it was kind of funny. He couldn't help it. He started to chuckle. The chimp did a series of somersaults, completing a circle and ending up where it had started. It bowed and then pinched two fingers and the thumb of its right hand together and pantomimed eating something held in them.

"Dude, I think he wants something to eat," McVeigh said, still laughing.

"He must have gotten separated from the others," Terry said. He bent down so he was closer to the chimp's eye level. "You lost?" he said, too loud. "Trying to get home?"

Confused, the chimp waddled up to McVeigh and tried to take his hand. McVeigh pulled it away, and the chimp stood there looking up at him.

"Maybe not all of them can talk," he said. "I don't know, what do you think? I feel kinda bad for the guy. We got some stale bread or something we can give him?"

Terry looked at the chimp for a long time. Then he said, "Go on, get out of here. Stupid monkey."

That was fine with McVeigh. Monkey gone, they wouldn't have to tell anyone about it, and they wouldn't have to clean up the mess and answer questions after shooting it. The perfect solution.

So he waved his gun toward the doorway. Then he noticed that the chimp seemed to be looking out that way, at something. McVeigh glanced over his shoulder and didn't see anything.

"You heard him," he said to the chimp. "Get out of here."

The chimp waddled out the door, waving bye-bye with big flapping motions of its hands. When it was gone, McVeigh decided to forget all about it. There were guns to check, and so many of them that he'd get to shoot all day.

35

Inside the mechanicals room, Malcolm and his team staged their equipment and got ready for the first big obstacle they'd have to surmount. That was getting water going *through* the dam again. Right now its sluices were dry, and the water pouring through the logjam at the top of the dam was ample evidence that the intake was not— as the professionals would have said—taking in.

Once they had that happening, they would be able to take a look at the wiring inside the mechanicals room and see what needed work. Then, with any luck, they could fire some juice across the hills, under the bay, and into the city.

To get water going through the dam again, they had to get to the flow mechanism in the dam's interior. And to do that, they needed to go through a series of tunnels inside the structure. Foster and Kemp secured ropes around a heavy vertical pipe mounted into the wall of the mechanicals room, and tested the knots, hauling with their combined weight until they were satisfied nothing would slip. Carver and Malcolm scraped ten years' worth of rust from around a hatch set into the floor of the powerhouse, and levered it open with a crowbar from one of the tool lockers.

Looking through the contents of the lockers, Malcolm thought that if nothing else, they would come away from this trip with useful supplies for the Colony—spools of wire, hand tools, unused lengths of pipe and conduit, all kinds of stuff. The powerhouse hadn't been looted, probably because it was in the middle of nowhere and most people had no idea where their electricity actually came from. So it wouldn't have occurred to them to go digging through a dam to see what might be inside.

When he and Carver got the hatch open, they dropped the ropes into the access tunnel. It was barely three feet in diameter, with metal rungs set into the wall. They were slick. Everything in here was slick. The water had enjoyed ten years to find ways in.

Alexander had the solar flashlights, all charged up yesterday. They were good for at least an hour of light. Malcolm hoped this first part of the dam operation wouldn't take that long. The teen handed each of the men a flashlight. They had carabiner clips, so Malcolm hooked his onto a belt loop. Kemp did the same. Foster and Carver had vests with loops, and attached their flashlights to those.

"Who wants to go first?" Malcolm asked.

Carver shrugged. "Doesn't matter. I'll go."

He flipped a belay rope around his forearm a couple of times and lowered himself into the tunnel, feeling for the first rung. When he got it, he bounced lightly, testing the steel's integrity. Then he took another step down. "Solid," he said, and started climbing down with the rope in a loop around behind him. As he reached from rung to rung, he flipped more slack into it. It wasn't a classic belay, since they hadn't brought climbing equipment, but if one of the rungs proved too slick, or snapped off, having the rope right there increased your chances of not taking a bad fall.

Kemp went next, then Foster. Waiting to give them a

little clearance so he wasn't stepping on Foster's fingers, Malcolm looked from Ellie to Alexander.

"This is the fun part," he said.

"I'll start testing some of the switches," Alexander said. He had a voltage meter and some other electrician's tools, along with a battery they could use to run test current through parts of the control panel.

"I expect a full report when we get back," Malcolm said with a wink. He looked to Ellie. "Dam spelunking," he said. "Life leads in unexpected directions."

"That it does," she agreed. "Be careful."

As he climbed down the ladder, Malcolm switched on his flash, and looked back up at the circle of light. He saw Ellie hold up one hand, fingers crossed. He shot her a grin and then had to concentrate on the rungs. Three points of contact, shift the grip on the rope, repeat. The tunnel was tight, and by the time they were thirty feet into it, the sounds of their breathing and the scrape of boots on metal rungs were the only things they could hear.

The roar of the waterfall was gone. Malcolm glanced down and in the swaying beam of his flashlight he saw that the other three men were already at the bottom, jammed together in a small landing area. He joined them and disengaged himself from the rope.

The next step was to see if they could get through the sealed door that opened from the access tunnel to the much larger penstock tunnel that channeled the water from the dam's intake down to the power-generating turbines below. The door was set into synthetic rubber seals that in theory should have survived sitting in place for ten years just fine… but they had no idea what might be on the other side of it in the penstock tunnel. Malcolm shot the bolts holding it in place and leaned against it.

It didn't move.

"Need a hand here," he said. Kemp and Carver braced themselves against the door. There was no room for Foster. They pushed again, and with a loud peeling crackle, as rubber seals parted for the first time in more than a decade, the door pushed open.

Malcolm leaned through it and shone his flashlight into the much larger penstock tunnel.

"Breathing room," he commented.

"Good," Kemp joked. "I was getting to know you guys a little too well."

The penstock tunnel angled sharply upward toward the flow mechanism, which was far enough away that their flashlight beams didn't reach it. Malcolm stepped onto a small level platform set into the angled tunnel wall. The interior of the tunnel was concrete, pitted enough to provide toeholds but slick enough that the best way to climb was close to a belly-crawl, keeping enough of your body in contact with the tunnel that friction had a better chance of keeping you in place while you searched for the next place to plant a finger or the tip of a boot.

They climbed, slowly and carefully, until they reached the flow mechanism at the top. Here was a level area, more than large enough for all of them to drop their packs and get a look at the massive shuttered door. It was engineered to open by degrees, regulating the flow, as well as the level of water left in the artificial lake the dam had created. On the other side of those shutters, Malcolm thought, there was a million tons of water wanting to get down the penstock tunnel and get back to the ocean.

The dam operators had shut it down for some reason, and now there was no way to mechanically open it—not after ten years. They didn't have the time or the expertise to take the control systems apart, clean them, put them back together, and then hope there was nothing wrong with the electronics.

He wished there was a way to make full use of the mechanism, but they weren't here to be perfect. If they couldn't operate it from above, they'd just have to force it open, and forget about regulating the amount of water coming through.

"So, you want to blow this?" Kemp said. "Have to be careful not to crack the dam, you know? Be a damn shame to come up here and accidentally breach it."

"It sure would," Malcolm said. "Foster. How much do you think we'll need? Conservatively. I'd rather do this twice than use too much the first time."

Foster reached into his pack and pulled out a brick of C-4. He flipped open a pocket knife, looked at the flow shutters, looked back at the pocket knife and set it about six inches from one end of the brick. "Give or take," he said.

"Okay," Malcolm said. "Conservative, like I said. We just need it open."

Foster started cutting the explosive as Kemp got a spool of wire from his pack and started unspooling it back down the tunnel. Foster molded the C-4 into a fist-sized blob at the bottom of the shutter assembly, right in the middle where the shutters came together. "I figure if we pop the bottom open, the water and gravity'll do the rest. Make sense to you, Mr. Architect?" he said to Malcolm.

"It does," Malcolm said. When Foster had the explosive set the way he wanted it, he took the wire ends from Kemp and stuck them deep into the blob. Then they made their way back down the tunnel, Kemp pausing frequently to unspool more wire. Malcolm was quietly terrified by this part of the operation. He imagined some kind of static buildup setting off the charge before they got back into the access tunnel. If the explosion didn't kill them—which it probably would, since the focused blast wave coming down the tunnel would probably turn their internal organs to jelly—the force of the water would batter them to death even before they had a chance to drown.

He said nothing about this, concentrating on getting back down the sloping tunnel without slipping. A long tumble down the concrete could well be fatal, too. There were so many ways to die.

But they reached the level pad outside the door to the access tunnel without incident, and laid the wire through the doorway. Then they hauled the door shut and shot the bolts.

"Okay," Malcolm said. "Time to see if it'll work."

36

In the mechanicals room, Ellie fidgeted with gear while Alexander ran through the tests his father had asked him to complete. It didn't take him long. The control panel fuses were all intact, and its wiring was in surprisingly good shape. People who built dams apparently over-engineered things like that, since they knew the equipment had to operate in close proximity to water. After a few minutes, he set down his tools.

"I'm done," he said. "As far as I can tell, everything's okay. But we won't really know until there's water going through again."

Ellie paused in the middle of going through one of the tool lockers. She was picking out supplies that met two criteria. First, she thought they would be useful, and second, they were light enough for the group to carry back across the logjam and to the trucks. It felt like busy work. She was frustrated, and irritated that the men had gone trooping off to handle explosives, leaving her here.

"We'll see," she said.

Alexander put his equipment away. He picked up a book out of habit—she had never seen a kid who spent every single waking moment reading when nobody was telling him specifically to do something else. Then he put it down again.

"I didn't know you had a daughter," he said out of the blue.

This caught her off guard.

"Yeah. I did," was all she could think to say.

"What was her name?" Alexander asked.

"Sarah," Ellie said.

She would have been twelve now, no doubt gangly and uncertain like Ellie herself had been at that age. At three, she was small for her age, a tiny bundle of bossy exuberance. She had already learned the alphabet. She could recognize her name when she saw it written down. Her favorite book was... well, there was a tie. She loved making Ellie read the tongue twisters in *Fox in Socks*, faster and faster, laughing when she stumbled. But she also loved to hear *Goodnight Moon* every night before bed.

Ellie had been reading *Goodnight Moon* when Sarah, nestled in her lap, sneezed blood all over the picture of the cow jumping over the moon.

A nosebleed, she'd told herself. Every kid gets them. But she knew it wasn't true. She was a nurse, she'd heard colleagues talking about the unnamed epidemic, and she'd heard stories on the news that got everything wrong except the growing sense of public unease. In her own hospital, several people had died of what would come to be called the Simian Flu.

She'd done everything she could, but thirty-six hours later Sara was gone.

Ellie couldn't tell Alexander any of that. Sarah was hers. She never talked to anybody about her, for fear of diluting her memory by sharing it. She knew it was stupid, knew that she was indulging in a coping mechanism that prevented her from completing her grieving process and moving on... But in a way she didn't want to move on, because what kind of a person could really ever move on from losing a child?

"I'm really sorry," Alexander said. Ellie looked back at him from the tool locker and smiled. What a terrific kid he was. Moody, introverted, scarred by growing up when and how he'd grown up... but he had a good heart, undamaged by everything he'd seen. And good hearts were in short supply these days.

"Yeah," she said. "Well... I have you and your dad now."

Alexander returned her smile. She thought maybe that was the first time she'd ever seen him really smile at her.

The moment passed, and he looked back at the open access tunnel hatch.

"You think they're going to take a long time?" he asked. "Those batteries don't last." They could hear the men down there, muttering to each other, the words made indistinct by their echoing trip up the tunnel shaft. Ellie wanted to go see how they were doing, but it was pointless. All that would do was prolong the time it took them to finish the job.

"You know your dad," Ellie said. "He's going to get through this part of it as fast as he can, especially with..." She trailed off, but she could tell he knew what she'd been about to say. Especially with the apes watching. Both of them—all of them—wanted to get down out of the mountains, out of ape country, as soon as they could.

Although she thought Alexander might not feel that as strongly as the adults. She'd seen him and the orangutan, sizing each other up that morning.

Who knows, she thought. *Maybe in ten years people and apes will all be living together.* It was kids like Alexander who could make that happen.

37

When they had the penstock door sealed and bolted, Kemp checked the wires, moving them gently back and forth to see if he could tell whether they'd been broken when the door shut. "They seem okay," he said, giving them a last tug. "But I guess there's one way to find out for sure."

The other three men pointed their flashlights in front of Kemp so he could see what he was doing. He unscrewed the end of his flashlight, exposing the battery terminals. He set the flashlight on the ground, terminals pointing up, and clipped the wires off the spool. He separated them and stripped about an inch of insulation off each. Then he looked up at Malcolm.

"You want to do the honors?" he asked.

"Doesn't matter," Malcolm said.

"Go ahead," Carver said. "It was your idea."

"Okay," Malcolm said. He handed his flashlight to Kemp and knelt, taking the wires and holding one end in each hand. Some of the fear he'd felt in the penstock tunnel was still with him. You never knew exactly what would happen when you detonated an explosive charge.

It might work exactly the way they'd planned, it might not go off at all, or the whole dam and powerhouse might come down on their heads.

Carver, Foster, and Kemp all stared at him, waiting. There was no turning back now, Malcolm thought.

"Brace yourselves," he said.

They all jammed themselves together against the wall across from the penstock door. Then Malcolm reached out and touched the exposed wire ends to the terminal nubs. A small spark arced in the darkness.

The sound of the explosion rolled down the penstock tunnel, reverberating through the tiny chamber at the bottom of the ladder. All four of them instinctively ducked and covered their heads. Malcolm wondered what the apes thought about it. He was going to have some explaining to do, the next time he saw Caesar, but what else was new?

As the initial boom echoed away, Malcolm heard Ellie call from the hatch.

"Is everyone okay?"

Kemp was closest to the ladder. He looked up and shouted.

"Yeah, we're okay!"

Malcolm heard something.

"Shh! Quiet!" he said. They all listened. "You hear that?"

Everyone strained to hear, holding their breaths… and they all looked at each other as from the penstock tunnel came the unmistakable sound of rushing water. Malcolm grinned like an idiot.

"We've got water." He reached out to shake Foster's hand. "Just right," he said.

"Hell, yeah," Kemp said, exchanging a cramped high-five with Carver.

Malcolm leaned across Kemp to shout up the access tunnel.

"Ellie! We've got—"

He stopped as they heard another sound. It was a long groaning rumble. Dust and gravel fell from farther up the shaft. "Oh, shit," Carver said. They all froze, then they all started for the ladder together, but it was too late. With a deafening rumble, the access tunnel collapsed around them.

Malcolm ducked and covered, crossing his arms over his head and hunching down to put his head between his knees. *Bend over and kiss your ass goodbye,* he thought. A piece of stone or concrete hit him hard on the back, not too far from where the rock had dug into his shoulder blade when One-Eye had dragged him up to the ape village. He cried out, but every moment he was still able to feel pain was a good thing.

The noise of the cave-in subsided to the sporadic rattle of smaller rocks and the grind of something larger, shifting somewhere out of sight. Malcolm coughed and started to sit up. He couldn't stand. Next to him, Kemp was coughing, too. Foster and Carver were silent. Malcolm saw one of the flashlights, partially buried in dirt and gravel. He dug it out and shone it around.

Let's see how bad this is.

Bad, but not as bad as it could have been. The wall on the downstream side had fallen in, huge slabs of concrete toppling to choke off the tunnel and smaller pieces jumbling below them... and, presumably, above. He and Kemp and Foster were okay. Foster rubbed at the back of his head and his hand came away bloody, but he was swearing with enough vigor that Malcolm didn't think he was badly hurt.

In an irony he would appreciate later—if he survived, he thought—the penstock door was clear. They could have gone right out that way if they hadn't filled the tunnel with water. He kept swinging the flashlight beam around and at last saw Carver, pinned under a rectangular piece of concrete as big as he was. Malcolm couldn't see his legs at all. Loose earth and small rocks cascaded around him as he struggled to free himself.

"Oh, crap," he moaned.

He heard Ellie's voice, very faintly, from above. He thought she was calling his name. Then he heard Alexander. He didn't want to shout back at them in case the sound of more voices might dislodge more debris. They were one little shift from being crushed or buried alive. Malcolm joined Kemp and Foster at Carver's side. Dust in the confined space gave the flashlight beam a ghostly quality, and also made it hard as hell to breathe. Carver coughed hard and rubbed dust out of his eyes.

"My legs, man, shit. I'm stuck."

They could hear Ellie and Alexander shouting from the other side. It sounded like Ellie was screaming. Malcolm felt rising panic, and choked it off.

No. Panic would kill them.

He breathed deep, in through his nose to filter out as much of the dust as possible, and set the flashlight on the ground near Carver so its beam illuminated the rubble pinning the man's lower body.

They got to work getting Carver loose. One of his legs was wedged under the other in a kind of figure-four. Malcolm got low to look more closely at which pieces of concrete were pinning him. He didn't see much blood, which was good, and neither of Carver's legs looked bent too much in the wrong direction.

"Okay," he said. "We'll clear the smaller stuff from around the bottom edge of the big piece. Then if it doesn't shift too much, the three of us might be able to lift one edge of it enough for you to get your legs out."

"Might, huh?" Carver said.

"No promises," Malcolm said. "We have to be careful. The more we move debris, the more likely it is we'll cause another collapse."

"Thanks, Sunshine," Carver said.

"I take my examples of good humor from you," Malcolm said. Carver laughed unexpectedly. "Hang in there. We'll get you out."

"Then how are we going to get *us* out? We're trapped," Kemp said, rising panic adding an edge to his voice. He'd found a second flashlight and was shining it up at the point where the ladder disappeared into the cave-in. "We're all gonna die down here."

"Will you *shut up*?" Foster snapped.

"Hell I will," Kemp shot back. "You did this. How much C-4 did you think we needed? Oh, enough to collapse the goddamn exit tunnel? You're a genius!"

Malcolm had already started scooping smaller pieces of concrete from around the base of the slab pinning Carver. Then he stood up and turned toward them.

"Both of you shut up!" he said sharply. "The more you shout, the more you breathe hard and thrash around, the faster we use our air."

Foster and Kemp backed down from the edge of what would have been a stupid fight. They both looked at Malcolm, who took his chance to go on.

"We don't know if any air is getting through from up there. We need to calm down and figure this out. Ellie and Alexander know we're here. They'll get us out."

"They will, huh?" Carver said. "A woman and a teenage dork. Some rescue squad."

"We could always just sit around and leave you pinned. How about that?" Malcolm offered.

"Hell, no." Carver grimaced. "Get this rock off me, man. I can't feel my foot anymore."

Working together, they cleared the bottom edge of the big slab on his legs. Then Kemp got under it, right next to Carver, on his back with his feet pressed against the underside of it as if he was preparing for a set of leg presses. Malcolm and Foster squatted at the exposed edge, both gripping it near one corner. There was no way they could actually lift it off the floor, even without all the other debris on top of it. The only thing they could do was try to maximize their leverage by tipping one corner up a little, and hope that was enough for Carver to get out.

Every so often they heard Ellie call from the other side. Malcolm couldn't stand it any more. He pressed his face up against the highest point of the cave-in and called out.

"We're okay!" he shouted. "Can you get some help?"

He heard her say something, but couldn't tell what it was.

"Anytime you're ready," Carver said, gritting his teeth in pain. Malcolm scrambled back over to rejoin Foster. "Okay," Kemp said. "One, two, *three*." He pushed. Malcolm and Foster pulled.

They heard a crumbling sound in the darkness and stopped.

"Whoa," Malcolm said. "That's what I was afraid of." He turned and picked up the flashlight, searching the walls around them to see if he could detect the beginning of a secondary collapse. Not that it would do them any good to know it was coming, since there wasn't a damn thing they could do about it.

He saw movement, at the upper reach of the space underneath the leaning slab of wall. Malcolm kept the beam there, motioning with his other hand for everyone to keep quiet… and still. More sounds came from the spot, and a head-sized piece of concrete fell to the floor.

"Oh, shit, here it comes," Kemp said.

Another piece fell, followed by a cascade of gravel. Then a hand reached down into the beam of Malcolm's flashlight, grasping the corner of a fallen block wedged against the wall slab. Malcolm's heart stopped for a moment.

It was the hand of an ape.

"Malcolm?" Ellie called. He could hear her more clearly now, and now he could also hear the sounds of more aggressive digging. A narrow shaft of light speared down into the bottom of the tunnel, then disappeared again as something moved to block it.

He couldn't believe what he was seeing. More ape hands appeared, lifting rubble away. The shaft of light broadened and three apes climbed down through the hole they had made. He recognized all of them. A chimp who was always near Caesar, a gorilla he'd last seen holding a club as thick as Malcolm's leg… and another chimp, with a bare spot in the hair on its shoulder around the unmistakable circle of a bullet wound.

Amazed, he watched as the two chimps dropped to the floor and the gorilla swung itself under the angled wall slab to hang onto the ladder. Malcolm pointed the flashlight at the bullet wound and looked back at Carver.

See?

Carver saw. He looked from the chimp to Malcolm and then away, down at his pinned legs.

The two chimps joined the humans trying to lift the slab off Carver. After a couple of tries, they got it heaved up just enough that he could drag himself out. The whole time he refused to look at either of the chimps. The gorilla studied the situation, looking at the injured human, then up, thinking. Then it wedged itself up into the narrow angle between the toppled wall slab and the wall, gripping the ladder with one foot and bracing the other against the wall. With its back against the slab, it pushed, and slowly the slab tilted toward the vertical. More rubble fell around it onto the humans and apes below.

"Hey, be careful," Carver grumbled.

The gorilla pressed until there was a two-foot gap between the wall slab and the ladder. The chimps scampered up and around it, disappearing.

"Malcolm, is everyone all right?" Ellie called.

"Carver's leg is hurt," he called back. "The rest of us are fine."

"She knows how to do stitches, right?" Foster said. "I'm gonna need a few."

"Yeah, she was a nurse," Malcolm said. "Go on up."

Foster climbed the ladder as far as he could without using the gorilla as a handhold. It looked down at him and nodded. He swallowed and grabbed a fistful of its fur, hauling himself up to reach the first rung beyond it and bracing his feet on its massive shoulder before climbing out of sight.

Kemp followed, doing the same and nodding back at the gorilla as he went by. Malcolm couldn't help but marvel at the creature's strength.

He got Carver's arm over his shoulder and helped the man stand.

"You feeling that foot again?" he asked.

"Damn right I am," Carver said. "How are we going to—?"

A rope dropped through the opening past the gorilla. "There's your answer," Malcolm said. He tied the rope around Carver's chest, snug under his armpits, and walked Carver to the ladder. Using both hands and one foot, Carver worked his way up to the gorilla. The rope grew taut and as he tried to reach around the gorilla without touching it. Someone—presumably the two chimps—

started pulling him up. He scraped against the concrete and swore.

"Damn, monkey," he said. "I guess I shouldn't have shot you, but take it easy."

Then he was gone. Malcolm looked around. He stuffed a few vital things into Kemp's backpack, which was the only one he could see. When he had stuffed the pack, he climbed up and paused before using the gorilla as a ladder. "You have a name?"

It nodded. With one finger it wrote in the air, concentrating hard. Malcolm saw it spell out L-U-C-A.

"Thanks, Luca," he said, and climbed into the light.

38

Twenty minutes later, Malcolm and Kemp had been back down and up the ladder three times recovering gear. After the third trip, he motioned to the gorilla.

"That's it, Luca. Couldn't have done it without you."

The gorilla eased the wall slab back into place. With a rumble, loosened debris fell to the bottom of the tunnel. A moment later, Luca squeezed through the opening the apes had dug around the side of the wall slab. Malcolm climbed up ahead of him and reflexively reached to give him a hand up out of the shaft. Then he caught himself, realizing how dumb it was for a human to lend strength to a gorilla.

Luca worked his way up through the hatch—a very tight fit—and knuckled his way up the stairs and out of the powerhouse. Malcolm and Kemp followed him along the catwalk and up onto the logjam. Seeing Malcolm struggle with the heavy pack, Luca stopped to lift him up. He did the same for Kemp. They got back to the open, rocky flat near the edge of the impoundment, with the logjam and waterfall below. The waterfall wouldn't last long now that the penstock tunnel was draining the impoundment.

Before a few days had passed, the top of the dam would be visible again.

The group of humans sat under the watchful eyes of maybe a dozen apes. One of them was Caesar, on horseback. He saw Malcolm and dismounted. Next to him, a younger chimp did the same, and then a baby—God, Malcolm thought, it couldn't be more than a few days old—reached out and rode the young chimp's arm down to the ground.

He paused on his way to talk to Caesar, checking on Carver. Ellie and Alexander were bandaging his leg. Sticking out from either side of the bandage was a stick she had used as a splint.

"Like this?" Alexander asked, holding the end of the roll of bandages.

Ellie nodded. "That's good."

He brushed a hand across her shoulders and ruffled Alexander's hair as he passed them. Then he met Caesar.

"Thank you," he said. "You saved our lives." Caesar nodded. Malcolm gestured toward the young chimp and the baby. "Your son?"

Another nod.

"Both of them?"

This time Caesar came close to a smile of fatherly pride. Malcolm waved a greeting at the young chimp, who kept his distance. The baby dodged in and out of his older brother's legs.

"Well," Malcolm said, "we got the water running. Now we just need to repair the generators, clear debris so the intake doesn't jam, and we'll be in business. I hope."

He was about to go on and explain the use of C-4, wanting to make sure Caesar knew why they'd had to use it, when the baby chimp bounded away from his brother toward the humans. He hopped on Ellie's back, startling a short scream out of her. Then she saw it out of the corner of her eye and quieted, allowing it to climb over her shoulders and tug at her hair.

"My God," she said. "You just couldn't be any cuter, could you?"

It dropped down in front her, looking up at Alexander, who stopped what he was doing with Carver's bandage to reach out and let the baby grab his finger.

"Dad, check this out," he said. Malcolm was watching. He saw Caesar was, too.

Building trust, he thought. Maybe this would all work out.

"Come on, wrap it tighter. It's gonna fall off," Carver said, irked by their attention to the chimp. Ellie shot him a look, but she went to work finishing the bandage. Nurses were used to the ill grace of their patients.

The baby chimp swung from Alexander's hand and let go, tumbling over toward the heap of supplies and gear. It poked into bags, jingled loose carabiners, and tugged the loose end of a coil of rope. Carver looked over at it just as it started to lift the latch on his toolbox.

"Hey! Get away from there!" he shouted, lunging over to swat the baby chimp.

It shrieked, and every ape within earshot was suddenly on high alert. The baby chimp scrambled away from Carver as he slapped at it again. Carver started to get to his feet and Caesar's son, enraged, leaped in front of him and shoved him back, screaming a warning in his face.

Caesar and Malcolm both stepped toward the confrontation, but Kemp got there first. He put himself between Caesar's son and Carver as the baby chimp scurried away to cower behind the heap of gear.

"Just take it easy—" he began.

Caesar's son shoved him, too, advancing toward

Carver. More apes closed around them, picking up the alarm. Some of them picked up weapons, too—rocks and sticks, anything close to hand. Foster got in the way, saying something to Caesar's son. Malcolm couldn't quite catch it. The young chimp son bared his fangs and Foster took a step back.

"Whoa, whoa!" he said. "Everybody just relax!"

Then the unmistakable ratcheting sound of a shotgun pump cut through the shouting and everyone, human and ape, fell silent.

They turned to see Carver, leaning heavily on his one good leg, wide-eyed and shaking. He held a sawn-off shotgun pointed at Blue Eyes.

"You touch me?" he said. "You fucking dare touch me? I'll kill you—"

Before he got out another word, Caesar crossed the distance between them, ripped the gun from his hands, and smashed it into the man's injured leg. Carver screamed and hit the ground hard, raising his arms to protect himself as Caesar held the shotgun by the stubby barrel, high over his head. One blow would break open Carver's skull, and Malcolm could see from the look on Carver's face that he knew it.

"Don't," Malcolm said.

Caesar turned to look at Malcolm over his shoulder, his gaze burning with anger at this betrayal of trust.

"Caesar, please," Malcolm said. There could not be a killing. All it would take was one, and it wouldn't stop until either human or ape was wiped from the earth.

For a long moment he thought he'd lost the battle. They'd made a deal and Carver had broken it. To Caesar it wouldn't matter whether Malcolm knew or not, especially not when Carver had tried to hurt his baby. Caesar held the gun high, his breath coming in fast, angry grunts... then he turned and hurled the gun away, out over the logjam and the waterfall beyond.

He took a step toward Malcolm, and Malcolm could see that Caesar was still teetering just this side of killing all of them.

"I swear to you, I didn't know he still had a gun," he said.

Stopping just short of physical contact, Caesar growled, "Humans. Leave... *now!*"

He turned his back on them and went to pick up his baby son, leaving Malcolm to wonder just how the hell everything had gone so wrong so fast.

After that, there was nothing to do but get back to the campsite before one of the more aggressive apes lost his temper and went after them. Kemp and Foster helped Carver while Malcolm, Ellie, and Alexander stormed ahead. When they got to the camp, Carver limped over to sit by himself near the ashes of the fire, pointedly doing nothing while the rest of the team packed up their gear.

Malcolm was nearly angry enough to kill Carver himself.

So much for peace between human and ape, he thought. *So much for trust.* So much for humans putting the general well-being in front of their own prejudices. It was only because Caesar had more self-control than any human that Carver was still breathing. He could have easily gotten them all killed.

And there was the spot Dreyfus had put him in, making Malcolm the focus of the whole dam project. *Damn dam,* he thought, *very funny.* He wanted the best for humans, he wished the apes well... but he also feared for his own safety. And what would Ellie and Alexander do if he was gone?

"No," he said, to no one in particular. He stood up and started walking.

"Dad?" Alexander said. His tone caught Ellie's attention. She had just shouldered her backpack to take it to the truck, but now she walked after Malcolm.

"Malcolm. Where are you going?"

He didn't stop. He knew if he stopped, she would talk him out of what he was about to do, and he couldn't have that happen. He could *not* accept this outcome.

He heard her call to Alexander.

"Just stay here," she said. "We'll be right back." Then she followed him through the forest, occasionally calling his name. He also heard apes in the trees, watching them. When they got to the gate where One-Eye had knocked him out the day before, Ellie finally caught up. By now she was freaking out and angry.

"Can I ask what you're doing?" she demanded.

"I've got to make him understand," Malcolm said as they passed under the arch.

Ellie hadn't seen it before, and now that she did, she figured out where they were going.

"Oh, God," she said. But she stayed with him and they walked on. Ape alarm calls sounded in the trees, relaying ahead of them to the looming gate of the ape village. Before they reached it, apes appeared closer to them, spears in hand. He was counting on the hope that they wouldn't kill him and Ellie without Caesar's go-ahead, but he wouldn't be able to count on that for long.

"Uh, Malcolm?" Ellie said. She was looking at a pair of apes who now stood right in front of them, spears ready.

Malcolm raised his arms, just as he had the last time. He wasn't as afraid this time around, maybe because he had nothing left to lose but his life, which was in danger whether he did this or went home... Or maybe because he was starting to understand the apes a little better, and thought they would respect this show of courage.

He looked up at the trees, deliberately ignoring the armed apes directly in front of them, and spoke out firmly, but not aggressively.

"I need to talk to Caesar."

39

Caesar had returned to the village still undecided about whether he should have killed the human or not. *Twice* he had given the humans a chance. And twice they had betrayed his trust.

He did not blame Malcolm, but Malcolm led the humans. If they did not follow his leadership, then Caesar could not speak to Malcolm as a leader. If the humans did not have a leader, there was no way to avoid a confrontation that was driven by fear. These thoughts stewed in his mind on the short ride back. He could not see a solution other than separating ape from human forever.

They would have to live without their lights.

His thoughts had been broken off when he saw the two midwives standing outside his dwelling, waiting for him with fear plain on their faces. He pushed past them, already knowing Cornelia was the source of their worry. Who else could it be? Blue Eyes and the baby had been with him.

When he saw Cornelia, he knew with terrible certainty that she was going to die. She looked around without seeing, making meaningless noises and rolling her eyes. They were yellow where they should have been white. The midwife with her saw Caesar enter and immediately signed.

She does not hear what we say. She will drink no water. She burns.

Blue Eyes and the baby had followed him in then, and Blue Eyes went to his mother, carrying the baby, who sensed the adults' concern and squeaked his own. He clung to his brother's hair and looked around in fear.

Caesar went to Cordelia. He stroked her head as he always did. She did not appear to notice. Resignation overwhelmed him. He realized that he had begun a deathwatch when he entered his dwelling, and he resolved not to leave until the last breath left Cornelia's body.

The humans could wait.

Or so he thought until a pair of apes entered a short time later, followed by another pair—each grasping the arm of a human. Malcolm and his woman.

Caesar rose from the bedside. This was the last time the humans would intrude.

Malcolm saw the look on Caesar's face, and he started talking because he knew he would only get one chance.

"If we go back to the city now, men will come back here with more than just a few guns. Men I can't control."

"Let them come," Caesar growled. "Apes will be ready."

"Ready for what, a war? I know that's not what you want," Malcolm said. "You're too smart for that. There must be another—"

"No!" Caesar roared. "Do not trust you."

I don't blame you, Malcolm thought. He was about to say as much when Ellie shrugged off the grip of the chimp holding her arm and walked toward the bedside, dropping her backpack from her shoulders and reaching into it. Their chimp escorts caught her immediately, pinning her arms as Caesar and Blue Eyes both turned to intercept her, as well.

Ellie kept her focus on the ape on the bed. Malcolm was no expert on medical issues of chimpanzees, but he could tell she was in bad shape.

"She's sick," Ellie said to Caesar. "I can help her."

Malcolm saw a chance.

"Caesar," he said. "Ellie was a nurse." Caesar looked at Ellie. He hadn't spoken to her before, and Malcolm saw him taking her measure, the way he had taken Malcolm's the first time they saw each other across the river.

"Nurse?" he said, trying to prompt the other apes. "Hospital?"

Caesar looked from Ellie back to Cornelia. She hooted something and then coughed, hacking up an ugly-looking phlegm. Caesar signaled to the apes that were holding Ellie's arms. They released her and she went to the bedside. From her backpack she took a small case and opened it. It held several small glass vials and a pair of hypodermic needles. The sight of the needles provoked a reaction from the older apes. God only knew what they'd been through when they saw needles before, Malcolm thought.

Sensing the reaction, Ellie showed all of the apes a needle and a vial in either hand. "It's okay," she said. Caesar came closer to her, close enough to stop her from doing anything to his mate, if that's what he decided. "Antibiotics," Ellie said. "Medicine. It will make her better."

Caesar hesitated. Malcolm took another chance, stepping forward and carefully placing a hand on Caesar's shoulder.

"Maybe I don't get to say this right now," he said, "but I'm going to anyway. Trust."

Caesar looked at him, then at Cornelia, then at his sons. He nodded.

With the smooth quickness of long practice, Ellie drew several milliliters of fluid from the vial into the syringe. She injected it into the sick ape's arm as Caesar watched. They all watched her on the bed, struggling for life— except Caesar's older son, who was watching Malcolm. He looked confused and hostile. Malcolm had a pang of sympathy for Caesar. That kid was probably a handful.

"One day," Caesar said, still looking Cornelia. Then he turned to Malcolm. "You stay one day."

Out of the corner of his eye, Malcolm saw the older son's reaction—incredulous anger. He nodded to Caesar, dipping his head to convey gratitude. But one day wasn't going to be enough. There was no way five people could get all the necessary work done.

"We might need more time," he said carefully.

"One day," Caesar repeated. Then, after a pause, he surprised Malcolm again. "Apes will help."

40

Caesar's offer was not without conditions, as it turned out. Number one was that Carver be removed.

"How about we just put him in the truck until we're done?" Malcolm suggested. Caesar went along with this, as long as there was no way for Carver to take the truck back to San Francisco himself. This made sense to Malcolm. Who knew what stories Carver would spin if he made it back without the rest of them? He would have a hundred men with rifles marching up the valley within a day.

So when he came back to camp with Ellie and a dozen or so apes—including Luca the gorilla—he immediately addressed his top priority.

"Carver," he said, "pack up your shit and get out of here. Foster, you mind helping him back to the truck?"

"What?" Carver was incredulous.

Foster picked up Carver's toolbox and shoved it into his gut so Carver had to grab it.

"Malcolm's trying to keep you alive, asshole. And he's trying to get electricity back on in the Colony so we can take a hot shower for the first time in ten years." Then he pointed. "Walk."

Carver took in the hostile glares from the assembled apes. Malcolm had never considered the possibility that he would just refuse to go, but for a moment it looked like that was exactly what was going to happen. Then Carver started walking. He also started talking.

"This is bullshit!" he said as he got to the edge of the camp.

"You knew the deal," Malcolm said. "You broke it. You're lucky to be alive. Now shut up."

"I don't take orders from monkeys!" Carver screamed, but he kept going, limping away into the woods with Foster next to him carrying the rest of his gear.

Poor Foster, Malcolm thought. *He's going to get an earful all the way back.* Then he turned to Caesar. "Okay?"

The chimpanzee leader nodded, and signaled to the assembled apes. They came forward and picked up all the gear and tools they could lay their hands on.

"Oh," Malcolm said. He hadn't expected this. "Okay. Thank you."

Alexander was watching the apes work, awed by what he was seeing. The orangutan from the day before slowed down as it passed him with an armload of gear. Alexander started to back away, but Malcolm saw him figure out that the orangutan was looking at the comic book in Alexander's hand. Boy and orangutan looked at each other. Then the orangutan moved on, getting back to work, and Alexander stood even more amazed.

Malcolm wondered if the orangutan was a comic-book fan. It wasn't impossible. People gave apes all kinds of stuff in the shelters and sanctuaries, not to mention the labs. But it was a question for later. Right then, there was work to do, and fast. One day was a tight schedule, even with an ape labor force to count on.

41

Carver was so far past his boiling point that he was practically steaming out the ears. All he'd done, keeping the trucks running, making sure Lord Architect Ape-Lover got all of his gear up into the mountains, busting his ass trying to help get water running and power on for all the people in the Colony who still thought they were better than him... and he was kicked off the island. Because that's what the lead monkey wanted.

"Bullshit," he said, for maybe the tenth time since he and Foster had left. And speaking of bullshit, Foster was treating him like he was the bad guy, too. He'd thought they were friends, but now he knew Foster was just another monkey-lover.

"Watch," he said as they trudged out of the woods to where the trucks were parked. "You guys go up there and get that dam working, and the next thing you know a million monkeys are going to show up and take everything they want. They'll see how the power works, and—" He made a throat-cutting gesture. "Then you'll know I was right."

Foster didn't say anything. He held onto Carver's arm until they reached the lead truck. Then he opened the door and pulled the keys out of the ignition. Carver limped past him and sat in the front seat. Foster shut the door.

"See you tomorrow, asshole," he said through the open window, taunting Carver with the keys. "Enjoy your stay."

Carver flipped him off. Foster just smirked and pocketed the keys as he walked away toward the camp.

Carver sat for a minute, considering the possibilities. He could hot-wire the truck in sixty seconds flat, and be back in San Francisco by nightfall. Without Malcolm, he could get the people good and worked up. He knew there were plenty of guns over at the old Navy base. It wouldn't take much to get folks picking them up.

The only downside was that he would look bad for running out on everyone. No way was he going to be the bad guy in this situation. Maybe there was a sole-survivor angle to play. He could pretend the apes had killed them all and he had gotten away... but could he make the story stick? Probably, at least for a while. But if he raised an army and they headed back up the mountain only to find Malcolm and the monkeys still one big happy family, Carver knew he'd be in a shitstorm of trouble.

It was almost worth trying. Almost. He put the plan in his back pocket for the time being. After all, he had twenty-four hours to decide whether or not to do it. The other thing was that if trouble really did break out, and he was gone, he would feel like a jerk for having bailed on the humans. They might be monkey-lovers, but they were still his species. He couldn't quite bring himself to run out on them, even if they were treating him like some kind of psycho just because he didn't trust the same monkeys that had started a plague and killed most of the human race.

It's like nobody has any common sense, he thought.

He climbed into the back of the truck so he could stretch out his bum leg. At first he'd thought it was broken for sure. Ellie had said there was no displaced fracture, and Carver was already feeling a little better. It hurt like hell, but it could hold his weight. That would come in handy if he had to make a run for it. He propped himself on a jump seat and got out some jerky and his canteen.

Looking at the canteen, he thought, *If I hadn't gone to fill you up, none of this would have happened.*

Except it would have, sooner or later. The apes weren't just going to stay in their dens forever, any more than the humans were going to hide behind the Colony's walls. Contact was inevitable. So, Carver thought, was conflict.

That was the thought uppermost in his mind when he heard the clip-clop of horses' hooves hitting stone. He craned around to look out the window and saw three apes on horseback. Leaning closer to see if he recognized any of them, Carver got a chill when one of the apes looked right at him. It was the one-eyed one, the one who seemed to feel the same way about humans as Carver did about apes.

The one-eyed chimp looked surprised to see a human in the truck. He looked at Carver like he was meat—or worse, some kind of bug.

What did I ever do to you, monkey? Carver thought. But it wasn't about him. That chimp had suffered at human hands. Nothing else could explain the loathing in its expression. It lingered on him for a long moment, and when it turned its head and rode on with its two pals, Carver exhaled a long breath, feeling like someone had just walked over his grave.

42

It was late in the afternoon, and they were up against a long list of stuff that had to be done, but Malcolm was starting to believe that they could do it—thanks to the apes. They dove in and worked hard, clearing debris from around the generators and the control panels, lugging heavy equipment and parts around, doing whatever Malcolm asked them to do. He was starting to wish he could have an ape crew on every job. They didn't gripe and they had twice the strength, it seemed, of the humans he'd worked with before.

Maybe, even after all the strife and Carver's idiocy, everything was going to work out. Even the golden light slanting in through the powerhouse's tall, narrow windows bathed everything in an optimistic glow.

Alexander, displaying more interest in technical, hands-on concerns than Malcolm had seen before, was helping Foster replace some of the burned-out and corroded parts in the huge generator blocks that would take the static electricity from the turbines and make it into current that could be transmitted across the miles to San Francisco. Foster's socket wrench slipped and he looked at it.

"Hey, pal," he said to Alexander. "Looks like I stripped out this socket. Find me another one, the same size?"

"Sure," Alexander said, heading for the tool closet at the other end of the control room.

The door at the top of the stairs slammed open and One-Eye barged in. Just like that, Malcolm's good mood evaporated. One-Eye slung himself down the three-story stairs in seconds and accosted an ape dragging a broken pipe across the floor. He signed something and the ape pointed across the room, past Malcolm. One-Eye dropped to all fours and raced across the room. Alexander, gaping at the violence of his entry, didn't get out of the way fast enough and One-Eye knocked him to the floor.

"Hey!" Alexander said. "What the—?"

One-Eye spun around and stalked back toward Alexander. Malcolm recognized that body language. *What did you say? You talkin' to me?* He vaulted over the railing separating the control panels from the main floor and got there before One-Eye did, interposing himself between the enraged ape and his son. He could see it wasn't going to do any good. Something had changed, and One-Eye wasn't going to hold himself back. If he'd had his harpoon, Malcolm would already be spitted on it.

Malcolm looked around for some kind of weapon. All he found to hand was the socket wrench Alexander had dropped. He picked it up, knowing it wouldn't be much help, but he was damned if he was going to sit there and let this ape come after his son.

Just as One-Eye got within arm's reach, the orange mountain of the orangutan stepped between him and Malcolm. He stood, making no sign and not saying anything, while Malcolm pulled Alexander a little farther away.

One-Eye wasn't about to take on the orangutan, Malcolm could see that. But he sure looked like he wanted to.

"Get Caesar," he growled. "Want Caesar!" He spun around and roared at the ceiling. "*CAESAAARRR!*"

Silence fell as his roar echoed away. The apes near the access tunnel stood aside, making room for their leader to walk up to One-Eye. Caesar was in no hurry, but he was also ready to fight. Everything about his pace and his body language suggested a spring wound just one turn too tight. Malcolm pulled Alexander farther away, all the way back to the control panels. He could feel the violence in the air.

One-Eye glared and stood his ground as Caesar approached.

"You make us serve humans? he said. "*They* should serve *apes!*"

Caesar squared off with him, stopping inches away and standing up straight, shoulders thrown back and chest out. This was serious.

One-Eye wasn't done.

"You shame us!" he growled. Then he pointed at Caesar's son, sullenly holding a long spool of cable at the far end of the room. "Shame your son!"

On the word *son*, One-Eye stabbed a finger into Caesar's chest.

That was one more provocation than Caesar was prepared to tolerate. He sprang and tackled One-Eye to the ground, rolling with him and grappling across the steel grille floor. At first the other apes hooted and shrieked, enjoying the show, but very soon it became clear that this wasn't an ordinary fight. Caesar and One-Eye were fighting as only old friends could fight—brutally, primally, with no quarter asked or given.

Malcolm had seen a video once, of chimpanzees hunting monkey. When they caught the monkeys, they twisted their limbs off and began to eat without bothering to kill them first. Malcolm wondered if this fight was going to end with one of them maimed. Or dead. They tore at each other with nails and teeth, gouging eyes, twisting joints. Then Caesar had a momentary advantage, and he started to pound One-Eye chimp-style, with both hands high in the air and falling one-two, one-two, as his whole body rose up and drove down, putting more weight behind each blow.

One-Eye struck back at first, but then his defenses were beaten down. Caesar pinned him down, squatting over One-Eye's chest and beating the scarred ape with a savagery Malcolm hadn't thought was in him.

What saved One-Eye's life was fear. Everyone, human and ape, saw the moment when he stopped fighting and started cowering, hoping only to defend himself long enough for his opponent's anger to burn itself out.

That fear registered with Caesar. For a moment it seemed to sharpen his fury. He reared up again, ready to deliver a killing blow... and stayed there, breathing hard, while One-Eye looked up at him, battered, making no attempt to escape or fight back.

Malcolm wanted to say something, but this wasn't his fight. The apes had to sort out their own business, if they and humans were going to deal with each other reliably. Caesar panted over One-Eye, visibly fighting the urge to kill him. The other apes in the powerhouse watched, but not one of them made a move to interfere.

Caesar's panting slowed, ever so slightly, and he mastered himself enough to speak.

"Ape... will not... kill... ape."

Releasing One-Eye, he stood and remained looming over his vanquished opponent. Malcolm thought he knew what came next—or at least what Caesar would want to come next. He didn't dare move, barely dared breathe. The other humans in the room didn't move either.

If One-Eye came after Caesar again, he was going to die. And from the look on his face, he knew it. Maybe, Malcolm thought, he even embraced it.

43

On his back, Koba looked up at Caesar, who stood a step away. The look on Caesar's face told him how very close he was to dying. He rose slowly, understanding that to move fast would be to provoke violence again. His head rang and he could feel the blows still, on his head and shoulders. He was in more pain then he had been at any time since leaving the research lab...

Because of Caesar.

Koba looked at the other apes. They all stared in shock, but as soon as he met their eyes they looked away. Humiliated, Koba turned to his friends. Grey and Stone had watched the fight from the stairs. Now, when he looked at them they, too, avoided his gaze.

He got to his feet and turned back toward Caesar. Further back he saw the human, Malcolm, and his boy. Then the woman who had helped Cornelia. The humans would look at him even though the apes would not.

He took a step toward Caesar, knowing what he had to do. He dropped to his knees and bowed his head, extending a supplicating palm but keeping his head down so Caesar could not see the burning hate on his face.

He knew Caesar would make him wait. He was prepared to wait… both for acceptance and for his revenge. Because the time had come for Koba to lead the apes. Caesar was weak, blinded, still wishing his favorite human was alive. Only Koba knew what humans were capable of. Only Koba could protect the apes from the humans… and, though he was sad to think it, from Caesar's weakness.

Koba felt the swipe of Caesar's palm across his own. He raised his face, wearing a mask of contrition. Koba knew how to dance, how to make faces, how to make others see him as they wished to, rather than as he was.

"Forgive me, Caesar," he said, making sure both humans and apes heard.

Later, as dusk fell, Koba, Grey, and Stone sat apart from the other apes near the fire pit as the entire village gathered for the evening meal. Grey and Stone were still with Koba, though he knew they would remember the moment when he had surrendered to Caesar. Let them. They would also remember the moment when Koba made sure the apes would survive on their own, whether the humans did or not.

He watched Caesar and Blue Eyes. There was anger between them, and Koba—who had worried about it before—was now glad to see it. Blue Eyes, too, would be important to his plan. Then Blue Eyes left his father, with no word or sign, and went to stand by himself closer to the fire.

Maurice sidled over to Caesar. Koba's eye narrowed. Maurice was loyal. An ape should be loyal. But Maurice was loyal to weakness. Koba would never be able to trust him.

Grey and Stone followed Koba's gaze. Keeping his hands low, Grey signed.

You did not warn Caesar about the guns we found?

Koba shook his head.

No. And neither will you.

Stone and Grey exchanged a look. Just like that, they were part of Koba's plan.

Still later, when most apes had gone to sleep, Blue Eyes remained by the fire. He had spent the evening after the meal repairing the spear broken in the fight with the bear. Now the point was retied onto the shaft, and he had chipped an edge back onto it. He sat, holding the tip in the flames to harden it.

Koba knew some apes believed that putting the stone in fire gave it a sharper edge. He himself did not... but there was no reason to tell Blue Eyes that.

When Blue Eyes looked up, Koba made a show of hesitating until the young one had looked back at the fire. He stepped closer and grunted softly to get Blue Eyes' gaze back on him.

Your father does not trust me now, he signed. *It may be up to you to protect him.*

Frowning, Blue Eyes set the spear down, to free him to sign.

What do you mean?

Koba took a step back. This was a time for small actions that would have large consequences.

His love for humans clouds his wisdom, he responded. *As long as they remain here, I fear for his life.* With that, he walked away. The plan was set in motion... and the finest part of it was that Blue Eyes would have a role to play.

44

In the morning, the first thing Malcolm noticed was the sound of the apes arriving in camp for the day's work. The second was that Alexander was not in his sleeping bag. He leaned forward and out of the bag he shared with Ellie to look out the tent flap. Behind him he felt Ellie stir and grab at the bag to pull it back.

Outside he saw Alexander, sitting with the orangutan, pointing at a page in his comic book. No, wait. The orangutan was holding the comic. Alexander was teaching him how to read it.

"Incredible," Malcolm said softly.

"What?" Ellie said from behind him. "That you never learned to get up without pulling all the covers off?"

"No, come here." Malcolm motioned to her. She held the sleeping bag close and scooched over next to him. He heard her catch her breath at the sight. "Can you believe it?"

"Can I believe what?" she said softly. "A fifteen-year-old kid teaching a talking orangutan how to read a comic book? Nothing unusual about that."

He chuckled, and they snuggled next to each other,

amazed that even in this world, where so much had been lost, moments like this were still possible.

Caesar arrived as they were about to head up to the dam site. He watched humans and apes working together. Malcolm had an internal debate about whether to approach him, and then decided what the hell, the direct approach had worked so far.

"We'll be done today. Like we promised," he said, coming close to Caesar's horse. Caesar nodded and looked away, tracking something one of the apes was doing. Malcolm wasn't quite done, though. "I just want to thank you," he said. "When we get back, I'm going to make sure everyone knows what you did to help us."

Caesar looked down from the horse. He reached out and dropped a hand on Malcolm's shoulder, exactly as Malcolm had done the day before in Caesar's tree house.

"Trust," he said quietly.

Malcolm nodded. There was a connection between them. Curious, he looked across the camp to where he thought Caesar's attention had been drawn earlier. There were Alexander and the orangutan.

"Caesar," Malcolm said, "do me a favor. What's the orangutan's name?"

"Maurice," Caesar said. "Good friend."

"Luca the gorilla introduced himself down in the tunnel after the cave-in," Malcolm said. "And your son?"

"Blue Eyes."

"What about the other one? And your... woman? Partner?"

"Baby is not named yet. Her name is Cornelia."

An ape of few words, Malcolm thought. He didn't want to push the chumminess of the moment too far, but it sure did help to have some names.

"Oh," he said. "And One-Eye…?"

Caesar looked at Malcolm. "Koba," he said. "Stay away from him."

"That's the plan," Malcolm said.

They'd spent the morning shooting more holes in the Jeep down by the water, and now McVeigh and Terry had decided that it was lunchtime, if "lunch" meant sharing a bottle of whiskey. They didn't do it every day, but today just felt like a whiskey day. They sat inside the warehouse, on the ground floor, looking up at the building's three levels, each jam-packed with crates.

"Man," Terry said. "We don't even know what's in half of those."

"Take us a year to find out," McVeigh said. He didn't care. Already they'd unpacked, test-fired, and inventoried enough firepower to put a gun in the hands of every man, woman, and child in the Colony. The rest of it, hell, it might come in handy someday, but they wouldn't need it any time soon.

He took what he considered to be a moderate sip from the bottle. Whiskey was one thing that was still available here in the ruins of all that was good and holy.

"This is the good stuff," he said. "None of that blended crap."

"What're you, some kinda connoisseur?" Terry asked.

McVeigh was about to tell Terry that there were three things of which he considered himself a connoisseur—women, guns, and whiskey—when they heard chimp noises.

They looked back toward the door facing the firing range and in came the chimp. Where had he been? McVeigh wondered. Did he disappear into the city somewhere?

He came hooting and shuffling in, making a big happy grimace and waving at Terry and McVeigh as if he hadn't seen them in a year. "

"Man, is this guy serious?" McVeigh said. "The rest of the apes must have left him behind because he's such a pain in the ass."

"What the hell's wrong with you?" Terry called out. "I thought we told you to go home!"

The chimp did a somersault, then another, rolling right up to them. He grinned at McVeigh and made eating motions.

"I think he likes you," Terry said.

"Shut up," McVeigh said. He slugged back a big mouthful of the whiskey and saw the chimp watching the bottle. He looked from one of them to the other, pantomiming with both hands a drinking gesture. McVeigh looked at Terry.

"You want a drink, Fugly?" Terry asked. He had a big false smile on his face. The chimp nodded and rocked back and forth from foot to foot. "Go on, V, give him some. If I had scars like that all over me, and I was blind in one eye, I'd hope someone would give me a drink."

McVeigh handed the bottle to the chimp, which brought it to his lips and sucked down a good fourth of the bottle. Terry started snickering.

"Whoa, take it easy," McVeigh said, mostly because he didn't want the chimp to drink all their damn whiskey, but also because he was feeling a little bad for the guy. Ape or no, he seemed like a harmless goofball. He reached to take the bottle back and the chimp let him have it right back. Something happened in his eye, a shift in the set of the muscles or something... and all that whiskey came right back out of the chimp's mouth, in a spit-take blast right into their faces.

"Ah, shit!" McVeigh cried, wiping the booze from his

eyes. He heard Terry crack up and was about to ask him what he thought was so damn funny about having a chimp spit liquor in your face. Shit, wasn't that how the Simian Flu had gotten started, from chimps sneezing on people? Terry's sense of humor was pretty damn weird, when you took a minute to think about it.

Then Terry stopped laughing, and McVeigh blinked the rest of the whiskey from his eyes, and there was the chimp, holding an AK47 in his hands like he knew how to use it. His teeth were bared and McVeigh thought, *That's what he looks like when he really smiles.*

The whole thing, the dancing, the grimaces, the somersaults. It was a game. It was a sucker play, and he and Terry had fallen for it.

"Come on, man," McVeigh said. "We were just kidding around with you. You hungry? We can find—"

The barrel of the gun came up.

He's not going to pull the trigger, McVeigh thought. No. *He's not—*

45

The apes had worked like dogs, clearing debris from the part of the access tunnel that had collapsed. Now a couple of them were looking down from the access hatch, one of them holding onto the rope that hung down and looped around Malcolm's waist. He'd done it to make Ellie feel better about the possibility of him surviving another tunnel collapse, and it had the side effect of making him think constantly that the tunnel might be about to collapse.

He needed to get this done and get the hell back up into the late-afternoon sunshine. If it was still late afternoon.

Pretty soon Caesar was going to come kick them out.

"Okay," Malcolm said. He was tired enough that he'd started talking to himself. "Almost got it. Let me..." He broke off because he needed all his breath to twist a rusty flywheel. It had been sitting in one place for long enough that it really didn't feel like moving. One of the apes could have done it must more easily, but this was the last thing. They'd rewired, they'd cleaned, and they'd cleared debris and replaced components. Now they had to see if the turbines would do their turbine thing. As he cranked the flywheel, that would create static electricity, and the turbines would take it from there, and the lights would come on in San Francisco.

He pushed, and the flywheel turned. He kept cranking it. The apes looked down from the hatch. Malcolm figured they were probably signing at each other about how weak he was. That was fine. He'd have the last laugh.

It was working.

He couldn't believe it. There was without question a thrumming beginning to come from the turbines. And if there was a thrumming coming from the turbines, they would be making electricity.

Malcolm cranked harder. The flywheel loosened up and its momentum started to take over. The humming started to get louder. If he could get it cranking fast enough, enough power would return on a loop from the turbines that the flywheel would turn itself. But how would he know? He was stuck down here in the tunnel.

He kept cranking, listening to the turbine hum and praying—really praying, the kind of prayer that only the non-religious can make—that it was really going to work.

"Alexander! Kemp!" he shouted. "Is it working?" He didn't know whether his voice would carry over the grind of the flywheel and the rising hum. His arms were like wet noodles, but he kept cranking.

Then he heard Ellie screaming from the powerhouse. He let go of the flywheel and scrambled to the base of the ladder. She was calling his name. He couldn't tell whether it was fear or elation pitching her voice so high until he saw her face in the hatch opening.

"Malcolm!" she said.

"What?" he panted. "What's happening?"

"You better get up here and see."

As he scrambled up the ladder, he paused just long enough to get another look at the flywheel. It spun along without his help, and it didn't seem to be slowing down.

He climbed fast, hearing a growing commotion above.

They could see it from the catwalk, a glow in the trees. But it wasn't until they got down to the bottom of the canyon, along the overgrown road that petered out somewhere in the resurgent forest, that they really knew what they were looking at. The orange ball of the gas station, the numbers glowing a warm indigo against the vivid orange.

Malcolm and Ellie got there with Alexander, Foster, and Kemp just as the clop of hooves announced the arrival of Caesar, Maurice, Rocket, and their group. All of them looked up at the orange globe, stunned. Ellie squeezed Malcolm's hand.

"You did it, Dad," Alexander said. Malcolm couldn't tell whether he was amazed at the sight of the globe, or surprised that his dad had pulled it off. Maybe both.

"We all did it," he said. As he spoke, he looked at Caesar and added, "Apes, too. We couldn't have gotten it done without you."

There was a loud pop, startling all of them…and then music started to play. It was an old song, a classic-rock chestnut that had been old when Malcolm was a kid. A wave of nostalgia hit him so hard that it brought tears to his eyes. There had been a world with music everywhere, and light when you wanted light, and hot water, and enough to eat…

All of that seemed to come through the old speakers set under the awning of the wrecked gas station, as a long-dead singer sang a song nobody had heard in ten years. Maybe this was where it started all over again. Maybe this was where they could begin to believe that the Simian Flu wasn't the end of humanity, but a hard and necessary corrective.

We can do better this time, Malcolm thought. *That's what second chances are for.*

Caesar dismounted and walked over to Malcolm.

"Can't believe it worked," Malcolm said. A thought occurred to him. "Up here at least. We won't know about the city until we're back."

Caesar considered this. He started back toward his horse, gesturing for the humans to follow.

"Come," he said.

Koba's plan took shape as they rode back into the mountains. He could not face Caesar directly. The apes had not come to his aid when he faced Caesar at the dam. and they would not do so now. So he would give them another enemy.

They slowed as they rode up the path leading to the humans' trucks, and dismounted. *Silence,* Koba signed. Grey and Stone nodded. They tied the horses far enough away from the trucks that their sounds would not reach the human. Then they crept to the edge of the clearing and looked. They smelled smoke, and Koba had another idea to add to his plan. He considered it and decided it would work. In fact, it would make everything that much easier.

When he heard the music, he froze. It took a little while for him to understand what was happening, and where it was coming from. Then Stone pointed, and Koba spotted the glow of the orange ball through the trees. He bared his teeth. The human, Malcolm, had done it. He had brought the lights back.

All the more reason to strike now, Koba thought. With lights, the humans would spread out again. They would find the apes, and with their building full of guns they would shoot until there were no more apes.

That was what would happen if Caesar led the apes.

That was why Caesar could no longer lead.

He left Grey and Stone at the edge of the clearing and approached the lead truck alone. In the truck's mirror he saw the human react to the music.

"Son of a bitch," the human said, and laughed.

Yes, Koba thought. *Laugh now. All of you humans, laugh now. You will not laugh long.*

The truck window was open and Koba saw the flare of fire from within. The human was keeping his... cigar— that was the word. Apes knew that word because many of them had been on television shows where the humans thought it was funny to make them smoke. The human was keeping his cigar going.

He walked right up to the window and stood, waiting for the human to notice him.

The human reached out to tap ash through the open window. As he did, he noticed Koba. His eyes widened and the cigar fell from his fingers. Before he could do anything else Koba reached through the window and dragged him out. The human tried to fight him, but Koba flung him to the ground. Before he could get up, Koba unslung the rifle from his back and smashed the butt into his head.

The human went down and his hat fell off, tumbling a few feet away. Koba hit him again. He tried to raise his arms and Koba raised the rifle like a club, bringing it down with all his strength. First he broke the human's arms. Then he kept pounding until the human's head broke open.

He stopped. From the edge of the clearing Grey and Stone were hooting with bloodlust. Koba looked back at them. His fury—with nowhere to go again now that the human was dead—began to build inside him. The music drifting through the trees just made him angrier.

Grey, Koba signed. *Pick up the... cigar.* He stumbled

over that sign, making the letters as best he could. *Keep its fire alive. Stone, pick up the hat.*

They went on toward the village, but did not enter through the gate. Leaving the horses on the path beyond the totem gate, the three apes ducked off and began the climb along the face of the canyon wall. They could not be seen. Not just yet.

46

The music carried better than Malcolm would have thought. Even up in the ape village they could hear it. The apes came out of their dwellings, looking around uneasily. Many of them were younger than ten, and had never heard recorded music before.

Or any music, probably, Malcolm thought. They were also nervous seeing the humans, after the rocky start to the human-ape relationship over the past couple of days. But he and Caesar walked together, and Caesar's calm assurance seemed to spread as more and more apes saw that they were together and united.

Caesar led the five humans and his closest apes through the gathering area at the center of the village and to the edge of the raised stone slab that seemed to be a kind of throne. The apes climbed up and reached back to help the humans. It was a pretty good view, Malcolm thought as he got his feet under him. The whole canyon was visible, with the river rushing down toward the dam impoundment. The dam itself wasn't visible, but the mountains to the west made for quite a vista. He turned to see what the view to the east was like.

"Oh my God," he said.

San Francisco, in the distance, glimmered and twinkled with a thousand lights. Lights from houses whose power had failed and whose occupants had died without bothering to turn off the switches. Lights from sources directly connected to the grid. Fort Point blazed, the airport runways were outlined in red and green, beacon lights at the top of the bridges shone into the deepening dusk as fog spread through the strait and across the bay. The elated humans hugged one another.

"Damn if you didn't do it," Foster said.

"All of us did it," Malcolm said. He wondered what kind of pandemonium was breaking out in the Colony right then. *How do you like that, Dreyfus?* he thought, gloating just for a moment. Alexander, who barely remembered electricity, gaped at the sight. Malcolm was overcome, partly with pride and partly with a joy that his son would grow up, not as one of the last survivors of humanity, but as one of the first generation who would make their way in this new world.

Even the apes seemed affected by the sight. Maurice studied it and signed something at Rocket, who signed back. Malcolm wished he knew their sign language.

"What did they say?" he asked Caesar.

"City looks alive," Caesar said. "Maurice is happy for humans."

"Humans are happy for humans, too," Malcolm said. "And listen, now that we've got power, we can help you, too. There's no reason we should keep on being afraid of each other, right?"

Caesar thought about this.

"Maybe not," he said. He saw Cornelia and Blue Eyes emerging to look at the city. Malcolm tapped Ellie's shoulder and nodded up.

"She looks a lot better," he said.

"The wonders of antibiotics," Ellie said. Cornelia held the baby in the crook of one arm. Caesar climbed up to her and greeted her, stroking the side of her face and then doing the same to the baby. Blue Eyes stood a little apart. Malcolm could read his body language as clearly as if the young ape was carrying a sign. He was contrite, but unsure whether his father had forgiven him for yesterday's outburst.

Then Caesar reached out and gestured for Blue Eyes to join his family. The young ape did, kneeling at arm's length and extending a supplicating palm. Caesar reached out, but did not swipe his son's palm. Instead he grasped Blue Eyes' arm and pulled him up, embracing him.

Now here was an unexpected bonus, Malcolm thought. Twenty-four hours ago, Caesar was on the verge of killing us. Now we got the juice going, and everybody's reconciling, human and ape alike. He started to envision a future where the two species intermingled, building a new civilization together.

Amazing, he thought. *Who could have predicted this?*

Koba watched ape and human celebrating together, and his rage and disgust grew. He had been right. Caesar had betrayed them. Now that humans had the lights, they would come for the apes. Koba saw clearly. He knew what he had to do.

He looked down the slope at Grey, who had the dead human's cigar in his mouth. He puffed to keep the fire alive. Grey looked at Stone, and they both turned their faces up to Koba. He nodded. Grey took a last puff. The end of the cigar glowed bright and hot. Then he tossed it into a cluster of dry bushes, with a litter of dead leaves and pine needles underneath it. Smoke rose instantly, and then fire.

Koba looked back up toward the mass celebration. Caesar and Blue Eyes broke their embrace and Caesar rubbed his son's head. Blue Eyes smiled back and both turned. Koba knew they were looking at the lights in the city. They smiled! How could they smile at *this*?

As he had seen the humans do, he braced the butt of the gun on his shoulder and looked down the barrel with his good eye. A small piece of metal stuck up at the end of the barrel. If that was on the target, that is where the bullet would hit. Koba waited for Caesar and Blue Eyes to separate a little farther. He needed Blue Eyes.

Below the flames grew. Soon every ape would smell the smoke and know it did not come from the fire in the courtyard.

The time to act was now.

Caesar turned, as if he sensed something, and walked to the edge of his perch, peering over the steep drop-off and into the canyon. He saw Koba, and Koba saw Caesar look first surprised, then welcoming. He smiled and started to beckon Koba to come up.

Then he saw the gun. In the split second before Koba fired, he saw Caesar's understanding.

Yes, he thought. *With human tools I kill you. With human tools I will kill humans. Then power will be Koba's. Power over apes, power that runs through wires.* But as his finger tightened on the trigger, the words from the wall ran through his mind. *Ape shall not kill ape.*

Caesar had saved them all. But now Caesar would let them be killed. Koba would survive. If Caesar had to die, if one ape had to die so the rest would not return to a life of cages and needles and scars...

He pulled the trigger.

47

At the crack of the shot, Malcolm ducked, gathering Ellie and Alexander to him as he looked to see where it had come from.

"Get down!" he shouted. Kemp and Foster hit the deck, too. Who was shooting? The apes had destroyed all the guns they'd brought with them... hadn't they?

Cornelia screamed from above them and Malcolm jerked back around in time to see Caesar fall from the platform built out from the trunk of his tree. He crashed through the brush and disappeared, the sound of his fall continuing for a terribly long time as his body tumbled down the steep slope into the ravine.

Blue Eyes stood, arms outstretched, watching. Slowly his arms dropped.

Rocket rushed past them up and up the tree. Other apes were shrieking and converging on the tree.

The gorilla, Luca, folded the wailing Cornelia into his arms as dozens of apes looked down into the ravine, searching for any sign of Caesar or whoever had fired the shot. Malcolm recognized some of them. There was one of Koba's closest apes, the gray one, climbing up from the other side of the tree to join the search.

Blue Eyes spotted something and jumped from the tree down onto a rock outcropping below. From behind them came a fresh burst of panicked shrieks. Malcolm turned to see fire spreading through several of the ape dwellings between the raised stone platform and the village gate. It was moving fast, running along the wall and through the brush. Terrified apes fled from it into the open space.

They don't know how to fight fire, Malcolm thought. *We can help—*

Then another ape charged from one of the dwellings and vaulted up onto the slab of stone, where he stood with the ape commandments behind him. In the smoke it took Malcolm a moment to recognize him, but when he did, he knew they were in trouble.

Uh-oh, he thought. *One-Eye. Koba.*

Pacing to the front edge of the stone slab, Koba raised his arms and roared, "Humans kill Caesar!"

"What?" Ellie said. "We didn't—"

It's a coup, Malcolm thought. It had to be. Carver didn't have a rifle and nobody else in the Colony knew where the ape village was. But there was no way to tell the apes that at the moment.

Blue Eyes came through the smoke then, holding a rifle over his head. In his other hand, he held Carver's cap. The apes parted before him as he made his way to the stone slab, sobbing without tears. Koba seized the rifle and raised it for all the apes to see. The fire still spread—it had caught on the other side of the village, leaping the dirt path on a breeze coming up from the ravine.

"You see?" Koba roared. "You see!" He pointed the rifle at the flames. "And now they take our home… with fire!"

The assembled apes erupted in primal screeches, with an undertone of basso roars from the gorillas. All eyes were on Koba, but Malcolm knew that wouldn't last. He linked hands with Alexander and Ellie.

Maurice leaned in close to Malcolm.

"Run," he said.

Malcolm didn't need to be told twice.

Koba stood before his apes. *His apes.* He held the rifle over his head and shook it, rousing them to a greater frenzy. Now was the time to unleash them.

He looked across the stone slab, but the humans were gone. Turning, he searched the village, and saw them, keeping low, running through the fire. He screamed, the sound piercing the rest of the apes' screeching, and pointed. A group of apes charged off after the humans, who were already through the gate.

Koba signed to Grey.

Females and children go down to the woods and stay. All others will follow me!

Grey started relaying the orders to other apes as Koba returned his focus to the assembly.

"Come!" he growled. "We fight! We fight... for Caesar!"

Over the roar of the flames came the renewed shrieking of the apes.

Fight for Caesar! Fight for Caesar!

Koba turned to Blue Eyes, who stood with his head down. Koba laid a hand on his shoulder. Blue Eyes looked up and Koba slid his hand around to the back of Blue Eyes' head. It was the gesture of a father toward a son. Blue Eyes hesitated. Then he reached around to cup the back of Koba's head.

Yes, thought Koba. *I am your father now. I am father to all apes.* He looked at the burning village. Groups of females and young moved up past Caesar's tree to the open field beyond, where they would climb down into the woods. War parties massed together at the other end of the village, beyond the flames, waiting for their leader.

Fight for Caesar!

It was time to end the human threat.

The five humans ran for their lives into the night, getting off the path as soon as the terrain permitted and cutting down into the woods. Behind them, they heard the crackling in the branches—the sound of apes pursuing them. Their only hope was to get somewhere and hide. They couldn't outrun apes, and the faster they moved, the sooner their sounds would give them away.

Just down the slope from the main path, beyond the totem gate, the ground gave way underneath them and they tangled their feet in dislodged vines. The shrieking of the apes was getting closer fast. Malcolm got Ellie loose and saw that Alexander was scooting farther down the slope, to where it leveled out in a small bowl. Ellie moved after him, and Malcolm saw where they were going.

He followed, making a beeline for a jumble of fallen trees, probably pushed together by a long-dead work crew on a job clearing the old road to the dam. He and Ellie and Alexander crawled under the pile, scraping through rotten wood and spongy masses of loam. Malcolm waited for Foster and Kemp to join them, but they were gone.

Had they split off in another direction? Had the apes caught them?

There was nothing he could do, in either case. They hunkered down as the sound of the apes grew closer, louder… overwhelming. This was more than the initial search party. This was hundreds of apes, stampeding along the ground, shaking the fallen trees as they leaped onto and over them. A storm of leaves fell from the forest canopy as hundreds more surged down the ravine. The three humans froze, not breathing, until at last the wave passed.

In the silence they could hear the fire in the ape village.

It was a long time before any of them dared to speak. Ellie was first.

"What do we do now?" she asked, very quietly.

At first Malcolm didn't answer. He had no idea.

48

In the Colony, there was jubilation. Every man, woman, and child surged through the market, marveling at the lights. So many lights! The children too young to remember electricity were awed, and some were terrified. Their parents explained with happy tears in their eyes. And word began to spread. Malcolm had done it! This was the start of a new day.

Almost literally, since it was nearly midnight.

The lights had been on for a few hours, and the celebration was just settling as a real party. Until that moment, everyone had been too shocked to celebrate, and too afraid that something would go wrong and the lights would go out again, crushing their hopes just when they had been raised. But belief took hold quickly, and soon they were dancing and drinking and raising hell from the pure joy of being alive.

Dreyfus's back stung from the number of times it had been slapped. His hands were scraped and aching from being shaken by what seemed like a thousand people. Finally he excused himself from the festivities, because there was something he needed back in his quarters.

* * *

It took him a while to find it, buried under a pile of maps on a shelf in the corner, but before long he was standing in front of an electrical outlet, an iPad in one hand and its power plug in the other. Moving with the care of a priest performing a mystic ritual, he plugged it in and closed his eyes when he saw the lightning bolt on its screen.

He watched it, hearing the joyful sounds outside but caring only for the tiny sliver of red that appeared on the battery icon. The tablet powered up, and Dreyfus tapped the photo icon. He swiped through photos of old Army buddies, fellow police officers, him at different social functions and fund-raisers... and there was what he had come for. Maddy and their boys, Edward and John. Standing on the viewing platform at the top of the Coit Tower, they smiled for the camera in that distant year of 2012, when the Simian Flu was just a public-health concern and nobody had imagined what the next ten years would hold. Dreyfus blinked tears from his eyes and looked, drinking in every last detail.

Electricity wouldn't just give them a future, he thought. It would give them back their past. He looked up and out his window, over the mass of revelers. Above them, blinking against the sky, was the light at the top of the antenna on the unfinished skyscraper. If the light was on, the antenna had power. If the antenna had power, they could make themselves known, and at last—at long last—they could hear other human voices.

If any were left.

He took another look at his family, kissed his fingers and touched them to each of the three faces in turn. Then he set the tablet on his desk and composed himself. It was time to be the leader again.

* * *

The radio room was set back in a corner of the Colony away from the market and near the edge of the workshop area. Dreyfus headed for it, enduring more backslaps and handshakes, smiling and high-fiving, and at last getting clear of the crowd. He entered the radio room, and the first thing that struck him was the sound.

Static.

Two men, Finney and Werner, were working with the transceiver. They sat at a table piled high with a wall of recovered equipment. They had everything from military-grade amplifiers to CB radios scavenged from old trucks. Those had taken some searching. In the age of the Internet, the CB had been almost as dead as the eight-track tape. But they had them. And they had everything else they could find that might send or receive a signal, all wired through stacks of drum-shaped signal boosters that gave them a broadcast range of hundreds of miles... in theory, anyway, and depending on the fog and atmospheric conditions...

Werner leaned into a microphone, headphones on, speaking over the thrum of current from the boosters.

"This is San Francisco, attempting contact. If anyone is receiving this message, we ask that you identify yourself and your location, over..." He noticed Dreyfus and nodded at the mountain of gear, proud of what they had done. "We're out on over two hundred frequencies now."

Dreyfus nodded. They all watched the speakers, looked from dial to dial on the dozens of sets piled together on the table. The static was broken by a sharp crackle and they all froze, listening harder. Had there been a hint of a voice?

The crackle lasted only a second. Then the static returned.

"Keep trying," Dreyfus said. Hell, static was a big step forward.

49

Koba and his army thundered over the bridge, not caring who knew they were coming. They were too many for the few humans in the fort, and once the apes were in the fort, the rest of the humans would be no match for them.

Carrying torches, they rolled through the fog, down the swooping ramp from the bridge to the road that ran past the brick building. They spilled through the open gate and headed to the firing range. Koba did not care what happened to whatever humans were there. If his apes killed them, fine. If not, it would not matter once they had the guns and they marched on the human settlement. There would be plenty of time to hunt down survivors.

What he wanted right then was a gun in the hand of every ape.

He and Grey and Stone rode past steel vehicles, some with wheels and some with metal tracks. Apes did not know how to use those, so he ignored them. They pushed through the firing range and Koba dismounted, leading his group into the warehouse. He glanced at a corner of the building, where the two humans he had deceived were folded into a pair of weapon crates. He had killed three more today, and the night would bring many more.

The apes stood gawking at the three levels of the warehouse, each stacked with endless crates of guns. They grunted and growled, keeping their voices low only because Koba had commanded it. He wanted them pent-up and boiling when the attack on the human settlement started.

At a gesture from him, apes scaled the walls and started breaking open crates. They formed chains, handing rifles down in armloads. Most of them were rifles like the one slung over Koba's back, but there were others, too. Some were shorter, with longer bullet boxes. Some were three times the size of a rifle, with hundreds of bullets in a long string. All of them went into ape hands as Stone moved among them with a pouch, dabbing war paint from it onto their faces. They looked at their weapons, eyes gleaming, rocking from foot to foot with the desire to hunt, to fight, to kill.

Koba saw Maurice and Rocket just inside the doorway. Of all the apes, only they seemed reluctant. He would keep an eye on them. They would submit. *Apes together strong.* He picked out Blue Eyes, watching the endless number of guns appearing from the darkened upper floors, and went to him. On the way he took a rifle from another ape. He thrust it in front of Blue Eyes, who looked down at it for a moment. Then he looked at Koba. Koba nodded.

Blue Eyes took the rifle, his face hardening.

Near them on the floor was a box full of bottles. Koba remembered the taste of the whiskey. He picked up one of the bottles and was about to drink when the inside of the warehouse lit up with muzzle flashes and the deafening sound of a heavy gun. One of the apes, careless, had accidentally fired many bullets up into the ceiling. Looking up, they could see the holes because beyond the roof, the fog was aglow with light.

Koba looked at his apes. They now saw what they held in their hands. For the space of a deep breath there was perfect silence in the warehouse.

Then it exploded with screeching and more shots as the ape army began to build itself into a new frenzy. Koba could not have stopped it if he'd wanted to... but he did not want to. Let them screech. Let them fire. Let the sound terrify any human who could hear it. He stood with Blue Eyes, letting the apes see them together, basking in the rising thunder of their hate, letting it grow to match his own.

Rocket and Maurice had no guns. Koba did not say anything, but he noticed. Yes, even with one eye, he noticed.

50

In the radio room, Werner was still broadcasting. He was tireless. Since the power had come back on, he'd been glued to the chair, repeating the same message, over and over.

"This is San Francisco, attempting to establish contact. If you are receiving this signal, please respond. Repeat, this is San Francisco—"

The door banged open and a rush of celebratory noise flooded in. Werner broke off, and Dreyfus looked up from pacing back and forth to see one of his officers, Dan DeRosario, gasping for breath in the doorway. Dreyfus had seen a lot of fear in the last ten years, but DeRosario was as scared as any human being he'd ever seen.

"What is it?" he asked.

"Apes," DeRosario said.

Dreyfus didn't need to hear any more.

He shoved his way through the celebrating throng, making a cranking gesture over his head as he tried to get the notice of the sentries on the parapet over the gate. On the way, DeRosario gave him a quick rundown.

"We got word from the fort. The apes went through and looted it. They've got every gun in the place and they're on their way here. All of them. Hundreds."

"Who else knows?" Dreyfus asked. "We need to get these people inside."

"I already put the word out to the militia," DeRosario said. "They're keeping it quiet for now."

One of the sentries finally noticed and started the siren. It cut through the celebration and the crowd looked toward the gate as Dreyfus got to the bottom of the stairs. He took them three at a time as the gate opened and the Colony militia spilled out to take up firing positions behind the Jersey barriers positioned between the gate and the street. Concrete walls about three feet high, placed end-to-end as used to be the practice when they were used along the highways.

"Keep them off the walls!" he shouted to the deploying militia. Then he looked up to the parapet, shouting louder. "*Keep them off the walls!*"

Back to DeRosario, he said, "How long?"

"We just got the call," DeRosario said. "Some of them are on horseback, but most of them are on foot. Not too long. A few minutes."

The crowd's energy began to transmute from ecstasy to aggressive uncertainty. Against the siren's howl, Dreyfus heard people on the ground shouting questions. He would have to make some kind of a statement, settle people down... in a minute. First he had to make sure their defenses were in place. If they couldn't count on reinforcements from Fort Point, that was bad. But he believed in the people of the Colony. They would hold out because they had do.

He wondered what had become of Malcolm and the rest of that group. If there was an ape army coming after the Colony, Dreyfus had to assume he wouldn't be seeing any of them again. It was a hard loss to absorb... but at least they'd gotten the power going first. The apes hadn't sabotaged it, either.

Dreyfus wondered if they were planning to take it over. But not on his watch, no sir. If the apes wanted peace, they could have it. But if they wanted war, they could have that, too.

Below him, recruits were adding material between the Jersey barriers, creating rough battlements. On the parapet over the gate, more recruits were finishing a wall of sandbags, adding a few feet in height and a lot more protection against either bullets or spears. They worked hard and they worked fast, but he could see they were also terrified. He couldn't blame them. Apes were monsters from their nightmares at this point. It was like being attacked by boogeymen.

At the edge of the parapet a young recruit, maybe eighteen or twenty, was shaking so badly he couldn't lock the belt into a grenade launcher. Dreyfus went to him, steadied his hands, and guided the belt into position.

"It's going to be okay, son," he said. "Believe it."

He stood back up and found his megaphone on the table next to the manual crank that drove the air-raid siren. He picked it up and signaled to the recruit who was running the siren. It quickly wound down.

"Listen to me!" he called out over the siren's dying moan. "Everything we've been through has prepared us for this night. Everything! We are survivors." He paced along the parapet, making eye contact with as many of his people as he could. "They may have gotten their hands on some of our guns—but that does not make them men. They are animals! We will push them back. Drive them down. Bury them!"

Some of the crowd shouted back at him, and the roar picked up. They knew they needed to fight, and led by the recruits and his cadre of more seasoned officers, they started to work themselves up to it. Dreyfus led them, raising his own voice and punctuating each phrase with a stabbing motion of his free hand.

"We... will... *not*... let them through these doors!" The echoes of his voice died away, and in the distance they heard the shrieks of the approaching apes. He left the megaphone dangling and said, loudly but calmly, "Fight with me. Fight for humanity."

Then he turned to stand with his soldiers and watch for the enemy.

The sound built, but because of the fog, it was difficult to pinpoint the direction. Dreyfus guessed they would be taking the direct approach, straight over the hill and down California Street. He looked that way, seeing lights here and there in the mist. More streetlights were coming back to life even now, hours after the power had started coming in. Still, illumination beyond the immediate vicinity of the Colony was patchy. He heard the sound of hoofbeats. Lots of them, and yes, coming from exactly where he'd expected.

"I can hear them," a sniper said, standing near Dreyfus along the parapet. He held steady, looking through his scope, but there was a tremor in his voice. "Where are they?"

Dreyfus looked through binoculars, trying to resolve any kind of detail. All he saw was the dimly diffused light of the Colony's illumination... then he realized something. The lights he'd seen out in the city weren't streetlights. They were torches, and as they got closer he could see their motion.

The apes' screeching intensified as they must have spotted the Colony's lights, and the torches started moving faster. They came on with frightening speed, and Dreyfus saw that they weren't just running along the streets. More were swinging from streetlight poles, in long lines stretching back into the darkness.

"There!" he shouted, pointing. All along the parapet, rifle barrels swung in the direction he indicated. They were waiting for his command, he realized, for a don't-shoot-until-you-see-the-whites-of-their-eyes moment. He took a deep breath, wanting the perfect phrase to present itself...

Then out of the fog, the apes began shooting.

The first sprays of bullets tore into the Colony's facade, breaking windows and punching into the sandbags along the parapet. The apes kept shooting, and their fire intensified as they got closer and could see their targets better.

Dreyfus forgot all about an inspirational phrase.

"Fire!" he shouted. "Fire now!"

They did, unloading from the parapets and from the makeshift fortifications in front of the Colony's gate. They had better positions than the apes did, and they knew their weapons better than the apes did, so their first volleys cut into the advancing apes and did more damage than the wild shots the leading animals had fired. But the apes were difficult targets, dark-colored and moving fast. Before the Colony forces could concentrate their efforts enough to make the streets too dangerous, the horseback vanguard of the ape army was practically on top of them.

The grenade launcher chuffed, and explosions scattered the closest groups of apes. The screeching reached a fever pitch. Dreyfus was amazed that individual creatures could make so much noise... and the screams of wounded horses added a painful dimension to the cacophony. Finney had set up a feed from the radio room on the siren table, and through it Dreyfus heard Werner, his voice getting desperate.

"This is San Francisco! If anyone out there can hear this, we are under attack, repeat, we are under attack!"

That we are, Dreyfus thought. He signaled to a small group of recruits at the other end of the parapet and they launched Molotov cocktails out over the Jersey barriers. They smashed onto the pavement and spread into a wall of flames.

Through the fire came apes on horseback. One, in the center, held a heavy machine gun. Dreyfus recognized him, the one with the blind eye who had looked so longingly at their guns when the ape army had made its first appearance. He did not see the other one—the one with whom Malcolm had talked. Seasoned political hand that he was, Dreyfus put two and two together. This ape had decided that Malcolm and the other ape were too chummy. He was taking matters into his own hands…

That made it even more likely that he had seen the last of Malcolm and the rest of the team which had gone up into the mountains. Hell of a sacrifice they had made.

The Colony would honor it.

He ran along the parapet, pointing at the one-eyed ape.

"That's the leader!" he bellowed, pointing to their target. "Take him out!" He repeated it all the way down the line. A spray of bullets tore into the wall around him, stinging him with masonry shards. "Shit!" he cried out. Right in front of him, a pair of recruits was blazing away with their AR-15s. They had a rocket-propelled grenade leaning up against the parapet between them.

"The RPG," Dreyfus shouted. "Give me the RPG!"

He lifted it to his shoulder, flipped up the sight, and tried to track the ape leader, who raked the parapet with his machine gun. Dreyfus recognized the weapon, and wondered what kind of world it was where apes on horseback shot M240s at you? Try as he might, he couldn't get a bead. The ape was smart, and didn't ride in a straight line. But tracking it, he saw a pickup truck with stacks of fuel cans lined up in its bed.

Now that's not going to move, he thought, and he fired.

The truck and its cans of fuel went up in a huge explosion that cut off the apes' direct approach to the Colony gate. The lead apes on horseback wheeled around and looked for another way forward, but the scattered debris from the destroyed vehicle burned in their way, and the other street rubble was catching. A few apes charged up and around the fire, using the building facades on either side, but they were cut down as they appeared.

The Colony had halted the ape advance.

"Keep it up!" Dreyfus shouted. His voice was getting ragged. "We've got them!" He hoped it was true. If they could handle the initial assault, they had the advantage. A good defensive position was their trump card.

51

The apes massed behind the wall of fire, shrieking and firing blindly through it as their frustration increased. Several of them lay dead in the flames, and others were badly burned, crying and rolling in the street. Ash lay stunned from the blast. Rocket gathered up his son and pulled him back, into the shelter of a car. Blue Eyes joined them, and after a moment so did Maurice.

Blue Eyes was trembling with fury and the energy of the battle. He wanted to charge back in, find some way through, lead the apes as his father would have done. But Maurice quieted him, putting both hands on Blue Eyes' shoulders and then lifting one to sign.

Wait.

Some of the apes, however, could not. Crazed with the battle, they leaped up onto buildings and rubble around the flames, but the humans were ready for them. Gunfire picked them off before they could bring their own weapons to bear.

Koba reined in his horse and looked for a way forward. He caught sight of a tangle of heavy wires, mounted to a fallen pole. They led through the flames. Koba shouted something to a group of gorillas and they went to the pole, hoisting it upright and pulling on it until the wires were drawn taut over the fire.

The humans were still firing from the other side, through the flames, keeping the apes from gathering... but now, Blue Eyes saw, there was a way over. Dozens of apes rallied to the base of the pole, climbing up and massing at the top. Koba held an arm up, commanding them to wait. Blue Eyes saw what he was thinking. It would do no good for a few apes at a time to use the wires. The humans would shoot them down as quickly as they appeared.

Apes together strong, Blue Eyes thought, recalling his father's words. Yes. Together they would go over the wires, and the humans would see how strong they could be.

Dreyfus ran up and down the parapet, pointing out individual apes as they tried to make an end run around the fire. The defenders of the Colony loaded fresh magazines into their weapons, and dragged their wounded back for treatment.

He shouted hoarse commands, making sure everyone knew that the battle wasn't over yet. The apes would not be broken. They would try again. But there was only one other approach, around the block and up the street from the other side. That was covered. If they apes tried it, they'd never make it to the gate.

As he had that thought, Dreyfus saw motion in the air over the blazing wall of wreckage. He looked, and couldn't believe what he saw.

"On the wires!" he bellowed. "Shoot!"

Apes came, not in small groups but in a single mass, swinging on the old trolley-car wires, using them as a trapeze to fling themselves over the fire. Even—incredibly— running across them, somehow avoiding the grasping hands of the apes swinging below. They fired as they came, more focused and deadly now as they got closer and had a higher vantage to see their targets on the parapet and behind the defensive works in front of the gate.

Dreyfus ducked out of the field of fire and picked up his own rifle. He came back up, sighting at the wires over the fire, and saw the apes dropping by the dozen onto the street, firing as they came. Gorillas, one at a time, swung behind them and picked up pieces of flaming debris as they dropped back to the ground. The debris crashed down behind the Jersey barriers, scattering the defenders and giving the chimps cover that enabled them to advance.

Dreyfus saw the leader, jumping through the flames on his horse.

"That one! He's the one! Get him! Get him!" He aimed and fired, but missed.

Near him, the teenager with the grenade launcher aimed at the one-eyed ape. Out of the corner of his eye, Dreyfus saw motion. On the roof of a trolley car across the street, an ape had spotted the grenade launcher. Dreyfus switched targets, but he was too late.

The ape fired and Dreyfus heard the bullets hit the boy. He spun back and dropped in a spray of blood, the grenade launcher falling over the parapet and down into the street.

The ape on the trolley car bared his teeth and screeched at One-Eye, who answered the cry.

For the first time, Dreyfus thought they might not survive. He aimed and fired, aimed and fired, but there were too many targets. The one on the trolley car dodged back and forth, mocking them. Apes leaped onto the facade of the Colony building and were shot down. But they kept coming.

Dreyfus was about to call a retreat when he heard a sound he hadn't heard since his days in the army—the unmistakable thump of artillery. A split second later the trolley car disappeared in a massive fireball that caught a dozen other apes and rolled up the front of the building across the street, shattering its remaining windows.

Dreyfus turned and saw a tank rolling down the street, smoke from its turret blending with the fog. From its hatch, a fire-control officer shouted commands, and the tank's .50-caliber machine gun opened up, tearing through the apes in the street.

Cheers broke out along the parapet and from below, in front of the gate. Help had arrived. Dreyfus shouted into the radio-room feed.

"Finney! Get that tank driver on the radio and tell him to park it right across the gate!" There was a crackle of static, and again Dreyfus had the fleeting sense he'd heard a voice. Then it was gone.

"On it, boss," Finney said.

The one-eyed ape turned and snarled at the tank as it fired again. This time the shell plowed up a huge section of pavement between the skeleton of the trolley car and the burning hulk of the pickup. Apes and pieces of apes tumbled through the air. The cheering on the human side got louder, and Dreyfus was right with them.

"Yeeeahhhh!" he screamed. "Let's go, let's go! Hit these bastards, now!"

Rifle and grenade fire from the parapet and the defensive bulwarks focused on the apes coming over the wires. They got a lot of them, but more and more kept coming. As soon as the tank got into position in front of the Colony gate, its .50-caliber would keep the apes off practically all by itself.

Dreyfus heard another crackle and the tank operator's voice blared out on the parapet.

"Bet our monkey pals wish they hadn't missed us out at the point," the man said, cool as could be. Dreyfus smiled.

Out in the street, One-Eye wheeled his horse around and charged at the tank. The .50-cal gunner was keeping his fire concentrated across the front of the defensive positions, making it harder for the apes to get close. He caught sight of One-Eye coming his way and tried to drop the .50's barrel down, but One-Eye blasted away at the turret and the gunner flinched down behind the shield. That gave One-Eye the moment of extra time he needed.

His gun clicked empty and he threw it away at the same moment as he threw himself off his horse, hurtling toward the gunner feet first. He hit the tank turret with one foot and gripped the gunner's neck with the other. The barrel of the .50-cal swung up and out, stitching a line of holes up across the facade of the Colony. One-Eye flung the gunner off the tank. Apes descended upon him almost before he hit the pavement.

They started to run parallel with the tank, watching One-Eye as he leered down into the hatch, and when he dropped down into the tank they leapt onto it and screeched, pounding their fists and the butts of their rifles on its armor.

From the radio room feed came Finney's voice.

"Boss?" In the background Dreyfus could hear screams.

"I know," Dreyfus said.

The tank lurched and turned, slowing down some but rolling steadily forward.

"Boss?" This time it was the sniper just to his right. He was pointing down to the tank, which crossed the street and angled straight toward the defensive emplacement in front of the Colony gate.

"I know," Dreyfus said again.

The tank crushed the outer part of the breastworks, ground its tracks against the Jersey barriers, and pushed over them, as well. The defenders scattered and the apes, adopting tactics used by soldiers since the invention of the tank during World War I, sheltered behind it. It rattled and bounced up the stairs and drove straight into the pillars dividing the Colony gate in thirds. Its engine roared and with a rolling boom, the columns collapsed into the Colony gate.

It held. For longer than Dreyfus would have thought, it held.

Then it collapsed inward and the apes poured through the breach into the Colony.

52

The parapet sagged, and part of it collapsed, spilling the defenders down into the rubble and the throng of apes. Outside, no organized defense remained. The apes owned the street. The tank stalled against the pile of rubble, and One-Eye climbed part of the way out, savoring the damage he had done. Then he realized the full extent of it, and a savage light seemed to shine in his empty eye.

Dreyfus, looking down at him, realized he had a perfect shot. He brought up the barrel of his gun, and at the moment of truth a group of fleeing humans rushed through his field of vision.

"Dammit," he growled, and held the rifle pointed at One-Eye. "Move," he said. "One of you, human, ape, I don't care. Just give me one… clear…"

"Dreyfus!" Finney screamed. "Let's go!"

There were too many people around. Dreyfus knew that, viewed from the distance of history, a dead bystander would be deemed a good trade-off for a dead One-Eye. But this was not history. This was life, right now, and he could not bring himself to pull the trigger.

So he ran after Finney as more pieces of the parapet

fell away underneath him. As he started to retreat, he saw apes climbing up the ruined gate. It was time to split up, guerrilla-style, and figure out how to fight. The irony of the term did not escape him.

The tank, he thought. *Who would have figured it would show up, and lose us the goddamn battle.*

Finney started climbing—well, mostly sliding—down an angled piece of one of the Colony gate's pillars. It sloped away from the main market area, which was a sea of hand-to-hand fighting. Absolute carnage, worse than anything Dreyfus had ever seen. He blotted it out, not because he thought he was above it, but because his people needed him to think. How the hell was he going to do that while seeing the beginnings of a slaughter? What he had to do was get out of there, bring as many of the Colony citizens as he could with them, and then turn the tables on the goddamn apes if it took a year, or ten years, or twenty to make it happen.

"Boss! Boss!" Werner's voice was screaming from the radio room feed. Dreyfus didn't have time to listen. He concentrated on the column, on getting down it without dumping himself into the midst of a sea of bloodthirsty apes. He couldn't tell if Werner was excited about something, or being dismembered by a pair of gorillas.

He made it down the column, putting his hands and feet exactly where Finny had. Then, from the scaffolding, they hopped across into the main building. Shortly after that, as they climbed down a steel ladder into the depths of the building's unfinished sub-basements, they got one more surprise.

Werner was down there.

"I grabbed the portable set and got the hell out of the radio room," he said before Dreyfus could ask. "There was fighting right outside the door, but I pushed through the back wall."

This was one of the virtues of living in a place where every dwelling was at least partly assembled out of scrap plywood, Dreyfus thought.

"But that's not the reason I brought the portable," Werner went on. Dreyfus looked at him. It irritated him when people said things, and then waited for you to ask obvious questions.

"What?" he snapped.

"This little guy has a recorder," Werner said, patting the transceiver hanging against his hip. "And I've got some sound for you, boss. I think you'll be glad to hear it."

"First we get the hell out of here," Finney said. He led them further down into the sub-basement. The apes would look up first—Dreyfus was counting on it. They weren't naturally drawn to dark or confined spaces. If he could avoid capture—or worse—for a little while, they might have a chance to figure out what to do next.

Dreyfus began to realize how exhausted he was. He needed to sleep. They all needed to sleep. So they picked a spot far into the corner of the deepest sub-basement, where a steel door opened—according to Finney—into an old Bay Area Rapid Transit maintenance tunnel.

"Couple hours of shuteye, and then we go into the tunnels," Finney said. "See if anyone else had the same idea. There are other ways to get in." Going underground, Dreyfus thought. It was bound to happen. He'd done just about everything else.

"Wait. First I want to hear what you got," Dreyfus said to Werner.

"Thought you'd never ask," Werner replied. He touched a button on the portable rig and rewound the digital recording a minute or so. When he hit play, the first thing that came out was his own voice, loud and strident.

"Jesus, turn that down," Dreyfus said.

Werner did, and then started it over again. Much more quietly this time, his recorded voice said, "This is San Francisco. We are under attack by... we are under attack and need help. We have a beacon marking our location! Please—we need help! We are under atta—"

A sharp crackle covered Werner's voice. Then came another voice.

Another human voice.

"...isco... we... you copy? Repeat... rancisco, do you copy?"

On the playback, Werner gave an audible gasp, followed by something that might have been either an oath or a prayer. Gunshots sounded in the background. One of the windows blew in, and they all heard the impact of a ricochet. Screams of humans and screeches of apes drowned out anything the responding party might have added.

Werner stopped the playback.

"That's when I got the hell out," he said.

"Yeah," Dreyfus said. They all sat, absorbing this new information. Two days ago—or was it three?—they'd all thought maybe they were the last humans, the last sentient beings, on the planet. Then along came a bunch of talking chimps, with the occasional gorilla, orangutan, or bonobo thrown in for variety.

Now came an answering *human* voice. But from where? Who was it? Were there cities somewhere, or at least thriving settlements? How many? Did this voice coming from the other side of the radio represent another scrabbling, desperate bunch of people... or was the world not gone quite so far to hell as Dreyfus had feared?

They have to be warned about the apes, he thought. *They won't believe us, but we have to do it anyway. And on the off chance they do believe us, and we survive the next couple of days, we'll ask them for a little help.*

"Did you talk to him again?" he asked Werner. "Before, after, or that was the only time?"

"That was it," Werner said. "But boss, there are people out there! Not just us. We're not—"

"You better keep your voice down, or there will be less people around," Dreyfus said.

"Alone," Werner said, more quietly. "We're not alone."

"Sorry," Dreyfus said. "I meant fewer." He reached out and gave him a slap on the back. "Good work, Werner. Really good work. Where do we need to get to, so we can send again?"

"Back to ground level, anyway," Werner said.

Outside, it was almost dawn. They couldn't risk travel during the day. At least not on the surface.

"Okay," Dreyfus said. "Here's what we're going to do."

As the sun rose over the city, Koba stalked among the highest beams of the unfinished building. He looked down on his conquest. The human settlement belonged to the apes now. It belonged to *him*. Fires still burned within it, and the apes pressed the humans into service, making them put the fires out... and learning so that they could do it themselves the next time.

Other apes lined these high beams, looking out over the city to the great orange bridge that had brought them here. As he passed, every ape bowed and offered a supplicating palm. He swiped them, not slowing down or looking each of them in the eye. He didn't need to. He ruled the apes now.

At the far end of the metal skeleton sat Maurice, who looked at Koba without supplicating. Koba waited. Maurice did not move.

How dare he do this, in Koba's moment of victory?

Koba felt his old friend—the rage he had carried with him since he first realized freedom might be possible—as it began to return.

Rocket pressed up next to Maurice and offered his own palm. Maurice looked over at him, and at last bowed his head and offered his palm. Koba swiped them both, slowly, making sure every ape within view was watching. Two of Caesar's closest friends—only Koba had been closer—and now they were his.

But as he swiped their palms, he looked at Grey, who understood the look.

Watch these two, his expression said. *They are defiant, and defiance must be dealt with.*

Blue Eyes sat alone, looking back toward the mountains where his father had died. Koba stopped next to him and, after a breath signed, *You fought bravely. Your father would be proud.*

Blue Eyes lowered his head and hooted softly, still in pain over his loss. Koba did not remember his own father, and had only the vaguest memory of his mother. He did not understand what Blue Eyes felt. But he did understand how to use it.

Blue Eyes looked up and offered his palm. Koba swiped it.

My apes, he thought. *Mine. Together strong.*

53

Sunrise came a little later to the deep forest than it did the ridges up above. The animals and birds came to life around Malcolm, Ellie, and Alexander, who against the odds were still alive. But they were also lost. They hadn't dared stay in one place long enough to sleep, not with apes tearing through the woods looking for them.

Maybe two hours ago, the ape sounds had died out as a mass of them gathered and headed down the mountain. Malcolm had a bad feeling about where they were headed, and what they were going to do. Of Foster and Kemp there was no sign. Malcolm hoped they, too, had made it through the night. But there was no way to know. At least they hadn't heard anything that sounded like a bunch of apes killing two defenseless humans.

"Does this look familiar?" Ellie said, walking behind Malcolm.

"I think... I'm pretty sure we parked around here somewhere," Alexander said.

Malcolm thought so, too. He recognized one of the rock formations that stood between the parking area and the river, at the base of a steep drop from the ape village, which was practically right over their heads. But anyone who didn't already know that would have been unable to detect it.

Well, that would have been true until last night. Now there was smoke still rising from the fire, and from Caesar's tree, burned to a charred skeleton that leaned out over their heads.

Using it as a reference point, Malcolm focused back in the direction of…

"I found it!" he called out. "Truck's over here!" He headed that way and heard Ellie and Alexander follow.

"Okay, we're coming," Ellie said. Then they stopped again.

"What is it?" Alexander asked.

Ellie's voice was low and scared as she replied.

"Stay where you are, okay?"

That got Malcolm's attention. He doubled back toward them and saw Ellie crouch over something in the underbrush.

"Malcolm!" she cried. He got there and saw that under the brush was an ape. A moment later he realized it was Caesar.

A moment later, Caesar's eyes moved, rolling in their sockets. They came briefly to rest on Ellie, then on Malcolm.

"He's alive," Malcolm said. "Can we move him?"

"We have to," Ellie said. "It's not like we can stay here."

Caesar weakly tried to sign.

"I don't understand," Malcolm said. "Just hang on. We'll get you some help."

There was no way Caesar could walk. The effort would have killed him before they got to the truck. So Malcolm squatted in front of him while Ellie and Alexander got him sitting up.

Caesar reached over Malcolm's shoulders while Malcolm stood, reaching back to lock his arms under Caesar's buttocks. The chimpanzee held onto his shirtfront. Malcolm stood, grunting with the effort. Chimps looked small, but they packed a lot of mass into their compact frames.

Nevertheless, he started walking.

Malcolm was in pretty good shape, since the past ten years hadn't afforded much opportunity for leisure. Even so, he was panting and soaked with sweat by the time they got to the trucks. Correction—truck. The second one was gone. Either Foster or Kemp or both had made it out of the woods. Malcolm hoped to see both of them back at the Colony, if it still stood.

Carver's battered body lay in the dirt by the lead truck.

"Alexander…" Malcolm said, about to warn him not to look.

"Dad," Alexander replied. "I have eyes."

So Malcolm let it go. He couldn't protect a teenager from everything. Hell, these days he wondered if he could protect his son from *anything*.

They got Caesar settled in the back of the truck, and Ellie climbed in next to him. As soon as she could, she began cleaning and bandaging his wound. It was bad, but not as bad as it could have been. Caesar's lungs were intact, and the bullet hadn't hit his heart. The wound was high in his torso and still bleeding freely, but if they could get the bleeding stopped, he might live.

"My son," Caesar gasped. "My family. Where are they?"

"We don't know, "Ellie said. She wiped blood away from the wound and tried to get a bandage in place. "I'm sorry. Try not to speak, you need to rest."

Caesar went limp again, his eyes rolling in his head. Ellie finished bandaging him and clambered forward to lean between Malcolm and Alexander.

"He's lost a lot of blood," she said quietly.

"Is he gonna make it?" Alexander asked.

"We have to get the bullet out, clean the wound..." Ellie paused. "What I need is back home."

"We don't know what's going on down there," Malcolm said. "There might not be anything left. Best-case scenario, I don't think the Colony's going to be welcoming if we show up wanting to treat a wounded chimp."

Ellie thought about this.

"What about Memorial Hospital?" she suggested. "It's right over the bridge. It wasn't completely looted. There might still be supplies."

Malcolm nodded and looked back at Caesar.

"I don't understand how this happened," he said. "How the hell did Carver get another gun?"

Caesar grunted from the back. All three of the humans turned. Malcolm thought he'd tried to speak, but he couldn't understand the words. Caesar tried again and this time they heard him clearly.

"Ape did this."

An ape? Malcolm was stunned. It could only have been Koba. The whole show of supplication after the fight in the powerhouse... it had been a ruse. Malcolm grappled with the implications. Koba had planned and executed a coup, using Carver as a patsy and killing him to make sure he wouldn't complicate the plan by telling anyone the truth.

"Apes?" he repeated, still not quite able to believe it.

Caesar nodded weakly.

Malcolm had even a worse feeling about what might be going on down in the city now. If Koba had pulled off a coup, and removed Caesar from power, his next move would be to consolidate that power. To do that, he would need to remove his other enemy.

The Colony.

They had to get back to the city. The only way to prevent an all-out war—if they could do that—was to make sure both humans and apes knew the truth. Malcolm started the truck.

"Buckle in, people," he said. "I won't be going slow."

He hoped the truck would make it.

54

With the sun higher in the sky, Koba gathered the apes. Numbering in the hundreds, they clustered on the highest girders of the unfinished building.

"While humans hide," Koba growled, "apes not safe! This... our home now. We must protect it. Find them... Cage them."

Blue Eyes watched the apes around him. Some were uneasy, looking away from Koba. Others hooted and danced from foot to foot, freed by Koba's hate, enabled to become animals again. Blue Eyes identified with the uneasy ones. He looked to Ash.

Everything happened too fast, he thought. Three nights ago, or was it four, he and Ash were chasing a speared fish. The wound on Ash's shoulder was still fresh, the hair just starting to grow back where the bullet had seared it away. Beyond Ash, Blue Eyes saw the long arm of the crane reaching out from the girders. A metal ball and hook hung from the end of it on a cable, swinging a little in the wind.

"They forget... what they did to us," Koba said slowly. "But Koba does not forget. We will make them remember. Go... Hunt them."

The body of apes began to move.

Ash shrugged. They got up and moved, but Blue Eyes was already wondering if he had been right to defy his father. But it made no difference now. Caesar was dead. Koba led the apes, and where he went, they would follow.

Blue Eyes and Ash went with a group sent to search the building they called City Hall. Koba said that this was where human leaders did their work. He told them he thought more humans would hide there.

A pair of gorillas battered open the heavy doors on the front of the building, and the apes flooded in, peering up at the high, domed space with staircases and balconies running around its edge. Blue Eyes admired what the humans had built, and the builders themselves. He thought he would like to build something more than dwellings of sticks and mud.

Most of the apes did not give the space a thought. They flooded across the floor, scaled the walls and banisters, hooting and screeching to flush out any humans who might be cowering within. Blue Eyes knew it would be dangerous to stand out, so he and Ash went with them, running along the balconies, banging in doors and searching rooms full of nothing but desks and shelves filled with books.

"Run! Run!" It was a human voice, echoing from a nearby hall, up another floor on the broad main staircase. Apes surged up the stairs, and Blue Eyes went with them.

There was a small group of humans at the top of the staircase, and they ran into a large hall, the morning light shining down through high windows. They ran the length of the hall and stopped short, as they found that the back stairs were suddenly full of apes. Blue Eyes heard those apes screeching in glee over the humans' panicked cries.

There was no need for Blue Eyes and Ash so they, with a few other apes, turned back to look through the level they were on. They ducked along a few narrow halls and offices, then came back to the stairs and started down. Blue Eyes looked over the railing. The floor was far away, polished and gleaming stone.

Noises from just above drew their attention. A group of humans ran out from the floor they had just searched. How had they missed them? The humans started to go up the stairs, but they heard the wild screeches of the apes up there and turned to come back down.

But Blue Eyes, Ash, and the rest of their group were there. They looked at the humans, waiting to see what they would do. One of them, an old man, his hair flying around his head like milkweed, suddenly lunged forward, swinging a metal pole at Ash.

"Gonna kill you!" the old human screamed. He kept swinging the pole in front of him, trying to keep the apes back. Behind him, an old human female huddled on the stairs. Blue Eyes could see that she was exhausted, and could run no more.

The old human swung the pole back for another swipe at Ash. Blue Eyes realized that he was no threat, and Ash was just waiting for him to get tired. But the old man staggered as the metal pole was jerked from his hands. He looked up and behind him, taking a step back when he saw Koba come out onto the staircase landing just above him.

The metal pole dangling in one hand, Koba looked down at the old human female. He looked back at the male and thrust out his arm, shoving him down the stairs to land in a groaning heap at Ash's feet. The old human looked up at Ash, terrified and in pain from the fall. Old humans, Blue Eyes understood, were like old apes. They were easily hurt.

Koba grunted for their attention. When they looked up, Koba tossed the metal pole down the stairs to Ash. Ash looked up at him and Koba nodded. Blue Eyes understood. Ash was to kill the old human as proof of his loyalty.

The old human understood this, too.

"Please," he said. "Please don't."

Ash looked from ape to ape. All of them looked away to Koba as soon as he met their eyes.... All of them except Blue Eyes. Blue Eyes looked at his friend. He did not know what to say or do.

Koba came part of the way down the stairs, cutting the distance between him and Ash in half.

"Kill this one," he growled.

Ash looked down at the old human, then at the metal pole in his head. He grunted something softly to himself. Blue Eyes couldn't hear what. Then he shook his head.

Koba's eyes narrowed. He came the rest of the way down to the landing, his gaze never leaving Ash. When Koba stepped off the last stair and was standing over the terrified human, Ash lifted his head. Blue Eyes was surprised to see a burning anger on Ash's face. He set the metal pole down and signed.

This is not what Caesar would want.

Blue Eyes too looked up at Koba. If Ash could face Koba, so could he. And Ash was right. Caesar would not have done this, and Caesar would never kill an old, injured human—one who was no threat.

Koba nodded, rumbling deep in his throat. Blue Eyes had a flash of hope that Koba would see that he was going too far. All of this had gone too far. Blue Eyes had been wrong to defy Caesar. By doing that, he had given Koba more strength. Now, how many apes were dead? How many humans?

Blue Eyes hoped Koba was thinking the same thing.

Koba reached out and seized Ash by the scruff of his

neck. Ash screeched in sudden fear as Koba dragged him up the stairs and around onto the balcony just above. Blue Eyes ran after them, and the other apes followed. If there was going to be punishment, they wanted to see it. Blue Eyes wanted to make sure Koba did not hurt Ash. Most likely he would make an example of Ash to cow the other apes. Blue Eyes understood that.

But Blue Eyes would not stand by and let Ash be hurt. He too would defy Koba, standing with his friend.

Yet he never got the chance. When he reached the top of the stairs and turned out onto the balcony, Koba lifted Ash into the air and threw him out over the railing.

As much as he tried, Blue Eyes could not look away.

Shrieking in terror, Ash flailed in the empty space and fell. The other apes were silent. Koba, too, watched Ash fall, and smiled when Ash's body hit the floor far below, landing with a wet crunch. Stunned, unable to know how to feel, Blue Eyes looked down at his friend. Ash had been hurt by humans, but had stood up for humans... because of Caesar. His death left an emptiness that could not be measured.

Blue Eyes had betrayed his father.

This was his fault.

He looked up at Koba, aching to fight him. But Koba was too strong.

"Caesar gone," Koba said into the silence. He spoke to all the apes, but he looked at Blue Eyes. "Apes follow Koba now."

Blue Eyes did not challenge Koba. He looked around him and saw that the other apes would not help him.

He was alone.

55

Malcolm drove over the bridge and saw smoke coming from the Colony. As they approached the checkpoint, a man with a rifle came out of the shack and flagged them down. Malcolm debated. They needed to know what was going on, how bad things were in the city, so they could make the right choice about what to do to help Caesar. The problem was that if things were very bad, they couldn't be seen with an ape.

Behind the guard came a group of armed men. They looked ragged and exhausted.

"Don't stop," Ellie said.

She was right. Malcolm didn't accelerate, but neither did he brake. He drove right through the checkpoint. As they passed the sentry, he waved wildly at them.

"What're you doing?" he shouted. "You gotta turn around, it's not safe! *Hey!*"

Malcolm ignored him, avoiding eye contact. If they recognized him, they would get word to Dreyfus if they could. If not, then it didn't matter. What mattered was getting Caesar taken care of without exposing him to a bunch of panicking men with guns.

He glanced back at the chimpanzee, who seemed to be holding on, and then flinched as he heard a burst of gunfire from behind them. In the truck's side mirror he saw the humans dodging into defensive positions at the checkpoint as a band of armed apes swung up onto the bridge from its underside.

"Oh my God," Ellie said. She was turned around and could see the battle through the back window on the truck's cap. Alexander was watching, too. The apes peppered the checkpoint with focused and disciplined fire, as if they'd been shown how to do it. It was an incredible sight. Malcolm hit the gas and got the hell out of there, racing off the bridge and down onto the Presidio Parkway.

"The hospital's out," he said. "We've got to get out of the area."

"Where are we going to go?" Ellie asked. She was still looking back up at the bridge.

"I don't know," Malcolm responded. He had a thought as he saw Divisadero coming up, and dragged the truck into a too-fast right turn. "Maybe Pacific Heights."

"Pacific Heights?"

"Nobody goes up there since the quake. There were gas leaks, fires…nothing to loot up there, either, unless you wanted to collect expensive furniture and contemporary art."

"I see your class consciousness survived the Simian Flu," Ellie said. One of the things Malcolm loved about her was the unpredictability of her sense of humor.

In the back of the truck, there was a dry gasp as Caesar tried to speak. They all heard it. Malcolm kept his eyes on the road. As they climbed into Pacific Heights, cracks in the road became chasms. He cut around onto side streets, looking for a place where they might be able to stop and do a emergency surgery on a chimp to stop the other chimps from killing all of their fellow humans.

Just another day in post-Simian Flu San Francisco.

"What?" Ellie asked. "What is it, Caesar?"

Caesar took a breath, then spoke, slowly and painfully. As he did, Malcolm started to see the outlines of a plan.

They had found nearly a hundred humans hiding in City Hall. Apes were now driving all of them across the plaza, where other humans stood under guard. The hunt was going well—Koba thought he had found most of them... and they had not killed any more than they had to.

He stood on a balcony outside the office for the city's leader. At the edge of the balcony was a flag, torn to rags and flapping in the wind that also brought the smell of smoke from the human settlement. MAYOR was the word on the door. Maybe Koba was mayor now. He watched as the guards drove the humans in a single group, away to a place where they could be held and watched while he decided what to do with them.

It would be simple to kill them. Koba wanted to. But he thought it would be smarter to learn what they knew first, to use them so he could understand what they did in the city, and how they used the power that turned on the lights. Then, when he had learned everything they knew, that would be the time to kill them.

Behind him, the office door opened. Koba turned to see a group of his apes bringing in Rocket and Maurice. Maurice did not resist. He was not the kind of ape to fight, especially when he could not win. Rocket thrashed and raged in the grip of two other chimps. When he saw Koba, he snarled.

"You... kill... my son!"

Yes, Koba thought. He had. Rocket was stupid. He had

challenged Caesar long ago, before the apes had been led to freedom. He had suffered at human hands like the rest. But when Caesar decided to make the apes weak by letting humans grow strong, Rocket had stayed loyal to him. Caesar's weakness had killed many apes, Koba thought. Every ape who had died in fire, or from a human bullet, was Caesar's fault.

So it was also Rocket's fault.

Koba bared his teeth in a grin. He had learned a new word and wanted a use it.

"Your son…" he said. "A traitor. Like father."

He nodded to the apes, who dragged Rocket and Maurice away. Rocket screeched all the way out of the building. Maurice never made a sound. Of the two of them, Koba thought Maurice was more of a threat. His patience made him dangerous. But neither of them would be a danger to him for long.

56

Malcolm drove slowly through the worst-hit parts of Pacific Heights, seeing house after house with leaning rooflines and spills of brick where their chimneys had been. Everything was overgrown with eucalyptus, wisteria, periwinkle... all of the invasive species that grew fast and didn't care what other plants were around. There were also fruit trees and what looked like gardens gone wild, just as in the other abandoned areas of the city. Entire blocks had burned to the ground, too, in the aftermath of the earthquake. Those charred remains were almost completely obscured by overgrowth.

He was waiting for a signal from Caesar, who was watching out the side window in the back of the truck. The ape had levered himself onto his side, and he grunted with pain each time the truck bounced on the neighborhood's ruined roads.

Even if they saw the house, Malcolm thought, they might never know it. It might have burned, or it might be so completely overgrown that Caesar wouldn't recognize it. He was beginning to worry they would just drive around Pacific Heights until Caesar died of blood loss and shock. What would they do then?

Caesar pounded his fist on the window. Malcolm braked the truck to a halt—not too fast, for fear of jolting something loose inside Caesar.

"What? Is this it?"

Sinking back to the floor of the truck, Caesar nodded.

They got out of the truck and looked up and down the street. Humans clearly hadn't been here in a long time, but there was no telling whether the trees hid a bunch of gun-toting apes. Malcolm popped the back of the truck open, and reached in to help Caesar out.

Before getting out Caesar paused, looking at one of the houses with an expression Malcolm almost wanted to call... nostalgic?

The Victorian must have been a real beauty ten years before, like all of the houses in this part of town. This one had been designed with great care, and despite its age, it was in surprisingly good condition—it had to have been renovated. One of those renovations had finished the attic, which had a beautiful round window facing the street.

They got Caesar up the stone stairs and onto the porch, and Malcolm rattled the knob. The door was jammed, so he kicked it open, and they helped Caesar inside. The interior was dim, thanks to the vines that had crept up the walls and covered the windows. The plants had worked their way through the siding and into the interior, too. The walls were water-stained, and everything was covered in dust.

"Here," Ellie said, brushing off a sofa. They eased Caesar down, and he lay back on the sofa, his eyes wide as he took in every detail of the house.

"Caesar, you okay?" Malcolm asked.

Caesar didn't answer.

"Think it's safe to stay here?" Ellie asked.

"Safe as anywhere else," Malcolm said. The only real

danger he could see was of an ape patrol finding the truck, but there was no reason for them to patrol up here.

Alexander, looking around the room, paused by a piano along the wall.

"Look," he said. Malcolm and Ellie joined him and he pointed out a photo on the piano. In it, a young man and a chimpanzee posed against the unmistakable background of the redwoods at Muir Woods. Malcolm turned to Caesar.

"You used to live here?"

Caesar nodded. He was still looking around the house, and now Malcolm knew for certain that the expression on Caesar's face, out in the truck, had indeed been nostalgia. *Amazing*, he thought. *He's about to die, maybe, and what he decides to do is go home.*

Ellie was watching him with deep concern. She drew Malcolm with her into the kitchen, where she started opening drawers, looking for anything she might be able to use to treat Caesar's wound. Alexander followed them in, and hovered in the doorway.

"He doesn't look good," she said quietly.

"We can't let him die," Malcolm responded. "He's the only one who can stop this. The only one they'll listen to." If they would even listen to him at this point, Malcolm thought. From the look of things on the bridge, events had taken on a momentum of their own. It might well be too late for the truth to matter.

Ellie stopped searching the kitchen.

"What if he doesn't make it? What do we do then?"

"I don't know," he said. "We have to help him. What do you need?"

"I was hoping to get into that hospital. I have a small kit back at my place, but that's—"

"I'll go," Malcolm said.

She looked at him, and he knew they were both thinking

the same thing. Going out into the city, by himself, with apes shooting at humans, heading down into the teeth of the battle to find medical supplies that might or might not be there… The outcome was, to put it mildly, far from certain. Ellie didn't like it, but she nodded. It was the only thing they could do. Malcolm turned to Alexander.

"Listen, pal," he said. "I need you to—"

"I know," Alexander said. "I'll stay here and help Ellie. We'll be okay."

What a kid, Malcolm thought. *Everything in his life turns upside down again, just when he's getting his feet under him… and here he is reassuring me.* It struck him then that once he walked out of this house, he might never see his son again. Or Ellie.

"I love you," he said.

Alexander nodded. "I love you too."

They embraced, and Malcolm thought *God he's getting big.* Dad thoughts—they came all the time now, while he was watching his kid grow up. He looked over at Ellie, and he could see that she was scared, but like Alexander she was trying not to show it.

All she said was, "Be careful, okay?"

Koba waited until Grey came to the mayor's office and reported that all the humans they'd found had been rounded up in one location. Together they went to the place Grey had chosen. It was a good place, a tunnel bored through a hill, with a fence across its mouth. Grey said they had blocked the other end of the tunnel, and on this end the fence was already there.

A gift from the humans, Koba thought. He knew they kept their sick apart. Probably they had put them here when the sickness came to the city. Now the humans were the sickness, and Koba was keeping *them* apart.

The area near the tunnel was covered in old signs and painted pictures. Many of them featured apes, or creatures that were part ape and part monster. Yes, Koba thought. He wanted the humans to think of the apes as monsters. Let them fear the apes while they lived. Let them understand what fear truly was.

He approached the fence. On the other side of it, hundreds of humans were pressed together. He could not see how many, because the crowd extended back into the darkness inside the tunnel. Koba climbed up on a car so they could all see him. The apes guarding the fence parted to clear the view.

"Humans," Koba said, his message simple. "You will serve apes… or die."

The apes hooted and stamped, waving their guns. Inside the fence, the humans looked to one another, scared and silent. They would want to know what it meant to serve apes, but Koba would not tell them yet. Let them live with their fear, inside a cage. Let them feel what it had been like for apes…

Until Caesar had freed them.

Koba pushed the thought away. Caesar had led when apes needed him. Now apes needed Koba. He turned his attention to his assembled troop.

"More humans out there," he said. "Find them!"

Immediately the apes started to move out.

Blue Eyes moved with the mass of apes around him, and they began to break up into search parties. A gap opened up, and across the space outside the fence he saw a bus with a pair of armed apes standing at each door. He looked more closely and saw the hulking shape of a gorilla inside. Luca. Other apes, too. Rocket was there, staring out the window, emptied by the death of his son. Maurice was pressed in the back of the bus, and in the midst of Blue Eyes' shock, the orangutan looked up.

He started to sign, keeping his hands tight against his belly so only Maurice would see.

I will—

But Maurice shook his head. He raised his hands and Blue Eyes saw they were bound together. Struggling with the bonds, Maurice signed back.

Protect yourself. Suddenly Blue Eyes realized eyes were upon him. He moved out with one of the search parties, not caring which one.

Apes together strong, he thought. Koba had led them for only a day, and already the old ways were dying. As he moved he started to ask himself whether he was Koba's follower, or Caesar's son. He knew he could not be both.

57

Malcolm moved as quickly as he could on foot, sticking to side streets wherever possible and coming down from Pacific Heights through Japantown and the Tenderloin, both of which were utterly deserted.

He got close to the Colony and began scouting, to make certain he knew what they were up against. Also, if he was going to get at Ellie's medical kit, he had to figure out a safe way in. Crouching out of sight, he heard ape noises and looked up at the nearby rooftops and light poles, then crept forward. He got to a corner a short distance from the Colony, and peered around.

What he saw shocked him. The gated archway had collapsed, a tank was stalled against one of the fallen pillars and apes were moving freely in and out. There was no sign of living humans, but there were plenty of dead. They lay in heaps where the apes had put them, just outside the destroyed defensive works.

Dozens of people, mostly men but some women and children, too.

Where are the rest of them? The Colony had held more than a thousand people.

An ape patrol started out into the street, coming more or less in Malcolm's direction. He ducked back out of sight and looked around for a quick to escape. He wouldn't be able to do Caesar—or anyone else—any good if he let himself be caught.

It had been stupid to come here, but the hospital was too far for him to reach. He'd never get there and back before Caesar died, and if there weren't any supplies there, it all would have been a waste of precious time. The sure bet was Ellie's place inside the Colony, now overrun with apes.

Back down the block was the entrance to a BART station. Malcolm headed for it, trying to move fast, stay out of sight, and keep quiet all at the same time. He got to the entrance and opened the glass doors, careful to keep his hands from leaving visible smudges in the decade's worth of dirt on the clear panels. He went down into darkness, following the wall when it got too dark to see, and moving by memory.

He followed a tunnel to a utility stairwell door. Once through, he saw a glow—a single light bulb at the bottom of the stairs still burned, surprising him. *Good thing someone got the lights turned back on,* he thought. *Ha.*

Further down there was a fire door that led into a construction zone. He was lucky. Though there was some smoke, no doubt from the fires above, it was exactly like he'd remembered. When the Simian Flu hit, BART had been in the middle of expanding this station so that it would connect to the lower levels of the new tower. The expansion had only gotten as far as tunneling and framing. The apes wouldn't know about it unless they'd decided to explore the tower's sub-basements, and Malcolm didn't think that was likely. From what he knew about apes, they preferred going up to going down.

On the other hand, these weren't ordinary apes. He was

taking a big chance, maybe even bigger than going back to the ape village and risking Caesar's wrath.

Hey, he thought. *That worked out. Why not press my luck?*

He stayed close to the wall, moving through the poorly lit space, skirting the edges of the pools of light cast by the few working bulbs. There was yellow construction tape everywhere, and abandoned equipment—concrete mixers, Bobcats, pallet jacks next to skids of cement bags and rolls of conduit. When he got to the wall on the far side, he found a door that—if he had it right—would open into the lower levels of the tower.

Malcolm passed through and continued slowly, listening at every corner. He went through the tower's sub-basements and up to the ground floor. He came up inside of the building, in total darkness. Moving by touch, he followed walls until he saw a glimmer of light ahead. He went toward it, and paused to listen. The only sound was his breathing, and he was trying to keep that quiet, too.

He opened a door and emerged into the back of one of the retail spaces the Colony had commandeered. It was trashed, and there was blood on the floor, but no sign of apes or humans. He skulked to the front of the shop, which the Colony had repurposed as a trading post. The shelves had been lined with all kinds of bric-a-brac, from needles and thread to glue and sunglasses. There had been medicines, hand-mixed by the Colony's few doctors. Now everything was all scattered on the floor—there was nothing he could use.

When he got to the front of the shop, Malcolm had a clear view of the market area, straight up to the destroyed gate. Bullet holes pocked the storefronts, the floor, everything. Piles of rubble and trash covered the floor. Their home was gone. Now it was just a ruin like everything else.

But where were the humans?

As desperate as he was to know, that was a question to answer once they had saved Caesar's life. So Malcolm cut across a corner of the market and headed up to Ellie's apartment. It was on the third floor of a smaller building that faced the main tower, across a street that was contained entirely within the Colony. He slipped in and started stuffing everything that looked vaguely medical into a duffel bag.

When he'd been in her apartment maybe two minutes, he heard a crash from outside and went to the window. There was a pair of apes, forcing two women out of hiding and onto the street. He pressed his face to the glass. The apes were sweeping the Colony again. Three of them were just going into Ellie's building, directly below him.

Malcolm stuffed a small first-aid kit into the duffel and headed for the door. When he came out into the hall, he hesitated. Left or right? There were stairs in both directions, equidistant from the apartment door.

Left, he decided, and headed for the stairwell. He let the door close softly behind him and started down the stairs, then heard apes below and turned to head back up. His feet scuffed a little, and the sound echoed down the stairwell, alerting the apes. They roared out an alert and Malcolm ran back up two floors of stairs without stopping. He paused to glance down, and saw them right on his trail.

So he kicked open the next door and rushed into a hallway that looked just like the one on Ellie's floor... only here, everything was wrecked. The apes had been thorough, smashing out walls and ransacking the apartments. Darting into one of them, he ducked in and out of holes between apartments, trying to put as many twists and turns as he could between him and the pursuing apes.

They crashed into the hall behind him. He made a last turn, into the interior of one of the units about halfway down the hall. Just on the other side of the wall, the apes smashed and screeched as they ran past, trying to flush him out. It almost worked, but just as he had done in the forest, he managed to hold still while they stormed past. Their clamor began to diminish as they moved into another part of the floor. Maybe they were far enough now that he could make a break for the stairs.

He took a deep breath, let it out, then went to turn and retrace his steps—and nearly walked right into an armed ape, standing right behind him.

Malcolm's heart stopped. He didn't dare move. With a thud he was sure the ape could hear, his heart started beating again, and in that same moment he recognized the ape.

It was Blue Eyes.

He and Malcolm looked at each other, the chimp's expression unreadable. Malcolm's throat went dry, but he started to try to say something anyway. Before he could make a sound, Blue Eyes clamped a hand over his mouth.

Malcolm froze.

Outside an ape patrol went past, smashing anything within arm's reach, still trying to flush him out.

Once they were gone, Blue Eyes lowered his hand. He had held Malcolm's gaze the whole time, but now he looked away, and Malcolm thought he saw shame on the chimp's face.

Take a chance, he thought. *Why stop now? After all, Blue Eyes just saved your life, and if the look on his face is any clue, he's not completely on board with Koba's Gestapo tactics.*

"Wait," he whispered. "Your father."

Blue Eyes froze. Then he turned, slowly, the barrel of his rifle coming up.

"He's alive," Malcolm said. "It's true, I swear. I can take you to him."

But only if you can get me out of here, he thought. Blue Eyes stared hard at him, the kind of stare you gave someone when you were trying to judge the truth of what they were saying. Liars broke under a stare like that.

Malcolm didn't break.

He let Blue Eyes prod him out into the debris-strewn hall, where the rest of the patrol screeched in Malcolm's face and feinted as if they were going to bite him. He looked down and ignored them. When they got tired of the game, Blue Eyes walked him down the stairs and then shoved him out onto the street, through the market, and out of the Colony. Malcolm saw other groups of apes leading human prisoners, some wounded or visibly beaten. But Blue Eyes kept up their ruse and held onto his duffel.

Ahead of them, he recognized another chimp, one of Koba's pals. The lighter-colored one. He looked up from smashing something—Malcolm wasn't sure what or why. When he saw Malcolm, he got a smile on his face.

I guess I'm a prize, Malcolm thought.

The gray chimp and Blue Eyes exchanged a look. The gray chimp looked as if he was about to come with them, and Malcolm had what was either a flash of insight or an episode of wishful thinking.

Blue Eyes has gotten himself into trouble, he thought. *Koba's buddies don't trust him.* The gray chimp stood and Malcolm staggered as Blue Eyes jammed the barrel of his rifle into his back, right where the rock had bruised his shoulder blade. *Three times,* Malcolm thought. *What were the odds?*

He let out a small groan of pain. The gray chimp hooted

his approval, and Blue Eyes shoved Malcolm forward, marching him up the street. When they were around the corner from the Colony, Blue Eyes grunted. Malcolm looked back and saw him heading down a side street. He followed.

58

It was late morning by the time they got back to Pacific Heights. Malcolm went in first, and saw Caesar where he had been that morning, flat on his back on the sofa, his bandage bloody. Ellie and Alexander were nearby.

"Thank God," Ellie said as she saw Malcolm. He held out the duffel bag and she took it, then stopped short as Blue Eyes came in, warily looking around like he still thought the whole thing might be a trap.

Caesar hooted softly from the sofa. Blue Eyes' head snapped around at the sound, and he set his gun down to cross the room and kneel at his father's side. The two apes touched foreheads, Blue Eyes' face contorted in an expression that would have been accompanied by tears if apes could cry.

"Your mother... your brother," Caesar said. "Safe?"

Blue Eyes nodded and signed something. Then he registered the bandage. He lifted it away and saw the bullet wound underneath. His body tensed and when he looked back at Malcolm, his anger seemed sudden and intense enough that Malcolm started to second-guess his decision to bring Blue Eyes here. Maybe he should have taken his chances trying to escape on his own.

"No," Caesar said. He reached up to grasp Blue Eyes' arm. Blue Eyes still glared at Malcolm, looking unnervingly like Koba. "Not humans," Caesar went on, every word an effort. "Koba."

Blue Eyes looked back down at his father, face blank with shock—and then the anger came flooding back in, only now it had a new focus. It was where it belonged, thought Malcolm. Maybe getting the truth out might still have a chance to do some good. Blue Eyes lowered his head, shamed and furious.

Ellie nudged Malcolm.

"We really need to do this now," she said. "Caesar?" He nodded, and she started to spread out the supplies from the duffel bag.

"Son," Caesar said. Blue Eyes turned back to his father and saw him reaching out with an open hand. Blue Eyes pressed close to his father, gripping the extended hand in both of his. Ellie leaned over him and started cleaning the surface of the wound, clipping away the surrounding hair to give herself room to work. She looked up at Caesar.

"Are you ready?" she asked.

He nodded again, holding tightly to his son.

When it was over, the three humans sat on the porch. Alexander was sketching, as he had been the entire time. Ellie and Malcolm sat on either side of him. Ellie looked exhausted. She hadn't slept in... how long? Going on thirty-six hours, Malcolm estimated. They all needed some rest.

"How is he?" Alexander asked.

Ellie gave him an encouraging smile.

"We'll see. He's very strong."

Twice during the surgery, Malcolm had thought they

might lose him. They were working with inferior tools, no anesthetic, no sterile conditions, on a bullet nestled between a nicked artery and the upper lobe of Caesar's lung. A lot could have gone wrong. Blue Eyes—to give credit where credit was due—had stayed through the whole procedure, not once flinching away as Ellie cut into his father's body. Malcolm thought he would remember for the rest of his life—however long that turned out to be—the expression on the young ape's face when Ellie reached into Caesar's chest with a pair of kitchen tongs and extracted the bullet.

He's just a kid, like Alexander.

As if he'd heard Malcolm thinking about him, Alexander leaned into his father. Malcolm mussed his hair, another one of those dad gestures that didn't make much sense, but felt good. Ellie leaned in from the other side and Malcolm dropped his hand from Alexander's head to rest on the back of her neck. Family, he thought. In the middle of all this, he still had his family.

Caesar stirred awake in the night, and saw Will's living room. He thought for a moment he was young again, three years or five years old, with Will and his father somewhere in the house and ordinary human noises outside. Then he came a little more awake and that dream fell away. The wound in his chest hurt a great deal, but he could handle it. He *would* handle it, for the sake of his son, who was sitting near the couch.

Blue Eyes saw Caesar awake and came closer. There was a silent moment while the young ape watched him. Caesar wondered if he looked weak. He must. Death had been very close to him.

I'm so sorry, Blue Eyes signed. *For everything.* Caesar had a little trouble following the signs in the darkness, but he understood them. He also understood what Blue Eyes meant, where this feeling came from. There were many things he wanted to say in answer. He wanted to explain his anger, his harshness toward Blue Eyes, his fear as he saw his son fall under the spell of Koba's unthinking hate.

Too many things to say.

Caesar raised his hands to sign, but he was too weak. His arms trembled and he lowered them back to his sides. He spoke in a strained whisper, saying only the most important thing.

"No. I am to blame."

Even in the darkness he saw the surprise on Blue Eyes' face.

But Koba betrayed you...

"I chose to trust him. Because he is ape." Caesar looked away from Blue Eyes' hands to his face. "Always thought... apes were better than humans." He paused for breath. "But I see now... how much like them we are."

Blue Eyes listened. Caesar realized how rare this was. His son had learned hard lessons in the past day. Something about him had changed. He had not told Caesar what it was, and Caesar would not ask. Apes had a right to their silence.

Thinking of his son's pain strengthened Caesar. He spoke again, a little louder.

"Where is Koba now?"

He's made the human tower his home, surrounded by the apes most loyal to him, Blue Eyes signed.

Caesar nodded. That was expected. Koba had taken the highest ground and made himself hard to reach.

"And those... who are not?"

Prisoners, Blue Eyes signed. *Maurice, Rocket...*

Fury rose within Caesar. Making prisoners of apes, for disloyalty? That was unworthy. Beneath them. Koba was a bully, a killer. Not a leader.

Blue Eyes kept signing.

The others only follow out of fear, he said. *But once they see you are alive, they will turn from Koba.*

"Not if I am weak," Caesar said. "An ape always seeks... strongest branch." He thought, turning over possibilities in his mind. "I must find a way... to stop him," he said.

Blue Eyes started to sign again, then let his hands fall. He spoke aloud, something he almost never did. "What can I do? Something... I can do?"

Caesar felt a rush of pride. His son was learning. He had stood with ten toes over the edge of a plunge that took many back into animal savagery. Now he was stopping. Only a brave ape was capable of taking that step back. He watched his son for a long moment, several breaths dragging in and out. His wound hurt him terribly, but he had to be strong. For apes. Maybe for humans, too. He started to think of a plan, and nodded at his son.

Yes, there was something he could do.

59

Maurice sat in the stinking bus and waited to die. That was the only thing he could see Koba deciding to do. He would not free them without a pledge of loyalty. Maurice and Rocket had already refused to make such a pledge. The other apes in the bus had either done the same, or had been imprisoned because Koba suspected them.

He watched out the window that gave him a view of the tower over the human settlement. They had opened the bus windows to let out some of the heat, and the sound of gunfire had been coming from the top of the tower all day. Koba and his friends were shooting just for the pleasure of shooting, enjoying their power. Maurice had also seen apes pass by carrying a box of bottles he remembered from the weapon storehouse. Maurice was old, and had seen many of the bad sides of human behavior. He knew what happened when humans drank from those bottles.

He guessed that the same would happen to apes.

Koba was moving the rest of the humans into the pen. He wanted all of them captured before the female apes and children came down from the mountains.

Maurice watched the guards sign to each other, passing

the word that they would arrive that evening. Some of them had already reached the far end of the orange bridge. Maurice thought it was strange that Koba—who hated humans so fiercely—was so quick to move apes into the human city. He preferred Caesar's way. Humans could have their cities. Apes could have the mountains.

But Caesar was dead, and soon Maurice would be, too. He sighed.

A fresh group of human captives arrived, driven violently by apes into the tunnel. Some of the humans fought, and the apes took every chance to beat them violently until they were still. Then the bodies, living or not, were dragged in and left inside the fence. The guards locked the gates again, and Maurice looked away, disgusted. They were animals.

Something caught his attention on the rear window of the bus and he looked over at it. His eyes widened and he immediately looked back to the other prisoners to see if any of them had noticed. They had not. All of them sat, staring out the windows or sleeping, resigned to whatever Koba would do.

Maurice looked back at the window. There, drawn with a finger in the grime, was a circular sign. Caesar's sign. He had seen Caesar draw it many times. Once he had asked him what it meant, and Caesar had explained that it reminded him of his home. Maurice had wanted to know more, but the sadness on Caesar's face had stopped him from asking.

Now the sign was before him. It was a message. But from whom?

He nudged Rocket, who had barely moved all day. Rocket looked back, and the despair on his face was wiped away by surprise... then hope. They both searched out the windows, looking for some sign of who might have done this. Some of the other apes saw them looking, and they too started looking without knowing what it was they were supposed to find.

Luca grunted. Maurice looked to him and saw him point at the mirror on the side of the bus. In the tall rectangle, Maurice saw a reflection of Blue Eyes. Astonished, he turned to look out the back window again, and then he spotted Blue Eyes' hiding place. It was between two abandoned cars where the guards could not see him. Blue Eyes raised a finger to his lips.

Luca nodded.

Maurice nodded, too.

Caesar awoke again in darkness. He looked out through one of the vine-covered windows and saw from the stars it was still early in the night. He could not sleep. His wound throbbed, but he knew now that Ellie had saved his life. He would survive. His strength would return.

He hoped it would return soon enough.

With great effort he moved through the house, past the bedroom where Malcolm and Ellie were asleep, and the other room where Will's father had once slept. Alexander was in Will's father's bed, mouth slack, a flashlight beam dimming as its battery ran out. In its beam Caesar saw the bright boxes of the picture books Malcolm's son loved. Maurice had been interested in them, too. Caesar wondered if Maurice still lived, or if any of the apes on Koba's prison bus still lived.

Quietly he pulled down the folding stairs that led up to the attic. He climbed them as a human would, not daring to test his muscles yet. In the attic he found everything, almost as it had been the last time he was there, ten winters before. His drawings. The puzzle of the figure Will called the Statue of Liberty, in a place called New York. Even the Lucas Tower puzzle Will had used to test his medicine that made apes smarter.

Caesar smiled over all of it, but sadly, thinking back to what had started his life on this path. Will's father, lost in the fog of his old age, trying to drive the neighbor's car. The neighbor threatening Will's father, and Caesar coming to his defense. The only act of violence Caesar had ever committed on a human was biting the neighbor's finger. The taste of blood had awakened something in him—an animal hunger.

After that, he had shut it away forever.

Koba felt that hunger, and embraced it.

Caesar saw his old chessboard. Then he thought of the chessboard in his tree, up in the mountains. Was it still there? Where were Cornelia and the baby? He moved one of the pieces forward, two spaces as Will had taught him... then he noticed Will's video camera, still sitting on the table. He picked it up and turned it over in his hands, remembering how it worked.

He opened the side of it to expose the screen and pressed the button to turn it on.

Light came from the screen and the camera beeped. On the screen a red rectangle flashed. Caesar knew that meant the battery would die soon. He pressed the sideways triangle and stared as an image came to life.

Maurice waited. It was almost time. Night had fallen and the guards were whooping and screeching at more human captives, forcing them into the tunnel. He looked up toward Luca, who was watching the mirror.

Luca nodded.

All of the apes reached up and grabbed the bar that

ran along the side of the bus over the seats. They lifted themselves up and swung, crashing their feet into the wall and pushing off. The bus rocked to the side, then back. The apes rode its momentum, swinging back as the bus groaned on rusty springs, and then on the return swing smashing into the wall again. They swung a third time, a fourth, and with each swing the bus rocked a little farther.

Between his feet Maurice saw that two of the guards had noticed. The others were too busy with the human captives. The pair of chimps left their post at the fence and came toward the bus. If the prisoners didn't get out soon, they would be at the mercy of the guards' guns.

Maurice growled, and the rest of the prisoners took up the sound, roaring and shrieking as together they swung back one last time and drove into the side of the bus, using all their weight.

With a loud groan the bus tipped onto its side. The two approaching apes had made a fatal mistake. They came too close, and were crushed as it toppled onto them. Their dying screeches were drowned out by the crash and the noise from inside.

Maurice heard a thump on the top of the bus and looked up to see Blue Eyes forcing the door open. The prisoners climbed out, still bound at the wrists. Maurice was the last one out and he stood on the bus, amazed at what had happened. Perhaps he would live after all. He looked back at the human pen, and was amazed all over again.

The humans, taking advantage of the guards' distraction, had forced the gate and were stampeding out of the tunnel. They flooded the plaza, running around both sides of the bus and scattering into the dark in every direction. The three ape guards fired their weapons, but then they were trampled.

Maurice turned to Blue Eyes. He made a circular gesture with one finger. Blue Eyes made a fist. He had a bag over his shoulder and he took a knife from it. It took him only a minute to cut the bonds while the humans kept pouring out of the tunnel, and the shrieks of alarmed apes echoed through the city. The sound was answered from the direction of the tower.

They had gained themselves a little time, Maurice thought. But not much. He looked to Blue Eyes and signed.

Where do we go?

Follow me, Blue Eyes signed.

This was a different Blue Eyes, Maurice thought. He was born of Caesar, but had seemed to want to be Koba instead. Now he was Caesar's son again, strong and good. Maurice was happy to follow him.

60

On the video screen Caesar saw himself, looking curiously out. The frame moved and he heard Will's voice.

"Caesar! Caesar, what are you doing? C'mon, give me that…"

The sound of Will's voice was a joy and a pain. Caesar reached and touched the screen as the view spun around and he saw Will sitting across from him with the chessboard between them.

"Okay, here we go," Will said. "This is called chess. This is the pawn. You can go one space…" He moved the pawn from one square to the next. "Or two spaces." He put the pawn back and moved it two squares. Caesar watched his younger self pick up the pawn and look at it.

The video cut and jumped. Now Will and Caesar were in the kitchen. Will made a sign.

"Home," he said, and he repeated the sign. "Home."

In the attic, Caesar mimicked the gesture and remembered learning it for the first time. On the screen, he also mimicked it.

"Yes," Will said. "This is your home. Good." Caesar leaned in to hug Will. In the attic, Caesar's arms moved

277

reflexively to do the same.

The viewfinder went black.

Caesar held still, keeping the memory close. He missed Will. He would always miss Will. He wondered what Will would have thought of the village. He wished Will had lived to see Blue Eyes and the new baby.

He reached out and picked up the largest piece on the chessboard, remembering that Will had called it the king. At the same time he noticed Will watching him...

No. That was Malcolm. Caesar closed his eyes. So much time had passed. He had lost much, and might lose more.

"Sorry," Malcolm said. "I didn't mean to..." Caesar nodded. Malcolm walked over to him, taking in the room and its contents. "Who was that? On the video?"

"A good man," Caesar said. After a breath he added, "Like you."

He saw Malcolm react to this. He *was* a good man, Caesar thought. He tried to do right even, when right was hard. And he was stubborn. It took stubbornness to be good.

"Your son's still not back yet?" Malcolm asked. Caesar shook his head. Malcolm watched him, worried. Caesar did not know whether he was worried about Blue Eyes, or about Caesar's strength, or both. All he said was, "I'm sure he's okay."

It was what a father said to another father when neither of them knew what was true. Caesar knew Malcolm was talking to himself about his son Alexander as much as he was consoling Caesar about Blue Eyes. He had too many thoughts in his head.

Koba had only one thought. That was why he had won so far.

Caesar picked up one of the kings from the chessboard. He placed it in the center of the board and started putting other pieces around it. He thought better when he had something in his hands. He looked at the pieces, shifted some of them around, and stopped when he had put the king in the center of a ring of rooks and knights, with pawns in circles around them.

"What are you thinking?" Malcolm asked.

"Koba will protect himself," Caesar said.

Malcolm nodded, looking from the board to Caesar. "You have to draw him out."

"But he must not see me coming."

Malcolm thought about this. If Koba was staying up on the tower where Blue Eyes said he'd gathered his apes...

"Maybe I can help with that," he said. He was about to explain about the BART station and the subterranean approach to the tower when the brush growing up the front of the house rustled. The sound was clear in the night silence. Caesar crossed to the round window—the one Malcolm had noticed when they pulled up to the house. Malcolm followed.

In the yard, figures were approaching through the brush and vines that covered the yard and part of the street. Malcolm felt Caesar tense next to him. Then both of them relaxed when they saw the orangutan.

"Maurice," Malcolm said.

Next to Maurice was Rocket, and with them was Blue Eyes. Caesar placed his palm on the window, filled with pride at the sight of his son. Many more apes, perhaps twenty, followed through the brush, picked out by a bright moon. Blue Eyes looked up and saw his father in the window. Both apes smiled. Malcolm couldn't help but smile, too.

Blue Eyes had pulled off his part of the plan. Now they would see if Malcolm could do the same.

* * *

An hour later they were moving fast through a BART tunnel, coming up on the station Malcolm had used to access the Colony. This time they'd entered the system one stop farther south, giving the Colony and Koba's patrols a wide berth. The time would come for fighting, but it had not come yet.

Malcolm's flashlight was their only illumination. He kept it pointed ahead of them, on the floor. The apes moved nervously around him. He was right. They didn't like being underground. They got to the access door leading to the utility stairwell and Malcolm halted them at the top of the stairs so they could listen.

"Down this way is the construction site," he said to Caesar, keeping his voice low in case Koba's apes had figured out about the basements, and were now guarding the entrance. "We go through it, and then up into the tower, but sound really carries in this kind of space. We have to be absolutely quiet."

He held his flashlight beam on Caesar's hands so all the other apes could see him repeating the instructions. Then they went down and into the construction site. Hanging sheets of plastic drifted in the breeze of their passage, but none of the apes made a sound—not even Luca, who moved with incredible silence, given his size.

At the edge of the construction zone, they paused.

"We're close," Malcolm whispered to Caesar. "How are you holding up?"

Caesar nodded. He looked pretty good, considering the fact that Ellie had dug a bullet out of him, just the day before. Malcolm started to move forward, then threw himself on the ground and scrambled back into the bottom of the utility stairwell as gunshots boomed from inside the construction zone. Malcolm killed the flashlight and they all waited for the echoes to die away.

Koba's apes were there, it seemed. Then a human voice cut through the darkness.

"Who's there?" Malcolm recognized the voice right away. It was Finney. "If you're human, you better say so, and I mean right now."

The apes looked at Malcolm. He held out a hand to keep them where they were, and called out.

"It's okay! It's me, Malcolm."

He turned to Caesar and pointed back up the stairs, then cocked his wrist to indicate a turn.

"Go back that way, how we came. Then find the closest stairs. You'll come up on the street there."

Caesar nodded. He reached out and cupped the back of Malcolm's head.

"Thank you," he said.

Malcolm was unexpectedly moved by the gesture. He nodded back.

"Good luck."

The apes vanished up the stairs, again moving with unnerving silence as a flashlight beam and the crunch of boot soles on rough concrete heralded Finney's arrival. He caught Malcolm in the beam, and then swept it up the stairs.

"Damn, Malcolm, we've been looking for you," he said. "How'd you find us?"

"Us?" Malcolm repeated. "Who else is down here?"

Finney gestured with the flashlight beam.

"Come on, I'll show you."

He led Malcolm through the construction zone to another part of the tower's unfinished basement.

"The apes are all over the tower," Finney said as they walked. "They don't know we're down here." Malcolm nodded, letting the man talk and feigning ignorance for the moment. He wanted to know what was going on before he gave away too much about his last couple of days—especially the fact that Caesar was still around.

Malcolm realized then that when he'd crossed through this space the day before, Finney had already been there. But since the footprint of the building covered an entire city block, both of them had remained unaware.

And he wasn't alone, Finney said. There was the radio engineer Werner, and Dreyfus himself. They were in a makeshift fort made of construction materials, piled together, with lit flares strewn on the floor nearby. There was a fan running to blow most of the smoke away. Malcolm had noticed it before, but thought it was smoke from the fires above, circulated down somehow through the building's ventilation system.

There were crates of weapons and boxes of ammunition stacked inside the makeshift bunker, even though Malcolm saw only the three of them.

"We got this together over the last day or so. Made runs up top and dodged monkeys the whole way," Finney said proudly. "And that's not all we got, but I'll let Dreyfus tell you the rest."

As they approached, Werner had his portable set plugged in and running, using the steel frame of the skyscraper as an antenna.

"I had them back for a minute, but they dropped out again," he was saying as Finney and Malcolm appeared.

"Keep at it," Dreyfus replied. He looked up at Malcolm and, without smiling, walked over and clapped him on the shoulder. "I didn't know if you made it out," he said.

No thanks to you, Malcolm thought. He held his tongue, though. This wasn't the time to pick a fight.

"Don't worry," Dreyfus said with a wink. "We're about to turn this around."

"What do you mean?" Malcolm asked. Something about Dreyfus's tone made him nervous. "How? And who's 'them'?"

"What?" Dreyfus said, and he looked confused.

"Werner said he 'had them back'," Malcolm said. "Who?"

"Tell you later," Dreyfus said. "First, follow me."

This level of the basement held the seismic damping equipment once required of all skyscrapers in California. Malcolm couldn't see all of it in the poor light, especially with the smoke from the flares, but it looked like a pretty ordinary base-isolation setup. The building was designed on a table that would absorb the lateral force of an earthquake. Its floor design would also be earthquake-conscious, with a heavier core surrounded by lighter beam structures that allowed it to flex more easily.

The builders might have even planned to add a mass damper of some kind on the upper floors, but there were only girders above thirty stories, so no one would ever know without digging blueprints out of the city planning office.

The building foundation itself, resting on the table with some kind of damping material between them, looked fairly standard. Concrete pillars stretched across the space, no doubt reinforced with rebar. Malcolm hadn't worked in large buildings, but he knew enough about the principles to see...

"Oh my God," he said.

That was when he noticed the gray bricks stuck on the sides of some of the pillars. Then he saw the open crates, filled with similar blocks. Some of the C-4 already had bridgewire trailing away from it, presumably to a detonator.

Dreyfus looked at his work like a proud dad.

"We take the tower down, and we get almost all of them at once," he said, bending to pick up another brick of C-4. He tossed it to Malcolm. "Welcome to the war."

Malcolm nodded, staring at the brick in his hand. He had to delay this plan. Caesar might be in the building right now, and if he wasn't, it wouldn't be long.

"When's the big boom?" he asked, trying to sound both casual and anticipatory.

"Soon as we get a brick on every pillar," Dreyfus said. "Then we'll wire the rest up in the crates just for good measure, get to a safe distance, and watch the show."

61

Caesar took a long time watching the apes moving in the naked girders of the tower. He saw them pass in front of the lights on the higher floors. Once, long ago, he'd asked Will why skyscrapers had lights on the top, and Will had told him it was so planes did not crash into them. Caesar remembered thinking how ridiculous it was to think that a plane could not notice something the size of a skyscraper.

He steeled himself to fight. His wound was deep, and his strength was less than it should be. But he would not back down from Koba. Surprise would be his ally, and he thought the nature of apes was on his side, too. When they discovered what Koba had done, many of them would return their loyalty to Caesar. Not all, but many. Once that happened, all would depend on Caesar's ability to defeat Koba in a fight. One of them, he thought, would not live through the next day.

He thought of Blue Eyes, and Cornelia, and his tiny new son, and he grew stronger.

"It is time," he said to Blue Eyes.

There were fewer patrols around on the side of the

skyscraper away from the Colony gate. The hundreds of apes on the beams and girders were mostly looking down on the site of the battle, or preoccupied with their daily routines. Caesar led his apes around. They scaled the walls of the Colony and rested a moment at the base of the skyscraper itself.

Any ape may leave this fight, Caesar signed. *It is not yours. It is mine.*

No one moved. Blue Eyes, standing in the middle of the group, looked strong. Calm and resolute, rather than angry and nervous. Caesar took this as a good sign. He smiled, and ducked his head to them, showing respect for their loyalty and their courage. Then he turned to the wall, and they began to climb.

The apes gathered on the beams above the finished part of the building started to notice them when they were only a few stories below. They screeched down at the interlopers, and the sound drew more apes, until the border between the finished and unfinished parts of the skyscraper was lined with them.

The escaped prisoners climbed together, in ranks of five or six. Rocket, Blue Eyes, Maurice, and Luca were in the first rank. They reached the edge and climbed over it, as the screeching of Koba's apes grew louder and higher-pitched.

But those apes backed away when the escapees held themselves strong, shoulder-to-shoulder with the massive gorilla and orangutan in the middle, flanked by Blue Eyes and Rocket. More of Koba's apes dropped down from the higher beams, adding to the shrieking and posturing. When the mood began to shift and the defenders had just about worked themselves up to attack, the escapees parted, and Caesar, alone, walked through the gap to face them.

He willed himself to stay tall and strong as he walked, his steps measured even though he was already tired from a climb that should have been child's play. Caesar hid his pain. The raging apes immediately fell silent, shocked, eyes widening as if seeing the impossible. On the levels above, more and more ape heads looked down. They, too, were stunned, and could not believe what they saw. None of them rushed to attack. None of them asked him a question.

Each of them, he thought, *has something to answer for. They know it.* But at that moment he did not care. He had one thing on his mind, and only one.

"Where is Koba?" he asked.

He waited for a challenge, but none came. First a few, then all of the apes looked up at the top of the tower.

Yes, Caesar thought. It was as he had expected. The first part of his plan was working. He was through the outer ranks of pawns. He walked along a beam toward the nearest girder that extended to the highest level of the building. The apes parted to allow him to pass. Few of them would meet his eyes, and those who did looked ashamed.

He reached the girder and began to climb, feeling the eyes on him as he passed each floor. His loyal troop climbed with him, and a strange thing happened after Caesar had climbed five or six floors. He felt the steel structure begin to sway as more and more apes climbed with him.

He did not look back. The ape who thought of only one thing, would be the ape who won. His gaze fixed above, on the top of the tower, Caesar climbed, feeling the pain in his body and turning it into strength. He had thought he needed to draw Koba out... but perhaps he already had done so, by stripping Koba's army away from him even though Koba himself had not moved.

Only time—and another fifteen stories—would tell.

* * *

Malcolm helped place bricks of C4 throughout the foundation while he silently debated how to forestall the explosion. He had a couple of choices: active resistance, or passive delaying tactics.

From time to time he dropped a couple of bricks, or made a show of hemming and hawing over placement. It only worked because Finney and Dreyfus knew he was an architect, and paid attention to what he said. They were glad to listen to him at first, but they were getting impatient.

"Let's get out of here and blow this fucker," Finney said. "How many more do we need?"

"Well, you tell me, Finney," Malcolm said. "You want to try it and have it not work?"

Finney grumbled, but he went back for more C4. They were most of the way across the basement level. Back in the bunker, Werner was doing whatever he did with the radio. Dreyfus was planting C4 in still another area. The idea was to have at least one brick on every pillar—the higher the better, to cause an immediate sag in the entire floor. The building would pancake straight down, and the ape problem would be solved.

At least that's what Malcolm had told Dreyfus, to strengthen his trust. The truth was that he wasn't a demolition expert, and he had no idea what the building would do if a hundred bricks of C4 went off simultaneously.

Fall down? Certainly.

Fall in a controlled and predictable manner? Not a chance.

Deciding that the passive delay approach had just about run its course, he judged that the time had come to take a more active role. He hated the thought of what he was about to do, but lives were at stake... perhaps including his. The problem was, they were armed, and he wasn't.

"Finney!" he called out. "Can you give me a hand?" Then he pointed up.

Finney walked over and looked. The ceiling was a little higher here, and there was a heavy crossbeam marked by a mending plate. "See the rivets there?" Malcolm said, pointing at the mending plate. "That's a good spot for a charge, but I can't reach that high."

"Sure," Finney said. He reached up, stretching as far as he could to work the brick onto the lip of the beam and press it in place. Malcolm saw the gun tucked into the back of his pants.

"Whoa, steady," Malcolm said. He braced Finney with one hand, and lifted the gun with the other.

"Nah, I'm okay," Finney replied.

"You sure."

Finney nodded, and Malcolm let go. Holding the brick in place, Finney reached back.

"Hand me some wire," he said. "No sense doing this Mr. Fantastic act twice." Malcolm didn't answer. "Hey, Malcolm—" Finney said, turning his head, and that was when Malcolm cold-cocked him with the butt of his own gun.

Finney dropped without a sound. Malcolm turned him on his side because he'd read somewhere you were supposed to do that to unconscious people so they didn't swallow their tongues. Then he got his bearings.

"This is San Francisco…" Werner was repeating his monotonous call for help. Malcolm listened, and when Werner paused to take a drink of water, he heard Dreyfus scraping around toward the other end of the cavernous space. Looking in that direction, he saw the beam of Dreyfus's flashlight, clearly visible in the smoky air. Without further ado Malcolm walked that way and found

Dreyfus affixing a line of charges onto a concrete shelf, just under the ceiling. He was standing on an upended crate, using it to reach the shelf.

"Dreyfus," Malcolm said.

Dreyfus turned around and peered at him in the gloom. Then he saw the gun.

"What are you doing?" he asked. It was a real question. Dreyfus didn't scare easily, and he'd had guns pointed at him before. He really wanted to know what Malcolm was doing. Sincerity radiated from every part of him, even the concrete dust in his hair.

"Listen," Malcolm said. "You have to stop. You can't do this."

"What are you talking about? Put that gun down." Dreyfus stayed up on the crate and pulled another brick of C4 from his coat pocket. Something about that struck Malcolm as funny, but he didn't laugh.

"They're not what you think they are. They want the same thing we do," Malcolm said. "To survive. They don't want a war."

Then Dreyfus started to get angry.

"What? Are you out of your—where the *hell* have you been?" he spluttered, almost overbalancing the crate as he leaned forward and jabbed a finger in Malcolm's direction. "Those animals attacked us!"

"Only because they thought we attacked them," Malcolm said. Dreyfus was a rational man, a smart man, but he didn't like apes, and he thought he had good reason not to like them. It was going to be an uphill struggle convincing him. But Malcolm kept talking. It had worked with Caesar, it would work with Dreyfus.

Or they'd all end up dead.

"They think he's dead, but he's up there right now—this fighting can stop, we can finish what we started, everything we've been working for." He would have gone on, but he could tell from the expression on Dreyfus's face that he was hung up on something Malcolm had said.

Malcolm paused. Dreyfus blinked, catching up.

"Wait," he said. "Who? Who's up there?"

62

Ten stories from Koba's perch at the top of the skyscraper, Caesar saw Grey look down. The face disappeared, and Caesar kept climbing until Grey and Koba's other closest loyalists came climbing down to meet him.

Blue Eyes, right behind Caesar, called out to him and Caesar slowed, planting his feet on a beam and awaiting their arrival. Caesar was grateful for the brief rest. He did not see Stone, and wondered what had happened to him as Koba's loyalists dropped onto the beams around him.

Each of them in turn looked stunned to see Caesar alive. They hesitated, wavered—then Grey raised his gun and pointed it at him. The sight brought back Caesar's memory of Koba's bullet, tearing into him, stealing his breath and the strength of his legs, dropping him down the rocky slope through the trees. He would have died had it not been for humans.

Now he stared at Grey as around him first a dozen, then a hundred, then a hundred more apes flooded up onto the beams. They surrounded Caesar. Grey looked at them— Luca, Rocket, Maurice, Blue Eyes, all the rest—and he looked uncertain. The other Koba loyalists, unnerved by the return of so many apes to Caesar, raised their own guns.

Caesar peered at him and did not waver, but he breathed deeply, wondering which would be his last breath before Grey pulled the trigger.

At his side, Maurice grunted. *Maurice!* The last ape Caesar would have expected. The orangutan stared hard at Grey and signed.

Koba's fight... Not yours.

If Maurice could be roused to action, Caesar thought, Koba had no chance. He kept his gaze steady on Grey, who looked at Maurice for a long time. Almost long enough that Caesar thought he might yet fire. Then, slowly, Grey lowered the barrel of his gun. Koba's other loyalists did the same.

And so, Caesar thought, *the king stands alone.* He thought of the chessboard, and of Malcolm sitting in Caesar's old room where Will once sat. He stared at Grey until Grey looked away. Then Caesar called to his apes, and resumed his climb.

A minute later he was on the top level of beams, whipped by the chill wind from the harbor. It hummed around the cables that were hanging from the end of the crane, swinging the hook and ball back and forth.

Caesar got his feet onto the highest beam and looked up at Koba, who sat alone on a girder that reached up. It was higher than the distance from the ground to the top of Caesar's tree. He was looking at Caesar, and then he looked around as the rest of the apes swarmed up over the edges of the building and massed around an open area left at the base of the spire. Koba shifted, a bottle in his hand. Slung over his back was his gun, and crossing in the other direction was the strap of his harpoon.

He looked back at Caesar, and Caesar smiled up at this king, alone in the kingdom he had never really had. He could see Koba's shock that Caesar was still alive. Would he be smart, or would he fight?

Leaving his weapons behind, Koba dropped down the girder, using one hand and both feet. He got to the grid of beams and looked at the assembled apes. Grey was nowhere to be seen. Koba leered and looked Caesar up and down. He knew Caesar better than any ape, and he could tell Caesar was weak.

"Caesar has no place here," he said. "Apes follow Koba now."

"Follow Koba to war," Caesar growled.

Koba made a sweeping gesture to the surrounding apes, the bottle sloshing in his hand.

"Apes win war! Apes together STRONG!" He did a pantomime of a kooky-chimp act, mocking as he repeated Caesar's own words to the assembled apes. Then he looked back to him and added, "Caesar weak."

Caesar looked at the bottle in Koba's hand and made sure that the assembled apes all saw him looking at it.

"Koba...weaker," he said.

At that, Koba snapped. With a roar he charged at Caesar, who leaped at him, meeting him in mid-air with a bone-jarring thump. They slammed down to the nearest beam. Around them, the assembled apes started to hoot and screech. Below that noise was a rhythm, a chant, wordless but powerful. The apes saw their once and future leaders, and they chanted to give strength to the ape who deserved to win.

Caesar and Koba grappled and bit, kicked and swung, leaped and punched across the grid of beams with a drop of three hundred feet below them. Caesar took the measure of his opponent. He was strong and he was fueled by his hatred… but he was also drunk. Caesar was strong and he was fueled by belief… but he was also torn by a bullet. Every time he swung from the arm on his wounded side, he felt something tear a little inside him. This could not be a long fight. He would not survive it if it lasted.

Then, Caesar thought, *I must end it quickly.*

"Okay, Malcolm," Dreyfus said. "I don't know what happened to you up there. What got into your head."

"I know how it sounds," Malcolm said.

"Do you?" Dreyfus shouted. "I don't think you do." He stepped down from the crate and took a step toward Malcolm, who took a step back. "You think stopping me will even matter?" Dreyfus said. "They're coming! We made contact! A military base up north. They're already on their way."

Malcolm couldn't believe this, but it fit with Werner's offhand comments from before. *Other humans*, he thought. *We aren't alone—*

Dreyfus charged him, taking advantage of Malcolm's surprise. He slapped the gun out of Malcolm's hand and knocked him over backward, jamming a forearm down on his throat. Dreyfus had been a soldier. Malcolm was an architect. He'd inadvertently started a fight he couldn't finish, and he knew it.

But he tried anyway, thrashing around and getting lucky when he drove a knee up and landed it squarely in Dreyfus's gut. Dreyfus gagged and Malcolm sprawled across the floor after the gun. He got it, spun around… and saw Dreyfus getting to his feet, covered with concrete dust and holding the detonator tuned to the wires leading to God only knew how many bricks of C-4.

"Don't," Malcolm said.

Werner had heard the scuffle and come running just in time to see the standoff.

"Dreyfus, what're you doing?" he said. Malcolm could see him trying to figure out the situation, and deciding that Malcolm was trying to stop Dreyfus from blowing them all to hell. Malcolm hoped Werner didn't ask himself too many questions about how he had ended up with Finney's gun.

Dreyfus looked at Werner, and back to Malcolm.

"I'm saving what's left of the human race," he said.

Koba was getting stronger as they fought, riding the crest of his hate. Caesar fought from will more than strength, still feeling the deep wound in his chest and the loss of blood. When both were healthy, Caesar was more than a match for Koba. He had proved it in the powerhouse. But he was not healthy, and he would only be able to hold out for so long.

He grappled only when he had no choice, preferring to swing and dip around the beams and girders, landing a blow here and a two-footed kick there. Koba shrugged them off and kept coming. He was trying to maneuver Caesar out onto a beam that extended toward the frame at the core of the building. The opening extended unbroken all the way down to the basements.

Caesar feinted a fall, then swung under a beam and came up behind Koba, striking him hard in the small of the back. Koba lashed around but Caesar ducked away, feeling his bullet wound tear a little more. Koba leaped after him and Caesar jumped up onto a girder, springing over his opponent's head and landing on the beam near where he had started.

Screeching in frustrated fury, Koba pounded the

girders, which transmitted the sound throughout the steel skeleton. Something rattled behind him and both he and Caesar saw the abandoned crane cab at the same time. It sat at a beam junction not far from the core. Its arm stood up at an angle, ball and hook drawn tight. Koba was closer to it than Caesar. He stepped to it and snapped off a piece of the crane arm, a six-foot length of steel with a sharp end. It was not a harpoon, but it would serve well enough if Caesar didn't stay clear of it.

He charged after Caesar, who evaded him and counter-attacked as best he could. He was getting weaker, though, and Koba landed two heavy blows with the metal bar. One numbed Caesar's arm for a moment, and the other opened a bloody gash on the side of his head. Then, jabbing at Caesar with the sharp end, Koba forced him to the edge of the core.

Caesar charged at him in desperation, grabbing the length of steel and jumping off to the side. Startled, Koba instinctively fought to keep his grip. That resistance let Caesar use him as a pivot point. He swung around and dropped back to the beam on the other side, a little farther from the drop into the core.

When he let go, Koba overbalanced—just for a fraction of a second. Caesar took his chance, leaping up to grab the ball and hook hanging from the crane arm. He kicked back and then forward, flinging himself feet-first.

Koba was recovering his balance, but the impact toppled him off the beam. He caught it with the fingertips of one hand and hung there, glaring hate up at Caesar.

Caesar returned the glare. If Koba tried to climb up or tried to attack him, Caesar would kill him. Both apes knew it. Caesar stood over Koba, waiting for him to make his choice. Koba had one last chance to be forgiven, one last chance to supplicate and rejoin the community of apes. But Caesar did not intend to wait forever.

* * *

"Put it down," Malcolm said.

Slowly Dreyfus shook his head.

"You think we can just go back?" he said. Malcolm saw Werner starting to freak out. He held the gun leveled at Dreyfus, who brandished the C4 detonator.

"Dreyfus, *put it down*!" Malcolm shouted.

Dreyfus raised the detonator, a haunted look in his eyes. He wasn't really there any more, Malcolm realized. He was gone, back into the world that had died with the Simian Flu.

"There's no going back—" he said.

Werner tackled him from behind, cutting him off. The detonator flew out of Dreyfus's hand. Time slowed to a crawl, as the options flashed through Malcolm's mind. One, he could try to grab it before it hit the ground. Unlikely to succeed, and it would result in Malcolm being vaporized.

But there was a short countdown, which was included as a failsafe. Two, he could try to stop that. Unlikely to succeed because he had no idea how to do it, and it would also result in Malcolm being vaporized.

Or three, he could run like hell and hope the countdown was just long enough to save his life. Unlikely to succeed, and Dreyfus was a good man. So was Werner. Neither of them deserved this. But Malcolm could not save them.

He ran.

63

Caesar was out of patience. If Koba would not yield, that was the same as choosing to continue the fight. Their gazes were locked, neither of them speaking or signing. There was nothing left to say... but Caesar could not quite bring himself to take the final step.

The building shook, as if there was an earthquake. It rocked to one side, then swayed back, the top floor moving fifty feet or more. Groans and pops sounded throughout its frame. The sudden motion pitched Caesar off the edge of the beam over the building's core. Koba, already hanging by one hand, barely kept his grip.

Caesar managed to arrest his fall at the crossing of a beam and girder two stories down. The impact jarred the bullet wound, and for a moment the pain almost overcame him. But he hung on, and looked down to see a fireball churning up the core shaft. Simultaneously he and Koba hunched into themselves, averting their eyes and waiting to burn.

The fireball dissipated before it reached them. All they got was smoke, and a passing wave of heat as if they had sat too close to the bonfire.

Caesar opened his eyes and clambered up onto the beam, squinting through the haze. Around him, other apes regained their footing and their bearings. Some had fallen fatal distances. He could see them on the last finished floor, thirty floors below, or dangling broken over beams. The last swaying quieted. Caesar started looking around for his opponent again.

Koba appeared, launching himself from the next floor up, metal spear raised over his head. Just five days before, Caesar had seen him in the same pose, in the air coming down on the back of the brown bear. Now, seeing it again, he was ready.

At the last moment Caesar dodged out of the way and tore the steel shaft from Koba's grasp. It pinged from girder to beam, spinning away down into the darkness. Tumbling past, Koba grabbed Caesar's arm, nearly pulling both of them into the abyss of the building core... but Caesar, with the last of his strength, gripped the lip of the nearest girder with one hand and locked the other around Koba's wrist. He cried out in pain as Koba's weight pulled on his wound, but he did not let go.

The steel spear tumbled and clanged away into the depths.

Now Caesar's grasp was the only thing keeping Koba from dropping.

I hold Koba's life, Caesar thought. He looked down, teeth bared from the strain, his wound tearing open again inside him... and saw Koba, too, realizing that his life was in Caesar's hand. The one-eyed ape grinned, looking up at his old friend, taunting him with the words of Caesar's own creation.

"Ape... will not... kill ape," Koba sneered.

Caesar hesitated. If ever an ape had deserved to die, it was Koba. But where did that leave apes? If every rule had exceptions when it became hard to follow, what good were rules at all? He stared down at Koba, the grimness he felt in stark contrast to Koba's mocking grin.

Caesar looked up, seeing all the other apes watching him. What he did next would make the difference between apes living together, and dissolving into warring tribes. He saw Blue Eyes, and felt the burden of doing the right thing as an example for his son. He saw Rocket, and felt the burden of easing Rocket's pain by taking revenge on his behalf. He saw Maurice, and wished he had the orangutan's placid strength, of both body and mind.

Other apes looked down at him, too, more than he could name. All of them saw Koba swinging from Caesar's arm. All of them waited for Caesar's decision.

He realized something then. Koba hungered for guns and liquor. He hungered for power. He desired revenge. He had turned on the most sacred law of the apes, betraying Caesar and using human weapons like a coward. Even now he smirked, dangling over the hole that dropped all the way down into the underground floors of the tower.

He turned his face back to Koba, his face grave.

"You are not ape," he said.

Koba's expression changed. One moment he wore the taunting leer of someone waiting for an enemy to realize his defeat. The next he was the schemer, realizing that his schemes had fatally undermined, not his enemy, but himself.

Caesar let him go.

Koba roared, his last act in life to scream out the rage and hate that had driven him to acts that no ape could forgive. His body grew smaller and smaller, then disappeared into the darkness below.

Caesar closed his eyes. It was a hard thing he had done. Once he and Koba had been brothers. They had fought together, saved each other's lives... but he who won this battle was he who thought of only one thing. Caesar thought only of the laws of the apes, which existed to keep them unified and strong in a world that had tried to eradicate them. Around him was silence, save for the wind humming through the naked steel.

The apes mourned Koba, as they should, Caesar thought. As he did. Then he heard a hopeful hoot from nearby. He located the ape making the noise and saw him looking away and down, toward the street. Stiff and aching, the wound in his chest bleeding again, he pulled himself up and loped across the beams, joined by other apes curious to see what could interrupt so solemn an occasion.

Coming over the hill and down toward the Colony was a throng of apes, moving in small groups but all together. The females and children had arrived. They were too far away for Caesar to recognize any individuals, but the sight of them filled him with a restored sense of purpose. He had done what needed to be done. Now was the time to begin rebuilding what Koba had tried to destroy.

Ignoring the pain radiating from his wounds, Caesar raised his arms and gestured for the rest to follow him. He dropped over the edge of the steel frame and began the long climb down to reunite with Cornelia. Blue Eyes cut through the crowd to climb with him.

Together, Caesar thought. *Apes together strong.*

They reached the courtyard at the base of the skyscraper, on the other side from the wreckage of the Colony gate. Some apes ran north to meet their families and guide the group in. Caesar waited. He did not have the strength to run, and even if he had it was more fitting for him to stay where he was. The leader of apes could not run around like an adolescent.

He rested and thought about what he had done. He had broken the law that ape shall not kill ape... but he had done it to save other apes. How many were dead because of Koba? Their village burned, the humans made into enemies, and deep divisions created within the troop... all those were Koba's fault. He had acted like the worst of the humans, making himself unfit for apes. Caesar had done the only thing he could, cutting out the disease to keep the body whole.

Several apes near the closest doors into the building started to screech and grunt. Caesar turned to see what they were doing, and saw yet another unexpected thing, here at the end of a succession of days that had brought one unexpected thing after another.

Malcolm, dirty and battered—blood smeared across his nose and dried in a trickle that ran down the side of his jaw—emerged from the building. The apes surrounded him, baring fangs and screeching. He did not react. Caesar admired his calm. It was one of the human qualities he admired.

"Leave him," Caesar said over the commotion. He crossed the stone plaza and saw on closer inspection that Malcolm was deeply anxious about something other than his immediate safety. "What happened?" he asked, pointing down. He knew there had been an explosion, and it looked like Malcolm had been a little too close to it.

"Dreyfus tried to bring down the tower," Malcolm said. "I tried to stop him." Regarding the hundreds of apes around them, he added, "I guess it worked. This building is built pretty tough. They have to be around here."

"It worked," Caesar said.

"What about Koba?" Malcolm asked.

"Koba is gone," Caesar said. He offered no details, and Malcolm didn't ask for any.

"Listen," Malcolm said. "You're not safe here." Caesar frowned in confusion. Koba was gone, the humans were scattered and now knew that the apes were under Caesar's control again... "They made contact," Malcolm continued. "There are others coming for you. Soldiers. You need to leave while you still can. All of you."

Leave, Caesar thought. Where? Back into the mountains, where they had almost died in their first months? Where the remains of their village still smoked at the edge of the canyon? Leave, while soldiers landed and the humans saw what apes had done.

"No," he said. It was too late to run. If there were other humans, no place on earth would be far enough away. Not when soldiers saw that a battle had already been fought.

"Yes," Malcolm said, his voice low and urgent. "Caesar, you have to—"

"Nowhere left to run," Caesar said. He looked up the tower, all the way to the top, where he and Koba had finally settled their differences. "Thought fight would end here," he said sadly, and looked back to Malcolm. This human had risked his own life for Caesar's, more than once. It pained Caesar to do what he was about to do, but he could see no other choice. "It is you who must go. I am sorry... my friend."

Malcolm looked as if he might say something. Caesar waited. Malcolm had convinced him to change his mind several times. Perhaps he could do it again. But then Malcolm nodded.

"I'm sorry too," he said.

They looked at each other, human and ape, knowing they were being torn apart, not by choice, but by events neither of them could control. Caesar stepped back, then turned and walked slowly down the stone steps into the large plaza beyond. A sea of apes, hundreds and hundreds, bowed and supplicated as he waded through them. He felt their renewed strength, and felt also the burden of what he would have to tell them. But not just yet. Let them be strong together for a little while, let them enjoy the reunion with the females and the children. He picked Cornelia out of the crowd, the baby clinging to her. Blue Eyes had already found her. The four apes came together and embraced. Together. Strong.

In the midst of this moment Caesar looked back toward the base of the skyscraper. Malcolm was gone.

EPILOGUE

It was just daybreak when they got to the bridge.

"Careful here," the captain said. "No telling what kind of debris is in the channel." He looked at an old chart. The water under the middle of the bridge was sixty fathoms at its deepest point, and the ship only drew six fully loaded. Now it was drawing maybe four. Should be plenty of clearance, but the captain knew better than to assume anything, after all the things he'd seen.

Next to him, the navigator was muttering a continuous stream of minor corrections, his instructions sent down to the engine room. The ship was a dinosaur, without any advanced electronics. They practically had to communicate with cans and string. But they got it done. The most advanced tech they had was the radio setup, and the captain glanced over to see one of his men coming onto the bridge.

"Still nothing on the radio," the man said. "Last contact was ten hours ago."

The captain considered this. The contact was confirmed. There were people in San Francisco. And judging by the tone of their communications, they were in trouble. They'd come all this way, so they might as well get a look at the city and see what kind of shape it was in. Surviving groups of humans were few and far between. If they could help these people, they would.

It wouldn't be the first time the captain had led a force against organized gangs or bandit groups. Slowly but surely, they were bringing order back to northern California.

He watched the battered central span of the Golden Gate Bridge as it passed over them, and ordered a little more speed as they came out from under it. Currents here were tricky, and would drag the ship all over the place if they didn't have at least a little head of steam to get through them.

Next to him, the navigator began scanning the city with binoculars. The fog wasn't as thick on the bay side of the bridge, but it still wasn't fully light.

"I see the beacon!" the navigator said, pointing. The captain saw it too, a bright light shining from high on an unfinished skyscraper.

"Get a closer look while we figure out if there's a place we can dock," he ordered. The ship started to clear the bridge and the captain looked along the waterfront. There were plenty of piers, but they would have to take the approach very slow. It might be best to send out scouts in a small boat, to look for wrecks around the ends of those piers. Wouldn't do the survivors of San Francisco any good if the ship tore its bottom out on a sunken ferry stack, and sunk a hundred yards from the Embarcadero.

The navigator looked through binoculars at the skyscraper. He adjusted the focus.

"What the hell is that?"

"What is it, soldier?" the captain asked. He reached for the binoculars and stepped around the navigator to get the best angle on the source of the beacon.

For a long moment he stared into the binoculars, unable to believe what he was seeing.

From the top of the tower, Caesar watched the ship come under the bridge, its outline indistinct in the morning fog. It churned into the bay, black smoke flowing up to darken the fog, and as it came closer, he saw that the deck of the ship was covered with humans. Soldiers, in uniforms, all bearing guns.

Malcolm had been right. He had warned Caesar that this would happen. In return, Caesar had made certain that all of the humans had supplies and were guided out of the city safely. What they did after that was up to them. Malcolm was his friend, but not every human would be.

Caesar's obligation was to his troop.

Around him, a thousand apes saw what Caesar did. He leaned out from the girder and roared. Apes had fought for this city. Apes had died. They would have peace if peace was to be had, but if not…

His apes joined his roar, raising their arms, thundering out their challenge. It rolled out across the city just lit by dawn, and they waited for the humans to choose.

ACKNOWLEDGMENTS

Thanks first to Pierre Boulle, of course, for the story that we're all still riffing on fifty years later; to Charlton Heston and Roddy McDowell and the rest of the cast of the first movie, for bending my head when I saw it on a Saturday afternoon Creature Feature; to Cath Trechman, Steve Saffel, and Alice Nightingale at Titan, for bringing me in and for perspicacious reading; to Josh Izzo at Fox, for answering some key questions at key times; to Michael Erard, for a fascinating conversation about language over beers one night; and to everyone involved in *Rise of the Planet of the Apes* and *Dawn of the Planet of the Apes*, for giving me so much to work with. I hope everyone enjoys reading this book as much as I enjoyed writing it.

ABOUT THE AUTHOR

Alex Irvine has written somewhere in the neighborhood of thirty books. His original novels include *Buyout*, *The Narrows*, and *A Scattering of Jades*. On the licensed front, he has written novelizations of *Pacific Rim*, *The Adventures of Tintin*, and *Iron Man 2*. Some of his other licensed fiction is *Transformers: Exodus*, *Batman: Inferno*, *Supernatural: John Winchester's Journal*, *The Seal of Karga Kul*, and *X-Men: Days of Future Past*. His comics work includes *Daredevil Noir*, *Iron Man: Rapture*, and *Hellstorm, Son of Satan: Equinox*. He currently writes the games *Marvel: Avengers Alliance*, *Marvel War of Heroes*, and *Marvel Puzzle Quest*. He is working on another game project as well as several new comics, novels, and scripts. He lives in Maine with his wife Lindsay, three kids, two dogs, a snake, a bird, and a fish.